The wrong world....

Along one wall were the comlines. He watched several people use them until he was fairly sure he had the way of it; then he moved in front of one, stepping forward until a ready light glowed.

"Your party, please?" said a light, metallic voice.

"Scholar Osrin Havard, historical and ethnic studies, College of Seleme Central," Tadko announced, somewhat more loudly than he had planned.

There was a bleeping sound, a click, then a different metallic voice.

"*Senior* scholar Havard is not presently in residence," it said, emphasizing the additional title. "He is on extended leave to the research center on Eilonsad. He will be returning on 8th Perian, Seleme Standard. Sub-space calls may be placed at the central terminal office, minimum charge one hundred duats. Will there be any further service, please?"

Tadko said nothing. The voice repeated, "Will there be any further service, please?"

"No, no further service," Tadko mumbled. "Nothing."

He moved away, and the eye-cell darkened. What now?

Many times he had wondered if he were doing the right thing in looking for his father, even though his mother's last words had urged him to do so. He had wondered if the man would even remember him and his mother; if he would want to have anything to do with Tadko, even supposing he did remember; but to arrive and find the man elsewhere—this he had never considered. Eighth Perian, he thought, and began working out how long he had to wait...eighty days, give or take a few. Somehow he would have to find a way to live...he wiped his sweating face on his sleeve and shook his head. *This is the wrong world for Elnakti,* he thought.

ABOUT THE AUTHOR

Margaret Howes is a retiree who has become a storyteller in the Society for Creative Anachronism (an organization which recreates the Middle Ages). She has drawn maps for the books *Murder at the War* by Mary Monica Pulver, *The Best of Leigh Brackett*, and the Underwood-Miller edition of *Showboat World* by Jack Vance. She has had short stories published in *The Tolkien Scrapbook* and *Sword and Sorceress VIII*. She is one of the authors of the novel, *Autumn World* (Stone Dragon Press, 2000), which she wrote in collaboration with Joan Marie Verba, Tess Meara, Deborah K. Jones, and Ruth Berman. *The Wrong World* is her first solo novel.

THE WRONG WORLD

MARGARET HOWES

FTL PUBLICATIONS
MINNETONKA, MINNESOTA

Copyright © 2000 by Margaret Howes. All rights reserved.

FTL Publications
P O Box 1363
Minnetonka, MN 55345-0363
http://ourworld.compuserve.com/homepages/FTL_Publications

Cover design and artwork by Terry Miller and Rita Miller at ImagiMation.
Cover copyright © 2000 by FTL Publications.

"Funerary Pyrolysis" copyright © 2000 by Ellen R. Kuhfeld, Ph.D.
Used by permission of the author.

Printed in the United States of America.

ISBN 0-9653575-1-1

This is a work of fiction. Names, characters, places, and incidents either are the product of the author's imagination or are used fictitiously. Any resemblance to actual events, locales, organizations, or persons, living or dead, is entirely coincidental and beyond the intent of either the author or the publisher.

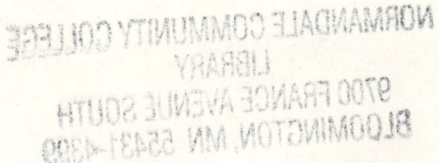

CHAPTER ONE

Tadko waited breathlessly in his assigned cubicle as the SS *Werauer* circled slowly in a holding orbit above Monna. He wondered when the ship would get clearance to land. Tadko felt oddly suspended, hanging between past and future: this planet Monna was his father's home. He had seen some old pictures, but had no real memory of his father.

His mother had done all she could to prepare him for a possible reunion. She had set up a school in a disused room in a storage cave. Table, two stools, styli to write with, stacks of paper bought every year at Port Town. (Grandfather had disapproved and frowned terribly, but Mother had her way.) There was also a helmet called a Tutorial, powered from a shiny box she called a persat, both brought from Monna, years ago. He had learned the Monnan language, and some basic education. So he had thought he would come to Monna someday, but not like this.

His door alarm sounded sharply.

"Tadko?" Jerely called. "May I come in?"

Tadko opened the door. Jerely looked him over and shook her head. "My father sent me to tell you you'd better wear your ship clothes for disembarking," she said. "He doesn't want you looking like an Elnakti, any more than you have to."

"Why shouldn't I look like an Elnakti? That's what I am."

"The router came on to give us our clearance," she explained. "When my father gave his last port of call as Elnakt, the router said, 'Are you bringing another load of Elnakti refugees? We'll have to refuse clearance, we can't accept any more.' So my father said no, he wasn't bringing a load of refugees, because one person isn't a load, you see." She grinned cheerfully. "But you'd better wear your ship gear for landing—I brought it—and here's a belt and pouch. Also here's a crew bag, you can pack your other things in this and take it with you."

Tadko looked with disfavor at the crew clothes he had worn on shipboard.

"Will I look like a Monnan in those?" he asked dubiously.

Jerely laughed out loud. "None of us could look like a Monnan! No, we hope these will make you look like a nondescript human who might have come off any ship, from anywhere. What you want is to look as inconspicuous as possible. You can put these on after landing—you won't have time now—then come up to the control room. You'll hear the signals—ah, there's the first warning."

The buzzer sounded through the ship and she was out the door, flinging herself up toward command level. Tadko closed everything into a locker to secure for landing, then strapped himself in to wait again.

Landing procedures dragged on much longer than he expected, but at last the bell sounded; he could get up. He joined Master Jaong and his family in the control room, dressed according to Jerely's instructions. His Elnakti jacket, breeches and boots, and the undersuit of smoothweave, were rolled and packed in the bag.

Jaong looked him over as Jerely had, and nodded approvingly. "You'll do, younker."

Tadko smiled at being called "younker." True, he was young enough to be Jaong's son, but he was 18 in Elnakti years, or 17 in standard years, after all. A man, at home.

"By the way," Jaong continued, "do you have any squares on you?"

Tadko looked blank. "Squares?"

Jaong fished in a pocket and pulled out a handful of squares, some large and black, some small and silvery, each covered with a complicated tracery of fine gold lines.

Then Tadko remembered one of his mother's lessons—he was small, then, just about old enough for his first shearing feast—and she, too, had held out a handful of squares like these. She explained their use, and told him, reminding him from time to time since, that he must be sure to take them if he ever went to Monna. He sighed.

"That would be Monnan money. No, I don't have any. My—my family had some, but there wasn't time to get it before I left."

Jaong shook his head. "You'll not get far without it. Not anywhere, I think. I, ah, hmm." He sniffed, rubbed his chin, and looked faintly embarrassed. "You'd better take these."

He clapped the squares into Tadko's hand, closed the young man's fist around them, and turned away to the port. Tadko looked at the squares in his hand. For a moment he was about to refuse them, unwilling to accept Jaong's charity beyond the passage on the *Werauer*. Then he remembered his mother telling him that he would be helpless on Monna without money. Jaong, for all his short manner, was a kind man.

Tadko put the money in his pouch. "Thank you, Master Jaong. I don't know that I'll ever be able to repay your kindness, but if I can, I will."

Jaong sniffed again. Elnakti promises had weight to them. "Never mind. All of your stories have entertained us. Think of it as wages, younker. You've made yourself useful. There! See the towers over there, with the smaller shaft beside them?"

Tadko went to the port, his eyes following Jaong's pointing finger. Then he found himself gaping, incredulous, at the sight of those towers, built on the top of an extinct volcano. They seemed to dwarf even the ship; on Elnakt, the ship had loomed big against the sky.

"Is that the terminal center?" He asked a bit shakily.

"So it is. Now they'll extend a tube from the side shaft, and we'll disembark that way. In the shaft we'll get on a lift platform that will lower us down to the crews' quarters. But on the way down, we'll pass ramp entries for the passenger areas. You jump off onto one of those. Once you get into the passenger concourse, you'll want the shuttle to the city center. You can use a comline from there, to call your father. Can you remember all that?"

"Could I call from the spaceport?"

"They'll charge you there. At the shuttle landing, in the City, you can call for nothing to anywhere on planet."

Tadko nodded and repeated the instructions word for word. He came from a culture that prized a good memory, and said so.

"Don't show off that talent too much," Jaong counseled. "Because if anyone wants to know what ship you arrived on, you must tell them you've forgotten." Jaong shook his head. "They'd find out soon enough if they wanted to, but as long as you keep away from the greens and keep your mouth mostly shut, you should be all right."

"Greens?"

"They're the law. Not bad sorts if you're not a lawbreaker, but if you are, they're not pleasant. Your father can fix things up about your entry, but until you're with him, be careful to stay out of their way. If you don't have a landing permit on you, you be in bad trouble."

Tadko nodded again. He straightened himself up, telling himself that, after all, he was Tadko Darusko, Mosor of Daruskan, a chieftain of Elnakt, and therefore a person of no mean consequence. The shakiness remained, however. He tried to ignore it, watching the tube slowly extend from the terminal building. It locked on with a clang, the airlock opened, and then they were all jostling along the tube. Jaong's crew—mostly members of his family—chattered loudly, discussing plans for their stay on Monna, goods they hoped to pick up for private sale, the probable profit from their cargo of Elnakti timber.

Tadko went with them silently. As the lift platform lowered them inside the terminal shaft, he watched the various openings closely, trying to conceal his nervousness.

"There!" said Jaong, pointing.

Tadko gripped his bag and leaped, staggered slightly but managed to keep his balance, and found himself riding a moving beltway that took him down at a slant into another section.

"Good luck, Tadko!" He heard Jerely call, and then Jaong and his family had disappeared behind him. Walls fell away on each side of the beltway, and there was nothing but a handrail between him and a long fall.

He clutched it tightly, braced his feet, and spiraled downward. The beltway curved past dormitory levels, with rows and rows of bunks stacked up in tens; signs along the beltway announced "For The Use Of Passengers In Transit." Smaller signs directed one to sanitary facilities for a bewildering variety of species, plus showers, tubs, and semibaths—whatever they might be. Other levels were walled off from the beltway except for luxuriously carpeted foyers; here the signs said, "First Class Accommodations Only; Please Display Ticket."

Another level was one vast restaurant; still another was devoted entirely to business transactions. Here luminous signs hung unsupported in the air, designating various areas as "Banking," "Offworld Currency Exchange," "Out Stars Freightage," or "Transtellar Communications Center."

People stepped on and off the beltway at all levels, a few managing it with a jump and a grab as he had done, but most of them making the transition with an ease and indifference that suggested long experience. He had a few moments of dreadful uncertainty when he noticed that the handrail he gripped disappeared briefly each time this happened, reappearing after the living body had passed out of the way. Yet it felt solid enough in his hand, and after he passed the first few levels he realized it would stay solid for him, as long as he stayed in place and held it. Nevertheless, he was glad enough to jump off at the end, on the floor of the concourse.

For a while he simply wandered around, aimlessly, gawking. He had lost count of the many floors above, and yet the ceiling of the first level was so high he would not have been surprised to see clouds caught in its height. Instead there were luggage floats, rising and falling, darting here and there, the luggage handlers seated on an edge with legs dangling as they maneuvered.

Spiral beltways like the one he had just used were spaced at regular intervals, carrying a continuous stream of people up and down. More luminous signs hung in the air, and announcements belled out of communicator nodes. Everywhere was noise, as thousands of people drifted, hastened, sauntered, gathered in eddies around a booth or kiosk, lined up at the great computer banks of the ticket rotundas, separated, crowded together again. Jaong's crew had told him that tourists came to Monna from half the galaxy, and now he believed it.

Most of the people he saw were human, from various worlds in the local group—Eilonsaders, Dorrans, F'thisk'k'zow—though their appearances showed great contrasts. He saw four men wearing only black kilts and boots, their skins bright scarlet, yellow hair standing straight up on their heads like crests. Was it dye, or their natural skin color? A couple passed by, followed by at least twelve children. All of them were bald, with blue-gray skins, prominent goggling eyes, ears reduced to tiny nubbins. All were dressed alike in form-fitting yellow coveralls. Parents and children both were almost as broad as they were tall, but the breadth appeared to be muscle and bone rather than fat. He had heard of high-gravity worlds and decided that this family must come from such a one. He stared with a mixture of pity and revulsion, wondering how his own people could ever have thought the Rhionny were alien, until the adults swiveled their bullet heads on nearly neckless shoulders and returned his stare balefully. Embarrassed, he turned and walked off briskly into the crowd. According to his lessons, all these were human—as were the Elnakti and Monnans—all descended from some (possibly mythical) single planet of origin.

He came to another stop at the sight of genuine non-humans. These two were just a few feet away, buying drinks at an automatic dispenser. They were half again as tall as himself, each standing on four thin stiltlike legs. Their long arms were articulated in two places, swinging forward and back with equal facility. Their torsos were draped in multicolored feathers; he could not tell if this was clothing or their natural integument. Their heads were triangular, vaguely insectoid.

The two had obtained globes of colorless liquid from the dispenser, which they proceeded to suck up noisily. Presently they were joined by a biped creature resplendent in bronze scales and crest, wearing a complicated arrangement of silver straps and tabs.

Tadko realized that he was thirsty, too. He approached the dispenser. All in transparent containers, it displayed liquids both colored and clear, some small pink ovoids that might be fruit, a grainy-looking black substance, pale green finger-sized nubbins, and stacks of red and white wafers that really looked appetizing. But the names on the various cells meant nothing to him and he moved on, deciding he had better make use of a dispenser patronized by Monnans.

The native Monnans certainly were the vast majority in the crowd. They were slender, graceful, and tall, with fine-grained, ebony skin, short black curls, and violet eyes. Men and women both wore elaborate sandals, and loose trousers and smocks in a multitude of bright colors. Soft pouches hung at their sides, suspended from ornamental belts. A handsome people indeed, with a poise, an easy elegance of manner, that made Tadko feel lumpish and stupid, a clod. In comparison, Tadko was short, stocky, with straight brown hair and brown skin.

As he walked through the building, he watched for other Elnakti, certain he could pick them out even in this crowd, but saw none. Jerely had told him they would have come in four or five days ago, but where were they now? Their absence worried him.

He found his way to another dispenser—a wide, squat column around which a good many Monnans stood sipping drinks. It took an effort to make himself pass through them, but he caught their attention for only a moment, and then they turned back to their own affairs. He watched, sidelong, while several of them operated the dispenser, noting how it worked and which drinks they received. Then he fished a silvery square from his own pouch, dropped it in the slot, and punched for a brown beverage in a tall container.

The liquid proved to be a mild, cool beer, and he drank it with pleasure, resting his bag of clothing on the floor at his feet. It came to him, watching the activity of this spaceport, that being Mosor of Daruskan meant little or nothing, here on Monna. He might as well be the 'nondescript' Jerely had spoken of, who could have arrived on any ship, from anywhere. Just another tourist, come to see the sights on a tourist planet. He finished his beer, pushed the container into the disposal slot as he had seen others do, hoisted his bag on his shoulder, and moved off, somberly, to look for an information booth.

He found one near a beltway descent, and presented himself in what he hoped was a confident manner.

"Shuttle to the city center?" He asked hopefully.

The young woman nodded, flicking an experienced eye over Tadko's clothing and features.

"Shuttle to Monna the City leaves every hour, Portal Twelve. Do you have a ticket?"

"No."

She turned to a machine and pulled levers. "One ticket to the City—that'll be six zinae."

Tadko dug six of the silvery zinae from his pouch, inwardly blessing Master Jaong's kindness.

"Right enough," said the young woman, accepting them. "You just arrived on Monna?"

"Uh, yes."

"All right, that's where you'll wait for the shuttle," and she leaned out of her booth and pointed. "Follow the black arrow to the portal and wait right there, don't let anyone push you out of line."

Tadko muttered his thanks and took his ticket. The young woman reached below her counter, brought up a black arrow made of smooth, faintly luminous material, touched it to a lens on her comp board, and set it in the air. It floated off through the terminal, an astonished Tadko hurrying behind it.

At the portal, the arrow disappeared into an opening beside the ticket window, and Tadko joined the line boarding the shuttle.

CHAPTER TWO

He looked out curiously as the shuttle left the terminal area. The cluster of dead volcanoes was left behind, and the land spread out. They flew over fields in every possible shade of green, low rambling hills, a slow river that merged in the distance into an arm of the sea. Everywhere were villages, clusters of buildings, smaller shuttle landings, a network of roads, the signs of human activity. It was too crowded, too cramped. Tadko thought longingly of the empty open plain of Elnakt. The air in the shuttle was hot. The sun Seleme blazed down unmercifully. He found himself sweating heavily, blinking and squinting in the sharp white light. He was glad, after all, for the lightweight ship clothing.

The houses along the roads began to huddle more closely together. The buildings were larger. Then there was no open space at all, and they were heading toward a cluster of towers again, the center of Monna the City. The shuttle landed on the flat top of one of these towers. Tadko followed the other passengers into a domed receiving room, smaller than the spaceport concourse, but still vast to his eyes. There were the same information booths, food dispensers, and other facilities. People wandered from place to place, looked out of the enclosing glass walls, and sat or slept on wide padded benches.

Along one wall were the comlines. He watched several people use them until he was fairly sure he had the way of it; then he moved in front of one, stepping forward until a ready light glowed.

"Your party, please?" said a light, metallic voice.

"Scholar Osrin Havard, historical and ethnic studies, College of Seleme Central," Tadko announced, somewhat more loudly than he had planned.

There was a bleeping sound, a click, then a different metallic voice.

"*Senior* scholar Havard is not presently in residence," it said, emphasizing the additional title. "He is on extended leave to the research center on Eilonsad. He will be returning on 8th Perian, Seleme Standard. Sub-space calls may be placed at the central terminal office, minimum charge one hundred duats. Will there be any further service, please?"

Tadko said nothing. The voice repeated, "Will there be any further service, please?"

"No, no further service," Tadko mumbled. "Nothing."

He moved away, and the eye-cell darkened. What now?

Many times he had wondered if he were doing the right thing in looking for his father, even though his mother's last words had urged him to do so. He had wondered if the man would even remember him and his mother; if he would want to have anything to do with Tadko, even supposing he *did* remember; but to arrive and find the man elsewhere—this he had never considered. Eighth Perian, he thought, and began working out how long he had to wait. He visualized an old Monnan calendar, hanging on the wall of his schoolroom, at the Daruskan steading. His mother had made him memorize it...but what was the date today? Surely that was a question any newcomer might ask. He went to one of the information booths.

"What is today's date?"

"Third Koried." The young man at the booth didn't even look up.

He pictured that calendar again and managed to figure it out—eighty days, give or take a few. Somehow he would have to find a way to live. He returned to the information booth.

"Is it possible to find employment on Monna?"

The young man seemed to wake up; he gave Tadko the same sort of appraising glance as the woman at the spaceport.

"Right enough, casual labor, you want the transient employment service." He dug into a pile of papers at the back of his booth and brought out a small map. "See, here we are on Seleme Way, this is our building. Take one of those lifts to street level—" He pointed. "—and go down *this* way, to the park. The service building is on the other side. Show them your entry permit, and they'll give you a work permit, and find you something."

"Thanks. Uh, thanks very much."

Tadko took the small city map and turned to the lifts. What else could he do? He thought he had better go down to street level, just as the young man said. It might look suspicious if he stayed on, after being given the information he asked for. But he had no entry permit. There was no use trying to find work. Once on the street he moved along in the direction of the park, for lack of anything else to do. Outside the building, the air was hot and moist again. Tadko had to slow his pace, as any exertion made him sweat.

The broad walkway was dark green, smooth, resilient under foot. The city glittered. It was made mostly of glass and plastic, with great blocks and columns of color, long transparent panels, occasional accenting curves of bright metal. Floaters moved through the air, around the buildings, under high arches, over the enclosed passages suspended between the towers. Ground cars hummed along the surface roads. All around him was a continuous blur of sound.

He thought of Daruskan and all the other steadings, built of stone and turf, half sunk into the rocky hills that projected above the long flat plain. The tall grasses, gray and brown, rippling in the wind, the purple bloom of the halm, under a gentler, dull orange sun. The great herds of oncas moving, grazing, through the cool, quiet days. Daruskan and its neighbors were the easternmost steadings. Past them the Ice River ran south, with the mountains rising sharply just beyond. Far more beautiful to him than all this color, noise and brilliance. As for the heat here on Monna—he wiped his sweating face on his sleeve and shook his head. *This is the wrong world for Elnakti*, he thought. *Mother did right, bringing us home.*

He turned a corner and discovered the park. An expanse of green, dotted with trees, beds of scarlet and yellow flowers, pools and fountains. The walkway narrowed, to become a winding path through the greenery. It was overly garish and bright, but still more grateful to the eye than its surroundings.

He could sit here for a while on one of the benches and think...odors of cooking food drifted through the air. His stomach growled in response. He hadn't eaten since the ship. The smells were not entirely appetizing, but he followed them into a small central plaza where people were buying food from a cart. In between sales the cart proprietor chanted, "Prime squelt and sauce, one zina; cold beer, two zinae; cold fizz, one zina; step right up and buy, siro, sira!"

Tadko took two zinae from his pouch and bought some squelt and a fizz. He was given a container of fizz plus a round of hard bread, scooped out and filled with—something. A bulb of sauce perched on top. He carried them to an isolated bench, preferring to try the strange food in privacy. This proved to be a wise thought. The fizz was delicious, an effervescent fruit juice poured over lots of ice. Very refreshing. The bread was quite good. The squelt was bad, tasting mostly of salt and fish. He doused it with sauce, which seared the inside of his mouth and made both eyes and nose stream while he choked. He had to dig into his bag for a cloth to mop his face and blow his nose, but he finally got the stuff down. Afterward he finished all the ice from the fizz.

He did feel better after the meal, when his eyes stopped watering, and he sat, chewing the last of the ice, pondering the next eighty-three days. The flavor of the sauce was tasty, aside from its heat. Used cautiously, it should make the squelt at least edible. Master Jaong had given him six black duats, besides the zinae he had now spent. According to his mother, one duat was worth thirty zinae. He shuddered at the thought of eating this squelt every day for the next eighty or more, but he supposed he would get used to it, and maybe he could find other cheap things to eat as he learned his way around the city. The grass right here in the park was as good a place to sleep as any. He knew there were public baths throughout the city; he would find the nearest, and use it to keep himself clean.

There was nothing he could find to eat that was as cheap as squelt. But on the sixth day he was unable to face another serving of it. He had stuck to his plan for five days, using the small map from the shuttle landing to find his way round nearby city streets.

Now, on the sixth day, he expanded his search and discovered a whole row of food carts. He splurged, feeling guilty, on a plate of fried reedfish and some fruit on a stick. It was indescribably delicious, after the squelt, but cost seven zinae. Back to the squelt.

On the eighth morning he was wakened by hard prods in his ribs.

"What's this? What's this? What are you doing, young man? You can't do this!"

Tadko sat up groggily, opened his eyes. Bending over him was an old man he had seen in the park before, apparently a functionary of some kind. His plain blue suit bore a distant resemblance to the uniform of the greens.

"I was only sleeping."

"But you can't do that here! Not allowed! You'll have to move along, move along! Don't do this again!"

Tadko stood, smoothed out his clothes as well as he could, and picked up his bag, while the old man made shooing motions with his bony hands.

"I'll be watching you, young man! Don't do this again!"

Tadko moved off with what dignity he could summon, thankful at least that the old man hadn't called for the greens. He had seen the green-clad lawmen, moving through the park, moving along the city streets. He had kept his distance. He wasn't the only offworlder among the crowds of Monnans, and he hoped that as long as he walked briskly, as if he had somewhere to go, he would be overlooked, especially among the tall Monnans.

The morning was cloudy, and soon it began to rain. Tadko took shelter for a while in one of the many arcades that penetrated the great buildings. Afterward the air was cooler for a while. The Monnans around him were shivering, but Tadko raised his head and breathed deeply, enjoying the freshness.

He left the arcade and walked on through the bright streets, wondering where to spend the night. He thought of the shuttle landing. The benches and chairs had looked comfortable, and some people there were sleeping when he came in. Nowhere to eat but the park, however. There were other cheap places, but nothing else that cheap. He made a wide circuit that day, into unfamiliar places. Colorful shops walled with lighted panels sold jewelry, elaborate clothing in a bewildering variety of styles, musical instruments, books, viewtapes, statuary, holograph pictures, exotic pets from offworld, machines and appliances whose use was totally unknown to him.

Tired and discouraged, he returned to the park for his evening portion of squelt. The old functionary was there, watching him closely. Tadko ate, pretending to ignore the old man's scrutiny, and left. At the shuttle building he rode to the top, finding the place just as it was when he arrived. The people coming, going, waiting. Two shuttles landing, another taking off, three plats empty, with luminous signs announcing future schedules. He looked around for the young man who had given him information on the first day, and was relieved to note his absence. Even so, he carefully chose a bench against a far wall, away from the booth the young man had occupied. Someone had left a printout news bulletin; he picked it up and tried to read, setting his bag beside him to help give the impression of a traveler on business.

Sunset, then night. Lights were turned on under the dome. There was a bustle as two more shuttles came in. Then, gradually, the pace of activity slowed. Tadko made use of the restroom, then moved to another bench, also well out of the main line of traffic. Some booths closed. A few remained open, with sleepy newcomers replacing the original staff. Now the lights were dimmed, and yes, some people were curling up on their benches to sleep. Tadko did the same.

Tadko didn't sleep as well as he had in the park. A few shuttles came and went during the night; each time he half-woke. Long before dawn the lights were turned up, and five shuttles arrived all at once. Debarking passengers streamed toward the lifts, and crowds of noisy people were jostling into line for boarding. Tadko sat up and watched for a while. Sometime in his half-waking state an idea had struck him, and now he rose and went to the bank of comlines. When the metallic voice answered, he asked, "Can a person find out about freighter arrivals and departures, at the spaceport?"

"A moment, please." A distant humming sound.

"Spaceport information here."

"I'd like to find out if a freighter is still in port."

"Name and point of origin?"

"*Werauer*, out of Eilonsad."

More humming, various bleeps and clicks.

"*Werauer* out of Eilonsad departed at 0836 hours on 6th Koried, next scheduled port, Innestan, on Dorra. Will there be any further service, please?"

"No—uh, yes. Is it possible to buy passage to Elnakt, and how much does it cost?"

A much longer pause this time.

"There is no passenger service to Elnakt," the voice said finally. "Passage may sometimes be available on freighters, cost between three hundred and five hundred duats. Do you wish us to check the freighter schedules?"

"No. That will be all—no further service."

He went back to his bench and sat down, his half-formed plan to give up and go back to Elnakt dead a-borning. Master Jaong might have taken him out of kindness, the next time Elnakt was on his route—but no telling when that might be. Elnakt was not a world the ships visited often. Only in midsummer for trading, or when a load of timber was wanted. He was tempted to go up to one of the greens and explain his situation. Only, he had no proof that he was Osrin Havard's son, or of his own Monnan birth.

He thought of Master Jaong's warning, and decided it was better not.

Time to go out to the park cart for a meal, but he lingered at the shuttle landing. It was cooler here. The five shuttles had left, and it was probably too early for the park; he might as well stay here, continuing his pretense of being a waiting passenger.

He wondered where the rest of his people were, here on Monna. In all his wanderings around the city he had seen no Elnakti. If their arrival had caused something of a stir, then it ought to be possible to find out, in the course of a casual conversation, where they had gone...he looked around thoughtfully, considering how to open such a conversation, trying to find someone approachable.

One young man caught his eye. About Tadko's own age, this young man was splendidly dressed in clothes of dark vermilion, his smock slashed at the sides with cerise inserts, his collar embroidered in gold. His pouch, belt and sandals were russet-colored leather. His small luggage case, finished in silver with black clasps, sat beside him. No, it wouldn't do. Too wealthy. Yet his round, handsome face, wide eyes, and expression of innocent ingenuousness made one want to trust him.

Tadko was debating over whether or not to do so, when a stir at the lifts caught his attention. Four greens came in, husky men with hard, alert faces. Two remained by the lifts and the other two began moving among the waiting people. Their voices carried clearly through the half-empty concourse, and Tadko heard, with horror, what they were asking.

"Where are you bound? What shuttle are you waiting for? Let's see your ticket."

The answers were usually indistinguishable, but the questions alone were enough to make Tadko turn panicky, not least because he was not quite sure what he had to fear. His impulse to confide in one of these men shriveled and disappeared. He glared around desperately, then sat still, trying to decide what to do.

Beyond him the young man in dark vermilion looked up casually from the bulletin he was reading, glanced mildly at the greens, and yawned. His gaze wandered indifferently around, over greens and other waiting passengers alike, and his eyes met Tadko's. For a moment they were fully aware of each other, and there was understanding in the young man's face. Then the young man turned away, stood up easily, and stretched. Carrying his case, he strolled over to a news kiosk, examined its offerings, looked around again sleepily, walked back to the benches in a different direction, and, as if by accident, dropped down beside Tadko. He lounged back in an easy position and said softly, "No ticket?" His lips hardly moved.

"No!" Tadko whispered. "What will they do?"

"Nothing, if I can work this," the young man murmured. "Lie down, pretend to be asleep, and let me talk. Don't move until I say so."

Tadko obeyed, thoroughly bewildered at this unexpected help, but very willing to accept it. He tucked his bag under the bench and stretched out with his arms around his head, doing his best to appear relaxed, as in sleep.

Time passed. Tadko began to hope he might be overlooked, but eventually the voices drew nearer, and he heard the men's footsteps.

"All right, what's this one doing here? where's he from?"

"He arrived last night, officer, from Kamerey. I talked with him earlier." The young man's voice was light, pleasant. Now he had a subtly affected accent. "He said he was waiting for the Polar shuttle, later this morning."

"The Polar Shuttle? Where's he bound on that?"

"Right to the pole, or so I understand. He told me he had signed for a contract in the mines—an offworlder, you know. I believe he has his ticket somewhere in that gray bag."

"A volunteer slot? More fool he. Ah, well, no use waking him, I suppose." Now the voice was distinctly deferential. "And yourself, siro? Not waiting for the Polar shuttle, I take it?"

The young man laughed. "Hardly, officer. Let me see.... Yes, the shuttle to Oceanside will be leaving at 0700."

"Good enough, siro, and thanks for your help."

The steps moved away. Tadko continued to lie quietly, for what seemed like a long time. The officer's voices dwindled and presently were heard no more. At last the young man said softly, "Stretch and yawn, pretend to wake up slowly. Don't look around."

Tadko did his best to act the part of a man newly awakened. He turned and looked at his rescuer, and the two of them examined each other briefly.

"What are you doing here without any ticket?" the young man asked.

Tadko saw no reason not to trust him.

"I came in eight days ago on—a little inter-system freighter. I was looking for my father, he's a senior scholar at the college, but he turned out to be offplanet. I have to get along until he comes back, on 8th Perian. I thought I could sleep here...I don't have much money."

"Why don't you go to the college anyway, tell them who you are?"

"I haven't any proof. It's been a long time."

"Ah." The young man nodded wisely. "Got an entry permit?"

"No."

The young man whistled. "You're lucky I was here. You'd have gone to the mines for sure."

"Why did you help me?" Tadko asked.

The young man grinned.

"I've no ticket either. It's a matter of sleight of mind. I vouched for you having a ticket, and they overlook that they haven't actually seen my ticket. Especially if you talk to them in that top-caste bleat. Wouldn't work if they had the scan out for someone special, but this was just a number one run, picking up casuals. Even so," he added, "they'll be back later to see if everyone has left when they were supposed to."

Tadko sighed wearily.

"I've nowhere to go."

The young man frowned a bit, then shrugged.

"You helped me pass off the grab. You can come along and stretch with me, tonight anyhow."

He cast another of his deceptively indifferent glances around the concourse. "Come along," he repeated, rising to his feet and picking up his case. "By the way, my name's Dacy Wile."

"Tadko Darusko," said Tadko. He hoisted his bag to his shoulder and followed Dacy into a public restroom. At the moment, it was empty. Dacy moved to a white wall panel, flicked a tiny instrument out of his sleeve, and applied it to a seam at one edge. The panel slid aside to reveal a small chamber. Dacy nipped inside, motioning to Tadko to follow. When the panel slid closed again there was a very slight sensation of motion. Tadko opened his mouth to ask a question, but Dacy shook his head urgently, gesturing around at the walls and ceiling. Tadko desisted, then watched in amazement as Dacy stripped off his elegant smock to reveal a lining patterned in yellow and white. He put it back on with the lining outside, then repeated the process with his breeches, managing very smoothly in spite of the cramped chamber. From a pocket he took a small bundle which opened into a gray bag not unlike the one Tadko carried, and his handsome luggage case went into this.

Tadko was still goggling at this transformation when the faintest of clicks broke the silence. Dacy pressed his hands on the panel, slid it aside. He stepped out, and Tadko followed into a cavernous area, lit only by glow-strips far above their heads. Boxes and bales loomed dimly, piled in rows far back into the shadows. Several ground cars were lined up in a row nearby. Off to his left he could see platforms raised at various levels above the ground, and heavy chains hanging from somewhere overhead.

"Where is this?" he whispered.

"Service and maintenance. They'll be starting work soon." Dacy jerked his thumb to the right and started off in that direction. They passed through the dimness, along a row of doors gleaming faintly, into a corner, and out through an unlighted door, into the Monnan dawn. Dacy looked around with an air of great satisfaction.

"Very sleek," he said. "I could work some of the hostels, I suppose, but I pulled a fair haul already tonight, might as well stash it now. We can take the trotline—do you have a couple of zinae?"

Tadko dug two of the silver zinae out of his pouch. At the corner of the street was a pillar box for the public transport in the city. Tadko had not used them, although they were everywhere along the streets; little two-person cars, each rolling on a single wheel in a depressed slot. He dropped his two zinae into the pillar, and presently one of the little cars appeared. It stopped at their corner and the doors sprang open. Dacy climbed in briskly, motioning Tadko into the other seat. When the doors closed, he spoke into a mesh at the side.

"Old Harbor."

The car rolled off, swaying slightly as it rolled. At first Tadko gripped the side. He could scarcely believe that the things would stay upright, balanced on a single wheel, as often as he had seen them; but presently he grew used to the motion, and relaxed.

Since they were alone, Tadko decided it surely must be safe to talk.

"What were you doing at the shuttle landing without a ticket?"

"Snaffling," Dacy said, grinning. At Tadko's look of bewilderment, he performed a set of rapid gestures, eloquently illustrating the slitting and rifling of a Monnan money pouch.

"You're a thief!" Tadko clutched at his own pouch, then bit his lip. Thieving on Elnakt was a terrible crime. He had never known it to happen. He felt himself shrink from Dacy, yet the young man had helped him out of a very bad situation.

But Dacy was beaming, as if he considered himself highly complimented.

"Right enough, and a fast dip, too. Do a little lifting also, some passing and such, but mostly snaffling. Nothing to get me into the mines if they do give me the grab."

"The mines," Tadko repeated, distracted from the question of thievery. "That's another thing. You said they would send me to the mines if they picked me up without a permit, but you told the greens I had signed up for the mines as a volunteer—how can that be?"

Dacy shrugged. "Simple enough. They can't send citizens to the mines except for violent crimes, so they pick up any no-permit offworlders and send them; but it still isn't enough, so they pay high wages to anyone willing to go and work voluntarily, and they get offworlders who come in on a permit just for that. But it isn't worth it," he added. "If the prisoners don't get you, the fumes will. Not many live to throw their squares around."

Tadko shuddered. "I'll try to keep out of the mines, then. But is there any way I can get a permit to do some decent kind of work?"

"There's a way—but it takes plenty of duats."

He said no more, and Tadko refrained from pressing for details. It seemed clear enough that the way would be illegal, and in any case he hadn't the necessary duats. Unless, of course, he took up snaffling, like Dacy. He turned the idea over in his mind for a while, then put it aside, knowing he would never have the nerve even if he could bring himself to ignore the dishonesty.

Few people were on the streets at this time. They rolled across a bridge above a long, narrow channel, with hovercraft moving along the water, each one still outlined in light. Riding lamps blinked from hundreds of smaller craft docked along the shores. The salt, iodine smell of the ocean, always present in the city, stung his nostrils here.

The lights were blinking out as they left the bridge and moved into an area of lower buildings, narrower streets. They passed through a district of small shops and street carts, just setting up for business. Here they came to a halt. Dacy pushed open the door and they jumped out.

"This way," he said. At a building in the middle of the block he pressed his hand flat against a luminous plate beside the door. It slid open slowly and Dacy led the way up a stair, into what he referred to as his "stretch." This was a fairly large oblong room with a window and ventilator overlooking the street.

The furnishings were sparse, but there were many drawers and recesses in the walls, a large holoscreen opposite the window, and a comline outlet in one corner. Dacy opened one of the wall bins, and closed his case up in this.

"Sit down," he told Tadko, waving his hand in a lordly gesture. "I'll find us something to chew." He took off his smock and hung it on a hook.

Tadko was glad to do the same, then drop into a low chair.

"Is it always this hot in the city?"

Dacy opened his eyes wide.

"Do you really think this is hot?" he inquired innocently. "This is mid-winter. Wait until the summer comes, when the sea boils up and they catch the squelt ready cooked!"

At the Tadko's horrified look Dacy threw back his head to laugh heartily.

Tadko managed a smile. "You should try my home. It's so cold we let ourselves freeze up in the fall, and wait to thaw out again in the spring."

It wasn't very good, but he had the satisfaction of seeing Dacy look startled for a second, before he grinned knowingly and turned to pull a cookshelf out of a wall slot.

Very shortly a now-familiar smell filled the air. Mound of cooked squelt, crispbread, bowl of cold pickled vegetables—it was much like the meals from the park cart, but when he tasted the squelt he realized the flavor of this was a great deal better. He said as much to Dacy.

"Why, where have you been eating?"

Tadko explained about the park cart.

"No wonder! They use scrapings in those places. This isn't top grade, of course, but it's better than you get at the carts."

Tadko had no idea what scrapings might be, but decided he would rather not know. When Dacy poured two tall mugs of cold fizz, he took a long swallow and leaned back in his chair, feeling truly relaxed for the first time since his arrival on Monna.

"There's something else I don't understand," he remarked, watching the bubbles rise gently in his mug. "We've always sold some Elnakti products to Monna—not as many as to Dorra, of course—but still some—leather, fleeces, smoothweave cloth, even some made clothes—and I thought I could sell the clothes I brought from Elnakt, if I could find a buyer. But it's so hot here, and they told me on the ship it's hot all over. Why ever would anyone on Monna want to buy clothes from Elnakt?"

"They were funning you," said Dacy with his grin. "Besides, ship people, not getting much away from City Island, might think that. It's colder at the poles, though *you* might not think so. There are resorts there, not in the mine areas, and resorts on Dorra too. It's the sort of thing the rich and the top castes go to, and they would buy Elnakti clothes, for show, you see. You're from Elnakt, then? How is it you didn't come in with the others? Some reason you had to wait and slide out quiet?"

At that Tadko sat up and leaned forward eagerly.

"You know about the others? where are they? I haven't seen another Elnakti anywhere in the city—where did they go?"

"Well, it was all on the news." Dacy gestured at the holoscreen. "They were all coming in on trading ships. There was a big storm about it, the Eleven arguing; some said one thing, some said another. I didn't pay much attention, but I know they ended up sending them to Sancy Island, that's on the other side of the world somewhere. I suppose they're still there."

Tadko was filled with a sudden hope. His own people, on Sancy island. If he could get there they would conceal him for as long as necessary, this he knew.

"How much would it cost to get to Sancy?"

"Couldn't tell. You'd have to call Transport Central, to find out."

Tadko's eyes turned immediately to the comline, but Dacy shook his head.

"Better call from a public outlet, just in case—can't be traced."

"All right." Tadko jerked a thumb at his bag. "Could I sell my clothes somewhere, then? I've been dragging them around ever since I arrived."

"Maybe. Let's have a scan."

Tadko considered. Yarron had given him a fairly decent outfit of supplies when he escaped from Daruskan, but he had taken very little of it on the ship. A good knife, some ends of cloth and cordage, a fire lighter, the clothes on his back—and three gold trade rings. These were tucked into his jacket lining. Should he show them to Dacy? He didn't want to. The young man seemed kind, but he *was* a thief. It might be necessary later, but for now he would say nothing. He did pull the clothes out, and spread them on the floor.

"Hum," said Dacy. He held up the clothes, felt their texture, turned the jacket part way out. Tadko held his breath, but Dacy was only inspecting the armholes for wear.

"Not bad," he said finally. "I'm taking my stuff to a passer today, and I think he'll pay for goods like this too. I can take them along with me when I go."

Tadko repacked his clothes, not too happy about the arrangement, but unable to think of a tactful refusal. He would have to slip the rings out somehow, conceal them in the bottom of his bag.

Dacy was slicing a melon to finish the meal.

"Why'd all you people come to Monna anyhow?" he asked. "Something happen there?"

It seemed incredible that this knowing young man should have learned nothing of the greatest upheaval on Elnakt in all its history. No doubt it had all been on the holonews, but Dacy, as he said, didn't pay much attention—it was no concern of his.

At first Tadko spoke slowly, marshaling his thoughts as he went along, but presently he found himself telling the whole story. How the Rhionny, those aboriginals of Elnakt long thought to be nearly extinct, had come down out of the mountains—those mountains his own people had never explored—to attack the Elnakti steadings. He told about the fighting all along the river lands, the overwhelming of Daruskan, and his own flight westward.

"Most of the trading ships had gone before I came to Port Town," he explained. "That's where the spaceships come, in the middle of the plain. The town was deserted, and so were the central steadings I passed. There was one ship left, they had come up from south continent, and they brought me to Monna."

Dacy was looking at him with an odd expression. The indulgent condescension was replaced by something almost respectful.

"You've fought in real battles? Killed men?"

"Yes." Tadko said briefly. He didn't intend to explain his very mixed feelings about that killing, still less why he had such feelings. He had said nothing about Yarron.

Dacy said thoughtfully, "We haven't had any wars on Monna for centuries, maybe more. There was one where some of our people tried to settle on Dorra, I think, we had to learn it in basic education, but I didn't pay much attention."

"We didn't expect this one," Tadko said.

"Hum," Dacy said, "I'll put up what I'm taking to the passer."

He opened the bin where he had stored his case, and began sorting the contents of both case and bin. Tadko watched in fascination. Dacy pulled a much larger bag from another bin, and packed his loot carefully in this. He finished, picked up the bag, and said casually, "You might as well come along, bring your own things."

"Right enough." said Tadko.

CHAPTER THREE

They took the trotline back across the bay, then east along the shore, to another district new to Tadko. Here the tang of salt and chemicals that hung in the city air was overwhelmed by an all-pervading reek of fish. The buildings were lower, and their bright colors had a blurred, frosted look, as if they had endured years of blowing fine sand. The walkways were less resilient; the shops were smaller, and dealt in an order of merchandise entirely different from that sold in the center of the city.

Many offered the fish and other sea-stuffs that gave the air its strong aroma. Front panels were swung back to display hampers of scaled, finned, or tentacled creatures, wet from the sea; some proprietors had braziers set up at the edge of the walkway where, for a price, passersby could choose an item and have it cooked right there. Groups of people were already examining these offerings, and every transaction was an occasion for loud haggling.

Children darted by occasionally, shouting at each other, and from time to time all other noise was drowned out by the hoarse bellow of a horn, from some watercraft moving up from the harbor.

Other shops sold melons, tubers, greens, and a whole assortment of boxed and packaged foodstuffs. Many small businesses announced their wares or services by printed window signs. "Net Crews—Get Perdeco's Top Quality Gear." "Certificate Qualification—Take the Next Step Up." "Eilonsad Cookery." "Licensed Bettor—Odds on Circumsolar Race, Milian Oceans' Run." "Public Baths—All Facilities Clean and Functional."

Dacy pushed his way along with skill and confidence, Tadko following close behind. They walked for some distance, passing a more imposing, sable-blue edifice called "Crale Ocean Mandate Hiring Hall," turned down another, somewhat quieter street, and Dacy stopped before a small shop under a sign offering "Repairs and Exchanges—Purchase of Oddments." The window displayed several shelves of timepieces, writing instruments, calculators of the type he had seen used on shipboard, and a collection of other appliances, mechanisms, and instruments.

"This is Unser's," Dacy announced, and led the way inside.

A tall man came forward, cadaverously lean, bald, eyes so dark they were almost black, looking sharply out of a wrinkled face.

"Ah, Dacy," he said. "New merchandise?"

"New merchandise."

The man nodded, glanced questioningly at Tadko.

"Friend of mine," said Dacy. "He has some merchandise too, the real goods."

Unser nodded again, silently, then stepped through an open arch at the back of the shop, beckoning them to follow. A panel slid shut behind them. The inner room was cramped but brightly lit. Dacy lifted his bag on to a high table and spread out the contents for Unser's inspection. The tall man examined each one with care, finally shook his head.

The Wrong World

"All these are fairly standard items, Dacy. I can give you—let me see—six duats, five zinae."

Dacy's eyebrows lifted.

"You know I'm not fresh caught, Unser, so don't try me with a bid like that. That's all quality merchandise, and I won't take less than thirty duats."

Unser smiled condescendingly. "I'm fond of you, Dacy, therefore I won't show you the door, even for asking such a nonsensical sum." He picked up some of the timepieces and re-examined them. "I will say these are—reasonable—I could raise it to ten duats."

Dacy shook his head. "Nothing less than twenty-five." He preened himself a trifle. "There are plenty of passers would pay better than that for a steady supply, and you know it."

"I'll say twelve and six, my boy, just because I don't want you cheated elsewhere."

Dacy became heated. "You're a slyhauling old fraud who'd cheat his own brother for a split zina. Even at twenty-three I'm giving you the lot."

Tadko was beginning to wonder whether the bargaining would be broken off completely, but Unser simply called Dacy an insolent young sprat, and offered fourteen. Eventually they settled on a price of nineteen and three. Dacy pouched his money. Unser pulled a deep drawer out of the wall, packed away his purchases, and then it was Tadko's turn.

Somewhat hesitantly, he stepped up to the table. First he took his jacket out of the bag. He felt for the slit in the lining, took out the trade rings, and laid them out for Unser's inspection. Dacy's eyebrows shot up, but his expression was unreadable.

Unser picked up the rings one by one, looked them over, inserted one into the bowels of a small machine at the end of the table, and read various dials.

"Pure gold?" he said dubiously. "Where did these come from?"

"I brought them with me from Elnakt. Is there something unusual about gold?"

"Yes, I would say so. Gold with no alloy—unheard of!" Unser dug a horny fingernail into the soft metal. "Too soft, couldn't sell them for jewelry, you see. But let me see—I could give you five duats, apiece."

Tadko considered. The softness of the trade rings had been a nuisance, especially when one tried to wear them as jewelry, but he and his people had never known gold in any other form. In any case, one ring was the payment for a prime fleece, and he felt certain Unser was offering too little, but what would be a fair price? Dacy's eyebrows had shot up again, but this was hardly enough to give him any concrete ideas. Set it high, he thought, and took a deep breath.

"I want fifty each," he said aloud. "Gold is gold."

Unser looked dumbstruck. He threw back his head, his eyes opened wide, his hands waved frantically.

"Fifty each! My dear young man, you're joking! Absurd! Impossible! Quite out of the question!"

Tadko said stubbornly, "One ring buys a prime fleece, and I want fifty duats for a ring."

Unser had regained his condescending smile. "No, quite out of the question, I'm afraid. Five is the best I can do."

"I might bring it down to forty, but I want a fair price."

"Sorry, young man. Still, since you are a friend of Dacy's, I'm willing to give six and five."

Tadko tried desperately to remember Dacy's facile arguments and casual insults, but he was completely out of his depth and he knew it. He finally accepted a price of eleven and two apiece, along with a firm conviction that he was being cheated. He pouched his duats glumly, then brought out the rest of his Elnakti clothing and spread it all on the table.

Unser examined everything with interest, rubbing up the thick fleece, tracing the fine tooling along the borders, and turning over a corner to feel the soft underside of the leather. He tested the weight and softness of the undersuit of smoothweave, inspected the seaming and finish of the boots.

"Fine goods," he said at last. "Very fine, but I can't look at them. Not at all."

"Why not, if they're fine goods?" Tadko demanded angrily. "There's a market for these clothes on Monna—I know that, anyway!"

"He's right, Unser," Dacy put in. "What's all this? Give us a fair bid, and stop fogging us."

Unser shrugged largely, spread his hands wide.

"Who buys such clothing?" he inquired rhetorically. "The Crales and Concoras, and such like types. And do they buy from poor old Unser? Of course they don't. Therefore, poor old Unser can't buy from you. Very simple."

"I might as well have left them on Elnakt," Tadko said disgustedly.

A faint look of surprise flickered across Unser's face. He inquired mildly, "These are your own clothes?"

"Of course they are."

"Well, now in that case I may be able to do something." Unser turned, pulled out another drawer, rummaged through the contents. He selected a card, read it over, and turned back to Dacy and Tadko.

"I charge a flat five zinae for items of information," he said.

"If you're sending us to Herenna's, we don't need your information," Dacy said coldly.

"Ah, but you don't know the name of the necessary person at Herenna's, now do you? Otherwise, Dacy my boy, I'm sure you would have taken your friend there in the beginning. Am I correct?"

Dacy nodded grudgingly.

"Right enough, I suppose. You might as well give him the five zinae," he added to Tadko.

Tadko counted back the five zinae even more grudgingly, and took the card.

"Herenna's Fine clothery," he read aloud. "Imports. Number Six Terminal Way. Ambert Finell, Special Purchase."

"Who's Ambert Finell?" Dacy asked.

"Ah, yes, you've never heard of him, have you?" Unser remarked. "At five zinae, I've given you a bargain then. An important man, and he doesn't ask questions. Such as when and how you arrived on Monna." He cast a sardonic glance at Tadko.

Tadko said nothing. He turned away to repack his clothes in his bag once again. Had Unser guessed, somehow, that he was here without a landing permit? Would he go to the authorities?

He put the latter question to Dacy when they were back on the trotline, rolling away from Unser's.

"No fear." Dacy sounded entirely positive. "Unser has his ways but you can trust him there—besides, he wouldn't bear looking at, either."

"What about the price he gave me on those rings? He cheated me, didn't he? I can guess that much."

"Well, yes, but that's the way of it, you see. You have to do your own bargaining, and Unser's a sharp one. He'll probably flog them to some back of the hand jeweler to be alloyed and reused. Where did you get merchandise like that?"

"The traders pay us for our fleeces and things." Tadko went on musingly, half to himself, "we use them for ornaments, and sometimes to trade with each other. We also use them to pay back to the traders for goods we buy, iron pots and harness findings and such." He looked at Dacy and said flatly, "The traders have been cheating us too, haven't they."

"Sounds like it. Where does the gold come from? The big mines for gold are on F'thisk'k'zow, that I know, but no sharp trader would haul it that far. Do you do much traveling in your own system?"

"Not much." It was really not any, but Tadko refused to admit that to someone like Dacy.

"Then I'd go bond some trader combine set up an auto-refinery in your system somewhere, to put out these rings, and they pick up what they need in system. They'd have arrangements and safeguards so they couldn't cheat each other—not much, anyhow."

Tadko grimaced, his mouth twisting with a bitter taste.

He thought of himself and his grandfather and all the other Mosori of Elnakt, proud of their great onca herds, of their long traditions, of their survival on a harsh world. Paid for their goods with gold mined in their own system, and very little of it at that. It sounded wholly believable.

Dacy saw his expression and clapped him on the shoulder. "Cheer up, friend Tadko. Now you're on Monna you'll learn to hold out for good old Monnan squares. Also before we go to Heranna's, we have to get you some Monnan clothes, you look too conspicuous."

Tadko took a deep breath and said carefully, "They told me on the ship I would look inconspicuous in these."

Dacy's gesture dismissed the ship.

"Right enough, at the spaceport, you look like crew, but here in the city you don't want to go on looking like spacecrew. You want to look like, hmmmm." He nodded to himself. "You want to look like a top caste Elnakti turned Monnan, you've kept your native garb out of sentiment, you hate to let it go—" He sniffed theatrically. "But you're in the round, you have to sell it."

He continued to develop his theme. "I'm your great friend, really top commercial caste but no name mentioned of course, helping you find the right buyer in your time of need."

Tadko laughed in spite of himself. It was impossible not to like Dacy, although he could probably be trusted no farther than one could see him. He offered an objection.

"I can't afford to buy new clothes, not the kind you're talking about."

"No fear. I know a place, right on the way. We're almost there."

A moment later he pressed the stop panel, and the car slowed to a halt.

* * *

This time the sign over the door said merely, "Clothes." Some hung on racks out on the walkway, with awnings to protect them from the frequent rains. Some filled the shop, on racks and shelves. Some were clearly well worn, not even clean; others looked, to Tadko at least, quite new and dressy. He was sure he couldn't wear the typical bright clothes with anything like Monnan flair, but finally accepted some green and white trousers and a dark red smock with green piping. Dacy grumbled at his choice, but eventually allowed that it would pass. The cost was one and six. Dacy attempted to haggle, but the proprietor said truculently that her price was her price, and that was that.

Then back to Dacy's room. His own quick change outfit went into the cleaner along with Tadko's new things, and, after Dacy had sniffed them a bit, all the rest of Tadko's clothes. They showered, washed their hair, and dressed in their finery, Dacy using what he called the flash side of his. He also added an ornamental clip to the top of one ear, and persuaded Tadko to accept one as well.

"You don't want to use your right name," he said. "Don't you have any really top caste Elnakti names, something with a title, maybe?"

Tadko had already thought of that. It had better be one not likely to show up on Monna. One of the steadings south of Daruskan should do.

"Call me Harkos Reskaro, Mosor of Reskarad."

Dacy tried this, with indifferent success. "Your language is all hisses and husks," he complained. "Isn't there a simpler name, maybe just a title? If I'm your great friend it'll sound leery if I can't say your name."

Ka Mosor, thought Tadko. My title is Ka Mosor. He remembered how the people had turned to him, after his grandfather died, first calling him Ka Mosor. He couldn't say it. It might mean nothing at all on Monna, but it meant something. He wouldn't use it for this.

"Call me just Reskarad, then, It's formal enough, on Elnakt. It's what someone from another steading would call me."

"Reskarad, Reskarad." Dacy listened to himself. He inquired solicitously, "Is this valuation acceptable, Reskarad?" A pause. "It'll do."

They left the trotline some distance from Herenna's, and walked the rest of the way, Dacy explaining that if they couldn't arrive in a private vehicle, with driver, this would look better. Herenna's was a building Tadko had seen before, a tower paneled in silver and pale sea green, with wide doors of frosted glass picked out in an open work pattern of sea flowers. The windows were wide and deep, lined with rose colored cloth; in each one stood a moving mannequin, unnervingly lifelike as it posed and turned to display its colorful garb.

Dacy assumed his air of languid hauteur; Tadko did his best to match it. He threw back his head, straightened his back, made himself stand like a Mosor of Daruskan, the heir of many generations. They entered the store.

A bright-eyed young woman in silver and green came to meet them.

"May I be of assistance, Siros?"

Dacy's tone was lofty. "We must see Ambert Finell, the Special Purchaser."

"You have an appointment?"

"Not necessary. My friend here is from Elnakt—just let him know."

Tadko couldn't believe that this ploy would succeed, unless Unser had some communication with this man, Finell; was it possible? The woman lowered her eyes and murmured softly, "Certainly. This way, Siros."

They followed her through the store. Tadko forced himself not to gawk, gaining only a vague impression of glowing lights and color, displays of robes, hats, ornamental draperies, jewelry, lengths of rainbow fabric. The carpet was like thick turf underfoot; hints of perfume drifted in the air. He pulled Dacy to a stop at one display. Here, on a raised platform, stood one of the lifelike mannequins, dressed in a complete suit of Elnakti clothing. He stepped forward, examined the suit for himself, said softly to Dacy, "Borusted. One of the western steadings." The price—three hundred and seventy-five duats. Dacy nodded, and they followed the woman.

The office of Ambert Finell was surprisingly plain. The same thick carpet, but unadorned white walls, a wide window, a desk, chairs, a bank of files, another of comlines. Ambert Finell came forward, a portly, gray haired man of immense dignity in the green and silver Herenna livery. He bowed courteously.

"Please be seated, Siros."

They bowed in turn, seated themselves.

Finell took a chair as well, looked them over thoughtfully, and at Tadko with recognition.

"You *are* from Elnakt."

Tadko managed to bow again, seated though he was.

Dacy went into his prepared speech.

Finell listened carefully. "You understand," he said when Dacy finished, "I cannot make a purchase from persons who might be of, shall we say, less than worthy position. However, I do understand the need for persons of high rank to remain anonymous in certain, ah, difficult situations. When rendering assistance to one who might be in distressed circumstances, as an example. This being understood, I will say that the firm empowers me to buy at my discretion from—shall we say—informal—sources."

What *is* he talking about, Tadko wondered. But Dacy smiled, inclined his head. He leaned toward Tadko deferentially.

"Siro Finell is clearly a man of sensitivity, Reskarad," he said in confidential tones. "I believe you may safely rely upon his judgement."

A flick of his eyebrow signaled Tadko's next move. Tadko inclined his head in turn. "Siro," he said to Finell. "For your consideration."

He opened his bag, once again spread out his clothing. Finell examined it even more closely than Unser had. He rejected the undersuit, pointing out spots of wear, a bit of raveling along one seam. Tadko reflected sadly that he could hardly have expected Yarron to have given him a new suit; who could have predicted that he would need to sell them? It was Daruskan clothing, but not his own. It might have belonged to any of the young men. Now Finell was discovering small snags in the fleecy jacket and trousers, received, no doubt, during some of the times when Tadko hid out in the halm thickets during his flight west. Would Finell reject the whole outfit? But no, the man was folding them carefully, nodding to himself, and seemed very well satisfied with the boots. He turned back to Tadko.

"Very fine work, Siro—uh—Elnakt," he said, echoing Unser's comment. "However, as you see it will require some preparation before it can be considered salable by our firm. I make you an offer of eighty-five duats."

Tadko turned to Dacy, who gave the very slightest shake of his head.

"Siro, the clothing is my own, my last memento of my native world. It pains me to part with it." The rehearsed speech sounded awkward to him, his own voice rang heavy and artificial to his ears. But Finell appeared touched, or at least pretended to be.

"Indeed, Siro. Truly, an exile must face great sorrow. I do of course possess some discretion in these matters. Perhaps an offer of ninety-five would more nearly meet your own estimation of these items' value."

Now Dacy entered the conversation.

"Siro Finell is generous, Reskarad," he said. "I believe you may find this valuation acceptable?"

No more bargaining, then. Tadko rose, bowed yet again.

"Indeed, Siro, you are most generous. My deepest thanks."

More bows all around. Finell left the room briefly, returned with 45 of the black duats and a larger blue square marked "50," paid them into Tadko's hand, and bowed them out of his office. Tadko was uncomfortably aware of the way the money filled his pouch. He thought of snaffling colleagues of Dacy's, and hitched it up a bit under his smock before they left the store.

Dacy insisted they stroll down Terminal Way for some distance before taking the trotline, pretending to be high-caste idlers, just in case someone from Herenna's might be watching.

"Would this Finell know Unser, or have gotten word from him?" Tadko asked as they paused to inspect a window full of enameled leather pouches.

"No chance. He wouldn't know Unser existed. Unser probably got to know of him, and got that card, through some back of the hand route."

"Then why the, uh, evasiveness?"

"Commercials have their own rules, see, things about buying sources and such; probably Herenna's isn't supposed to buy off the ship like this, but they'll do it anyway, *sometimes*, to get a nice piece of merchandise. Also they do favors for people they think are important. He probably wouldn't have bought if he thought we were just ordinaries."

"Is that why we dressed up, and put on this pretense? But how did you know?"

Dacy's gesture was offhand, his expression smug. "Instinct. Standard practice. If you're going to deal with *any* commercial, you want to make sure he thinks you're one step above him, at least. You want to try selling the rest of your outfit?"

"I would, but who will buy it if not someone like Finell?"

"We'll try old Bonu. She wouldn't give much, but she might give something."

Old Bonu was the proprietor of Clothes, a plump but sharp-nosed old lady, her hair yellowed rather than graying with age, her own clothes apparently chosen randomly from her stock in trade. She was not at all impressed by Elnakti garb.

"Who'd buy such heavy stuff, except they were going to Dorra, and not likely to stop in here? I'll give six zinae, not one more. You want more, you go elsewhere. That's my offer."

Tadko accepted the six zinae without a word, glad enough to hand over the last of his Elnakti suit. He was tired of carrying it around...in fact he was suddenly very tired. Too much had been happening, too fast.

"I'm hungry," he said as they left Clothes, "and is there somewhere I can sleep at night? Would the money I have now get me a place to stay for the next seventy-odd days?"

"We can eat round the corner, it's a fairly decent place, and you can stretch with me tonight, remember? I told you at the shuttle landing."

Round the corner was a small, crowded eat shop. Tadko was introduced to coppies, little fat fish the size of his thumb, wrapped in peppery leaves and baked. Somewhat better than squelt. The place also served cold ices, a pleasant finish to the spicy meal.

While they ate, he considered Dacy's offer. He was less sanguine about spending the night with the young man than he had been when the offer was first made. He had more money now, and Dacy *was* a thief. He wondered about the inns and hotels his mother had described; but in the end, sheer weariness decided him. He went home with Dacy.

Preparing to sleep on one of the low pallets Dacy pulled out of the wall, he rolled his pouch inside his ship clothes, placed those inside his bag, and used the resulting bundle for a pillow. In spite of his concern over Dacy's honesty, his sleep was sound.

CHAPTER FOUR

When he woke, Dacy was in the shower. He checked his bundle hastily, and was relieved to find it all in order, the money safe. He had no idea what he would have done if Dacy had robbed him during the night. Perhaps Dacy's code, however it worked, forbade robbing a guest, but he was uncomfortably aware of how little he knew, even now. At least he felt safe enough taking his own shower after Dacy had finished.

That morning Dacy served slices of melon, hot crispbread, and a hot, tart, dark red liquid he called froile. It was mildly stimulating. It made Tadko sweat, but after a cup or two he felt more alert, less fatigued, than he had since his arrival on Monna. He mused, frowning slightly, over the events of the day before.

"Didn't they cheat me at Herenna's, too, over the price of my clothes?" he asked. "You saw how much they wanted for that suit they were selling, and Borusted work isn't considered the best on Elnakt."

For the first time, he saw Dacy look uncertain. "Well, yours wasn't a whole suit, and it wasn't new, of course. I couldn't say, clothes not being my line, but one thing you can go bond on—commercials are sticky, buy cheap and sell dear, that's their line."

"Huh. Couldn't we at least have bargained a little higher?"

"Oh, we didn't bargain at all, and I'm surprised he upped the price at all. That line about your native world was sleek, very sleek, but we couldn't do any real haggling or he'd have guessed we weren't what we looked like. Top caste don't haggle, ever."

"Neither does old Bonu, and she isn't top caste, surely."

"That's just her. And she will sometimes, if you get her in the right mood." He gestured widely, his mug in one hand and a chunk of bread in the other. "Down on the street, with ordinaries, some do and some don't. It all depends if they've got enough trade and they can get their prices, they don't bother, but commercials don't, ever."

Dacy went on, clearly pleased at having such a willing listener, to describe the city. He seemed to know it as well as he knew his own room, from Overlook where the highest commercials had their homes and the Eleven met in the Rotunda, to Sweeper Beach, were they'd knock over a stranger just as soon as look at him. Beyond the city, his knowledge was slender or nonexistent. The scarlet-dyed men in black kilts whom Tadko had seen at the spaceport? From F'thisk'k'zow, where the gold mines were. Also there was Eilonsad, circling the third sun, where gems were mined and small electronic gear manufactured. Dacy would know these, Tadko thought wryly, because such things were his stock in trade. The stocky people who must come from a heavy planet, or the various aliens Tadko encountered at the spaceport? Dacy waved them aside. Just tourists, from somewhere or other.

The two were silent for a while. Then Dacy cocked his head and said abruptly, "You don't want to go snaffling."

"I'd never have the nerve," Tadko said quite honestly. "But what can I do? Do I have enough money now to pay for a place to stay? And what about a permit?"

Dacy nodded thoughtfully. "There is a place you might go. Students and Apprentices Protective League, it's called. I think you've got enough money to buy in now, and they'll find you—uh— 'honest work.'" He spoke of honest work in a tone that suggested it was something hardly to be discussed in polite society.

Tadko grinned faintly. "But what about a permit?" he repeated.

"I've heard they won't say anything. They say the people running it don't care about the mines policy, takes away workers they could use themselves. Tell them you're here for a while and you're on the round, and it ought to be right enough. But you'll have to step soft, and keep on the shady side, and mind your manners with the top caste types."

Tadko mulled it over for a while. It sounded less than appealing, but no doubt one had to allow for Dacy's attitude to "honest work." It might be his best chance, unless.... "First I want to find out if I have enough to take me to Sancy Island," he said. "If I don't, then I suppose I'd better try this League."

Dacy stood up briskly. "We can call Transport Central from one of the shuttle ports, not the one you slept at."

Passage to Sancy Island, much to his sorrow, cost one hundred and seventy-five duats by cargo barge, the cheapest transport available. Schedules irregular.

"Do you know how much it takes to buy into this League?" he asked Dacy as they left the shuttle port.

"Last I heard it was thirty-five. Two—three years ago, that was. If it's more now, it wouldn't be much more."

They walked for some distance across the bustling city center, out into a section that Tadko remembered from his previous wanderings. He recognized the large square building, walled with rust colored panels, occupying almost the whole of a city block. A narrow green lawn surrounded it, with benches under rather scraggly trees. He had rested here from time to time, never daring to stay very long.

"This is the place?" he asked Dacy.

"Right enough. There's the main entrance." Dacy pointed to a set of double doors. "Ask for—" he paused, searching his memory. "Ask for the novice proctor, that's it. Luck of the catch, friend Tadko. Maybe I'll see you again sometime."

It was goodbye, and it left Tadko feeling depressed and uncertain.

"Maybe you will," he said, "and thanks for the help." He walked up the path, braced his shoulders, and entered the building.

Poros Manderton was a solidly built man of middle age with a look of intelligence and competence.

"Your name and origin?"

"Tadko Darusko, from Elnakt."

"Are you here as a student or an apprentice?"

"I'm not a student, and I hoped to find work."

"How long have you been on Monna?"

Now was the time to find out if Dacy had been right about this league.

"Ten days."

Manderton said only, "Elnakti. Unless you can buy an apprenticeship, casual unskilled labor would be the only employment available. Membership in the League is fifty duats, apprenticeships run from two hundred and fifty to five hundred duats, conditional upon your passing qualifying tests. You speak Monnan very well; do you read and write it also?"

"Yes, but I can't afford an apprenticeship, I can only afford membership in the League." Should he explain that he only needed it for 80 days—no, less than that, now. Or that he expected to contact his father then? Maybe these people would even loan him the money to get to Sancy. He wished he had asked more questions of Dacy when he had the chance, if only he had known what questions to ask.

"I'd like eventually to get to Sancy Island, to join the rest of my people," he said hopefully. "Does—does the League make loans—or anything?"

Manderton's smile was understanding. "Loans are available to members after a three month residence; there shouldn't be any problem then."

After three months he shouldn't be needing it; ah well.

"Then I'm willing to work at whatever I can do."

"Very well then." Manderton leaned back, made a tent of his fingers, and launched into a speech that he had obviously delivered hundreds of times before. "As a member of the Students and Apprentices Protective League, you will receive certain benefits. You will reside here, sharing a room with two or three other young men. You may take your meals in our refectory, food is served four times a day, a schedule is posted in each room. Medical care is available if needed. There will be no charge other than your membership fee until you are employed; at that time you will be expected to pay 15 percent of each cycle's wages to the League. If you become a student, League members receive a reduction in tuition and the price of supplies.

"As for your obligations, we expect quiet, respectful behavior in the residences and courtesy to proctors, warders, and your fellow residents. We permit no thieving, destructiveness, fighting, or gambling. You may not bring in alcoholic beverages or any form of hallucinogen.

"Certain rooms are sound barriered for the practice of musical instruments, we do not allow their use elsewhere.

"Men and women may not visit each others' residences.

"You are expected to be in your room by 2100 at night; if you wish to remain away until later, or overnight, you must have permission from your house warder.

"A poor report at work or at school, or general misbehavior, will be cause for dismissal from the League."

Manderton ended his recital, and leaned forward again.

"Do you understand these requirements, and are you willing to accept them?"

By concentrating intensely, Tadko just managed to follow all this. He felt a momentary pang of regret for the—relatively—carefree life of a snaffler. This sounded fairly dreary, but it looked as if he had no choice.

"I understand, and I accept."

Manderton nodded. "And by the way, League membership is accepted in any work application."

At first this meant nothing; then Tadko realized what Manderton was telling him.

"I—thank you. Thank you very much."

He signed the membership agreement and paid out his fifty duats, receiving in turn a membership card and a silver badge to wear on his shoulder.

Manderton spoke into a mesh at the side of his desk. "We need to assign a new member, male, Lehnis."

"One minute."

It took less than that; a young man appeared from the next room, handed Manderton a key and a printed sheet, and withdrew again.

"You're assigned to room 824-A-10; your current roommates are Willen Eames and Kheer Rhenearr." Manderton pronounced the last name with aspirates and much rolling of R's. "Your house warder will be Gelmin Seronico, he will see you tomorrow." He handed over the key, then produced an arrow like the one Tadko had used at the spaceport. "Take the lift to the eighth floor, and the arrow will guide you to your room."

The eighth floor was quiet. Some of the doors he passed were open, revealing short hallways, leading to the residence rooms. He caught snatches of conversation as he went by, bursts of laughter, occasional snores of varying pitch and intensity, but all sounds were muted.

He found 824-A-10 at last, walked through the short passageway and paused in the entrance to the room. Before him on the floor two young men sat cross-legged, completely absorbed in a game, a business of three levels with circles of pyramids on squares of various colors. Tadko concentrated on the oddly assorted players. One was Monnan, a broad-shouldered fellow with large hands and feet, hair cut rather long for a Monnan, and an easy humorous expression. He wore comfortably rumpled clothes of bright green and yellow. The other was a pink-skinned, red-haired Eilonsader, but not such an Eilonsader as shipmaster Jaong and his crew.

This youth wore a tight-fitting tunic of shiny black material, laced up the front with scarlet cords. The sleeves were short, hugely puffed, and yellow. More scarlet cords covered his forearms from wrist to elbow, woven in a complicated basket weave pattern. His breeches were striped red and yellow, puffed out like the sleeves, gathered at the knees with brass buckles. Short black boots with inlaid patterns of purple and green finished off this costume. His red hair stood straight out all around his head, shining with an almost metallic gleam, each individual hair tipped with black. Even among the many races and costumes Tadko had seen since arriving on Monna, this one stood out for sheer gaudiness. Absurd.

Then the young dandy bent forward to move several black pyramids into a line.

"First circle," he announced to his opponent. "That evens us up, I think."

"So it does," said the Monnan. "Bah, my neck's getting stiff." He stretched, pulling his head back, and became aware of Tadko watching them.

Somewhat embarrassed, Tadko cleared his throat. "Are you Willen Eames and Keer," here he had trouble expressing the "kh" sound, "uh—Renar?"

"That we are," said the dandy. "Willen Eames there." He jerked a thumb at the Monnan. "And I'm Kheer u Rhenearr." He spoke his name with long sliding R's and a good many more syllables than even Manderton had managed. "And you?"

"Tadko Darusko. I've been assigned to this room."

"Come on in then." The two got up, and Willen picked up the game board. "New member?"

"Yes, Just today."

"Well then, this is it." Willen gestured around the large room. "These rooms are made for four people, you're the third one here. Those shelves on each side are for sleeping; we've each got a lower, you can pick one of the uppers. These doors on the inside wall are the storage cabinets—this is mine." He opened the first door to display rows of shelves, clothes racks, boxes stacked untidily on the floor, into one of which he pushed the game and its pieces. "This next one is Kheer's." He passed the entrance. "This first one on this side will be yours." Tadko opened the door and slung his bag on one of the shelves.

Willen continued his tour of explanation.

"This is the washroom, we share that." He opened the door to a large white walled chamber and pointed out its amenities. "Shower cubicle, waste closet, this cabinet here for cleaning clothes—you hang them on the racks—and the mirror and shelves are for personal grooming." A faint smile hovered at the corners of his mouth and his eyes gleamed, as if he found something highly amusing in the latter arrangement, but he offered no comment. His face was quite sober when he stepped back into the main room.

"Are you going to school?"

"No, they said they could find work for me."

Kheer had been lounging on his bed. Now he laughed.

"Unskilled casual labor, am I correct?"

"Yes."

Willen shrugged. "We all do what we can, that's all. Here, you'll probably need to know how to use the study center anyway."

He pointed to four large circles outlined in black on the floor. He stepped into the center of one, bent over and slipped his fingers into a recess in the floor, gave a quick jerk. A chair rose smoothly from the floor and settled in place with a sharp click. Willen beckoned to Tadko, who sat down a bit gingerly, but it felt quite steady and solid.

"This is the console," Willen continued. Another jerk in a floor recess, and a desk with various shelves, drawers, and attachments rose up in front of the chair. "This is your film projector, and this is where you insert the chips. It's simple enough. And this button here is for your sound barrier."

He pressed the button, and a shimmering veil appeared around the circumference of the circle, reaching from floor to ceiling.

"That way if you have three or four people studying at once, they don't drive each other to drowning. Sound doesn't travel in or out, except for the bells for meals and lights out. Air passes through, of course, so you don't smother."

"Can you touch those—sound barriers?"

"Oh, yes, no problem." Willen stepped in and out to demonstrate, then turned off the barrier.

"Very convenient," Tadko said. He stepped out and looked at the equipment. "How does it go back in the floor?"

"These little catches in the back. You have to get out and go in back to release them, so it isn't possible to do it by accident."

Kheer laughed again.

"It can happen deliberately, though. Nothing's more funny than creeping up and pulling the catch on some busy little swotter, and watching him wake up as he sinks."

Willen laughed too and Tadko joined in. It was a funny picture; nevertheless, he made up his mind to keep an eye on Kheer.

"Are you in school or working?" he asked.

Kheer said loftily, "I'm in the College of Seleme Central. qualifying for my fourth level certificate. Willen, here, is an apprentice."

His tone suggested that being an apprentice was a considerably lower level of being than a student, but Willen was unperturbed. His lips twitched slightly, his eyes gleamed with that look of secret amusement again.

"That's right," he said cheerfully. "I come from Many Dunes, up on the north coast. I didn't want to go squelt netting like all the rest of my family, or plankton harvesting either, and to get into the specialty boats you almost have to be born to the guild, so I worked long enough to save up the cost of an apprenticeship and came down to the city. The League found me a place with Interworld Transport, and now I'm apprenticed in the routing section, doing stubbing and batching."

"I see," said Tadko, having followed the general implications, if not the exact meaning. "I come from Elnakt." It struck him the next moment that he ought to keep quiet about his origins in casual conversation, but too late now.

Kheer had assumed a faintly bored expression. "And where in space is Elnakt?" he inquired carelessly.

"It circles Yan, not far from the three suns," Tadko said, feeling nettled, although he wasn't quite sure why. "You're from Eilonsad, aren't you?"

"That I am." Kheer pursed his lips, kissed his own fingertips and waved them in the air. "Lovely Eilonsad, garden world of the three suns. Have you ever been there?"

"No, but I came to Monna on a ship—" he stopped. If he admitted to a ship out of Eilonsad, might Kheer want to know the name? He *must* learn to watch his tongue. Would they notice his hesitation?

But Kheer was uninterested. "Obviously on a ship, we know you didn't fly." He turned to Willen and opened his mouth, but bells began sounding throughout the building, interrupting his next speech.

"That'll be supper," Willen said briskly. "Let's go."

"Not tonight," said Kheer. "I found out this morning it's going to be emmer pudding."

"You did?" Willen considered. "Then it's the House of Many Worlds for me. What about you?"

"What else?" said Kheer.

"What's emmer pudding?" Tadko asked.

"It's something the Monnans consider edible, for some unknown reason." Kheer remarked. "It has the texture of mud, and it looks like mud—yellow mud. Tastes like mud, too."

Willen only grinned. "It isn't bad if it's properly spiced. They don't know how to cook it here—it's a north islands dish."

Kheer shook his head. "Flavored mud is still mud. Let's be off to the House of Many Worlds."

Willen turned to Tadko. "Care to come along?"

Tadko inquired cautiously, "How much?"

"A couple of duats. Right enough?"

Tadko would have preferred something cheaper, but emmer pudding sounded even worse than squelt. "Right enough."

The halls, when they left the room, were full of young men. Most of them were headed in what Tadko assumed was the direction of the refectory, generally with resigned looks on their faces. The grumbling was loud, mostly variations on, "If I had anything left besides my trotline slug...."

A few, like Tadko, Willen, and Kheer, were bound in the opposite direction. In the big entry hall they found quite a crowd of young men and women, all discussing alternate places to eat that night. They joined a group of a dozen others, all bound for the House of Many Worlds. There were introductions all around, but the only one Tadko registered was Raul Saneko, a fellow who looked to be half Monnan, half Eilonsader.

Tadko watched him unobtrusively, as they left the building. Presently he got up his courage and asked, "Where are you from?"

"My mother's from Nurhio, on Eilonsad," Raul said easily enough. "She was commercial representative to the Ornibeck Interest here when she met my father. He went back with her to Nurhio three years ago, when her term ended, but I was already in school here, so I stayed." He looked at Tadko with friendly curiosity. "And you?"

"From Elnakt," Tadko said. Now was the time to announce casually that his father was also Monnan, but he found himself unwilling to do so even to someone like this Raul. Who could tell what other questions it might lead to? "I came to work," was all he said. "There are quite a few other Elnakti on Monna now, working too."

Raul nodded. "I heard about it. Bad lines for you, but Monna's a good world—you'll like it."

Tadko thought that was impossible but he had no wish to rebuff Raul's friendliness. They walked on in companionable silence, listening to the chatter of the others.

Some ten squares away from the League, they stopped at one corner of a structure paneled in cerise and lavender, with silvery arabesques in the center of each panel. The sign glowing above announced, "Independents Authorized." The main entrance was broad and high, framed with luminescent rods, but above a small corner door an even more brilliant sign announced, "House of Many Worlds."

Kheer pushed it open and led the way down a short flight of steps. The House of Many Worlds was in a single large circular room. A pleasant golden light came from glow-strips recessed in the ceiling. Around the outer walls hung paintings of landscape scenes from many different planets, chosen perhaps more for exotic detail and color—reds, purples, and electric blues predominated—than for pure artistic merit. A raised dais occupied the center of the room. The rest of the floor area was crowded with small curved tables; the patrons were seated along the outer curves, facing the dais. Men and women wearing scarlet smocks over black trousers moved through this crowd with remarkable agility, carrying loaded trays.

The group from the League made their way through a muted hubbub of laughter and conversation to tables along the outer edge of the room. Willen hailed a passing waiter. "What is it tonight, Juwenel?"

"Butterlets, fresh from Padriocosta. Two and six." She smiled broadly. "Emmer pudding tonight at the League?"

"You know it. Let's see, fifteen of us to serve." He looked around questioningly at the others. "And ale all around?"

A chorus of agreement, and the waiter moved off.

Raul nudged Tadko, seated beside him. "Look over there." He jerked his thumb at a section where the tables were much less crowded. Around it was a line of short posts, with a blue cord looped from post to post. The people there were different; they reminded him of Dacy, in his elegant clothes, using what he called his most top-caste manner. He had seen their like at Herenna's, moving casually through the store, flicking a lazy finger to summon the liveried clerks. Here, each one wore in his or her hair a complicated knot of many-colored ribbons.

He turned questioningly to Raul, who nodded.

"Commercial caste types. They wear their house colors to a place like this, so they won't be mistaken for ordinaries. The food is good, they come for that, and they also come for the entertainment."

"My brother knew a fellow from F'thisk'k'zow who performed here once." That was one of the girls, leaning over from Raul's other side. "Wore his kilt and stones and everything, and did one of their challenge dances. Anyway, someone from one of the Houses, Quelonnin I think, hired him, and the last we heard he gave up his apprenticeship and was just touring the houses."

"That's the way to collect squares all right," put in a spindly young man at the next table. "If I could only perform at something—"

"Yes, and get dropped like a burr eel as soon as they got tired of it." That was Willen, calm and practical. "Stick to something steady if you want to be safe for a long voyage."

Some voices were raised in protest at his pessimism, but then the food began to arrive and the protests were forgotten. Each received a bowl of tiny steaming shellfish with another bowl of the inevitable hot sauce and several rounds of flat bread on the side. Tadko managed to add just enough sauce to flavor the butterlets without burning his mouth, and found them, surprisingly, very good. The ale arrived shortly after. All this Monnan ale was bland compared to what they brewed at Daruskan, but at least it was cold.

The great room was already almost full, and when a few more customers had come in and seated themselves, a mellow gong sounded. A handsome man in black and silver robes, with silver-dyed hair, came down from the other side of the room and climbed the steps to the dais.

He raised his hands.

"An evening without entertainment is like a meal without hot sauce," he proclaimed. "Who will entertain us?"

Immediately six young Monnans rose from a table very close to the foot of the dais. Followed by laughter and some catcalls, they joined the silver-haired man. He spoke with them for a moment, then turned to the crowd.

"The Six Irreverents will share their views with us," he announced, bowed, and left the dais.

The Six—three men and three women—proceeded to put on a series of skits, satirizing the ancestry, manners, brains, and integrity of the governing Council of Eleven. It was all beyond Tadko, but the rest of the audience laughed hilariously, including, much to his surprise, the commercial caste types in their special section. When the six bowed and returned to their table, a graceful woman with a yellow, white, and maroon knot in her bronze-tipped hair rose from her place and came down to speak with them.

"They're all set for the season, anyway," said a voice from another table. "But you do have to have something different to go on with."

"Different!" the spindly youth exclaimed angrily. "Different as one squelt from another. Everyone's doing that sort of thing now, it's the rage."

"Well, why don't you do it too?" Kheer asked pointedly, and the spindly youth subsided, grumbling.

There was a pause, and then four figures approached the dais. Veiled from head to foot in floating robes of grey, they were taller than most Monnans and moved with a swaying, mobile grace that even a Monnan could not match. One carried a complicated coil of tubing tucked in among the folds of the grey robe.

The four mounted to the dais, followed by the master of ceremonies. He spoke to one of them, then another, at much greater length than to the Six Irreverents. Finally he turned to the audience with a slightly puzzled look on his face.

"Four—ah—individuals from —ah—a far world will perform for us," he announced, opened his mouth as if to say more, then thought better of it, bowed, and withdrew.

"That's one on old Naylor," Kheer sounded genuinely surprised. "I thought he could pronounce anyone's garble."

"Are they even human?" Raul asked in a low voice. "We don't see many non-humans here, but—"

A little ripple of whispers throughout the room indicated that others were also curious. Then there was silence, as the four began their performance. The one with the coiled instrument crouched over it, and presently the veils began to move slowly, the coils appeared to pulse slightly. A series of deep, solemn notes, in a ponderous rhythm, welled out into the room. The other three beings followed this somber music, rising, sinking, swaying together and back, in a deliberate manner suggesting ritual more than dance.

The effect was eerie. Tadko felt the music as much as heard it, for it was almost below the level of audibility. Glancing around surreptitiously, he noticed with some relief that the others were equally uneasy; even Kheer had a look of discomfort.

The performance ended at last. The four beings bowed and departed, in no way giving any indication that they cared about—or even noticed—the lack of applause.

"Brrr!" said Raul with feeling. "Something different there, and no mistake. My life, look at that!"

Tadko turned, and watched incredulously as an elaborately dressed couple made their way down and spoke with the four.

"They'd want *that* for entertainment?"

"You heard what Lehnis said—it's different. Besides, see their colors? That's Crale. They say Crales go for anything strange, the more alien the better."

"Crales are fairly strange themselves, they say," Willen put in. "I wouldn't know. Many Dunes tallies to Crale, but it'll be a dry ocean before any of us ordinaries meets one in person."

They fell to discussing the various commercial caste families, their vices real or imagined, their eccentricities, generosities, or lack of them. Tadko finished his meal, sipped his ale, and watched the entertainment.

The four in grey were followed by a charming girl with a flute, playing wonderful airy melodies like bird song. Strangely, he thought, no one went down to speak to her after her performance.

"What happens if she isn't hired?" He asked Raul.

"If she isn't tapped she'll at least get her meal free, so it's not a total loss."

The girl was followed by a team of acrobats, and they by a singer, a solemn-faced man with a deep voice. Tadko was growing sleepy. He was glad when Willen stood up, beckoning.

"Come on, you poor square chasers, time to go if we don't want to be locked out."

Kheer and several others objected. "There's plenty of time, you're always afraid of the doorwards."

"So I am," said Willen, not in the least embarrassed. "You would be too if you had any sense, always slicing it too thin. You can stay if you like. I'm going."

Tadko and Raul rose to follow Willen; the rest came after, a few hanging back and muttering to themselves as they went. Darkness had cooled the air a little when they left. It made the others shiver and hurry along willingly enough, but Tadko was tempted to linger. The dampness made him cough a bit, but he wished he could sleep outside again.

The lights in their room had already been turned off when they came in, but Monna's large moon shone in the window, giving enough light to undress by. Having a choice between sleeping above Willen or Kheer, Tadko chose Willen.

CHAPTER FIVE

Once he was up there, sleep was impossible.

It was too hot, and he was painfully conscious of the drop to the floor. At home, he slept in a bed closet, or on the ground during the long migrations with the herds; here he wished for a pallet on the floor, like the ones at Dacy's. He turned carefully on his stomach, laid himself along the wall, and tried to think about his two roommates instead.

He disliked Kheer already. Kheer had a way of narrowing his eyes, pinching his nostrils; the curl of his mouth seemed always on the verge of a sneer; his voice held a permanently contemptuous tone. Willen was decent and reliable...he slept, dreamed of falling, and woke gasping, clutching at the bed.

It was no use. He climbed down and pulled off the mat, lowering it slowly from one end so as not to wake Willen. He pushed it against one wall, stretched out, and was soon asleep.

Bells brought him awake in the morning, sitting up blurrily on his mat. Willen was still flat on his face in bed, one hand trailing on the floor, but Kheer was up immediately. He yawned and looked around sleepily, then noticed Tadko on the floor. First he looked incredulous, then the curled lip became an unmistakable sneer, and finally he laughed out loud. He passed on without speaking and disappeared into the washroom.

Tadko's first impulse was to follow Kheer, seize him, and beat him to the floor. How dared he! To a Mosor of Elnakt, a herdmaster! He remembered the League rules and forced himself to sit still, to unclench his fists, to calm down, before starting for the washroom himself. At the door he stopped in amazement.

Kheer stood naked in front of the large mirror; reflected in it Tadko could see his frown of concentration, his lips caught between his teeth. Beside him on the shelf was an array of small brushes, combs, applicators, bottles, and jars, including a pot labeled "INSTANT BLACK HAIR GLISTEN." He was drawing out his hair a few strands at a time, applying a clear liquid from one of his bottles, drawing a fine comb through to separate the hairs, then tipping each strand with black hair glisten on a little swab—the whole business apparently requiring the nicest care and precision.

Tadko only just managed to keep from laughing. He waited until Kheer noticed him, then allowed his own lip to curl in what he hoped was a properly contemptuous smile, turned his back, and stepped into the shower cubicle.

He had finished dressing by the time Kheer came out, hair finished to perfection, and began lacing himself into a purple tunic with orange sleeves.

A second bell sounded. Willen sprang off his mat all at once, and rushed like a shadow into the washroom. There was a loud splashing and gasping, the whir of the drier, and he was out again. He pulled open his closet and snatched out his clothes, tossed them on while he slipped into his sandals, then belted on his pouch and ran his fingers through his tight black curls. He was prepared to go almost before Kheer had completed the final touches on his costume.

"Ready?" he said briefly. "Come along then."

The hall was full of hurrying young men, some sleepy and silent or yawning terrifically, others already talking full speed.

"Is the morning meal likely to be any better than the evening?" Tadko asked.

Before Willen could answer, Kheer asked mockingly, "Where in space did you learn to speak Monnan? You talk like a turtlehead."

Tadko clenched his teeth, realizing that it had been a mistake to challenge Kheer.

"My mother tutored me," he said defiantly. "I speak well enough for the Monnans."

"Your mother! You mean you didn't go to school? Unschooled savages, coming to a civilized—"

Tadko turned, fists raised, but Willen caught him by the shoulder in a surprisingly strong grip.

"Enough of that!" he told Kheer sharply. "You know the rules. I could list you for provocation. Do you want to keep your own membership?"

Kheer subsided, his expression sullen.

"I withdraw," he said grudgingly.

Willen turned questioningly to Tadko.

"Do you accept?"

It sounded like a necessary formality of some sort; Tadko liked it no better than Kheer.

"I accept," he said finally.

Kheer stalked off ahead of them with a defiant twitch of his shoulder.

"I wouldn't let him bother me, if I were you," Willen said quietly. "Most Eilonsaders are decent types, but the ones from the diarchate are all popinjays, and all think they ought to own the universe. Also, his people are some sort of tattered-smock relatives of a diarchal family, and he was someone at home. Here it doesn't mean a thing of course, and he has a hard time being an ordinary."

Tadko said nothing. He, too, had been "someone" at home, but he felt no more kindly toward Kheer because of that. After all, he didn't go around offering gratuitous insults to strangers he had only just met. He mumbled something he hoped Willen would take as agreement, and followed him to the refectory.

Breakfast was very good, the same foods he had shared with Dacy the day before—melons, crisp spiced bread, and mugs of froile. He ate with good appetite, then watched the crowd of young people disperse to schools and apprenticeships and work before returning to his room.

Back in the room, he just stood for a moment. Then, moved by an impulse he didn't fully understand, he went into the washroom and stood before the mirror as Kheer had done, regarding himself critically.

Medium height, stocky frame; well-knit, but distinctly lacking in Monnan grace. Medium brown skin and almost-matching straight hair, cropped on the ship just below his ears but now beginning to straggle over his shoulders. Blunt features with wide mouth and broad, rather high cheekbones. He thought of Raul, last night. Raul's triangular, foxy face and green eyes were definitely Eilonsader, but he had the long-limbed Monnan build; his curled hair was dark bronze, his skin light brown with a purplish sheen. Tadko himself had nothing of his father, unless some quirk of the latter's heredity had given him his curiously light eyes, neither Monnan violet nor Elnakti brown. Otherwise he looked entirely Elnakti and had never thought of himself as anything else.

The door buzzer sounded, and he went to answer it with something like a sigh.

The man who entered was short and plump for a Monnan. His hair was thin, his countenance cherubic. His expression was one of such kindly benevolence that Tadko, remembering Dacy, felt uneasy.

"I am Gelmin Seronico, your house warder," he announced. "You are Tadko Darusko, from Elnakt?"

"Yes, er, please sit down." Tadko made a rush at the study blocks to pull up two chairs, seating himself after the warder had done so.

Seronico fussed with some papers.

"You didn't go with the rest of your people to the south coast of Sancy? I believe the climate there is more salubrious for Elnakti."

"No, I was told the League could arrange work for me."

"Ah, yes. We have very little call for casual unskilled labor, but I'm sure some type of employment can be arranged."

Tadko was growing bitter about the constant repetition of the phrase. He'd like to see one of these smooth people try to shear an onca, or cut one up for drying. Or drive a herd near going dormant the last lap of the way to winter cover.

Aloud he said flatly, "I understand."

"Let me see; who was it accepted you into the League?"

"Poros Manderton."

"I see. And when did you arrive on Monna?"

"Eleven days ago."

Seronico's face changed. His mouth tightened, his eyes congealed into purple pebbles. It lasted for a breath; then he hitched the smile back into place but now it was the smile of one who had scored in a game.

"Ah, yes, yes," he said effusively. "Well, then, if you will just sign these applications—" He proffered them along with a stylus. "It may take some time, you understand, it will be necessary for us to search our records, but some time this afternoon you will be notified. You will wait here for the notification, of course."

Tadko's heart had gone "plob" against his ribs.

"Of course," he said, hoping he sounded properly matter-of-fact. He signed, returned the papers, and saw Seronico out with suitable courtesy. Then he rushed to his closet, blood pounding through his body. *The mines*, he thought frantically, *the mines! Seronico will get me sent to the mines!* Out, out and away before it was too late! He was afraid to take his bag. He hung his sheathed knife from his belt, inside his trousers, rolled his few other possessions in his ship clothes and tied them around his middle. He left the League membership that would now be wasted, but took the badge, maybe it could be sold.

With a snarl he went to Kheer's closet. Kheer had half a dozen pouches in fancy embroidered or tooled patterns, hanging side by side. Tadko felt in each one, discovering a whole handful of duats in the third. He felt bitterly ashamed and could not bring himself to rob Willen, who was friendly and kind.

Then out into the corridor, almost shaking with tension—would someone be waiting to make sure he didn't leave? But the corridor was empty. Perhaps, he thought hopefully, Seronico believed that a stupid Elnakti hadn't caught on to his change in attitude, and would wait patiently in his room for a work-notification.

Along the corridor, down in a lift, along another corridor, down in another lift; presently he knew he had missed a turning and was lost. He forced himself to go on, walking briskly but not running, taking the lifts down, trusting that he would be able to find his way out when he reached the lowest floor. The last lift took him down to a totally unfamiliar cross-corridor. A faint hum of machinery came from behind closed doors. Down one corridor, a turn, down another, and there were a pair of wide glass doors with sunlight coming through.

He glanced quickly behind him, then ran the rest of the way. For a few horrible seconds he thought the doors were locked, but with a heave he managed to shove them open, and found himself out on a narrow back street, of the type he and Dacy had used to leave the shuttle port building.

There was no one in sight. He moved away from the door and risked changing into his ship clothes, rolling the Monnan outfit around his waist instead. He ran down the street, turned a corner, slowed to a walk as he came onto the thoroughfare, and started off in what he hoped was the direction of the harbor.

A trotline car came swaying down the street. He ran to the corner and got his zinae into the kiosk in time to stop it. Now what was the name of that district where Dacy took him to sell his things? Yes. "Seawrack Bay," he said into the mesh, and rolled away.

His first reaction, back at the League, had been to think Dacy betrayed him. Now, mulling it over, he didn't think so. Dacy had admitted that he knew about the League only from hearsay, and he was right about Manderton, certainly. Tadko guessed dimly at rivalries, intrigues, within the League. Dacy would know nothing of such things, and probably lumped everyone in the League together as "honest workers." He wondered if Dacy would be willing to help him again, but decided not; not when the greens might really be after him. He was on his own.

As far as he knew, no Elnakti before his mother had ever come to Monna the City. Since all the others had been shipped off to Sancy as soon as they arrived—or so he assumed—he might not be recognized. Especially that Seronico person, freeze him. Would they call all over about something like this? He must have a disguise.

He jumped off the trotline not too far from the Crale hiring hall. Moving through the noisy crowds with their numerous population of offworlders, he felt a good deal safer and much less conspicuous. People swarmed the walkways and spilled over into the streets, infuriating the trotline riders who went past shouting and shaking their fists. People strolled as if they had hours to spend, or dodged along through the press at top speed, or clustered around the shop fronts, or collected in groups to argue and talk.

There were Eilonsaders of a type very different from Kheer, in shabby garments of all sorts, scarlet-dyed F'thisk'k'zows in kilts or Monnan garb, milky-skinned, pale-haired Dorrans in long white clothes and broad-brimmed hats to protect them from the sun, and mixtures of many other races. Greens patrolled these streets, but he watched for them and avoided them. For the first time, he was grateful that Monnans were taller than Elnakti; in spite of the sun dazzle that made it so difficult, he always managed to see them and keep his distance.

He began making certain purchases, choosing busy shops of the kind Dacy described, where they got their price and did no haggling. He made sure each place was so crowded they could do no more than glance at his selection and collect his money, and bought only one thing at each store. Presently he had a set of second- or third-hand Monnan clothing, slightly stained, in a pattern of bright blue, light green, and red. Also two small pots of the black hair glisten he had seen Kheer using, a cheap map of Monna and one of the city, a palm-sized sewing kit, and something he had not planned on but was delighted to buy—a long-tipped bulb labeled, 'Ultima Dark Retina Screen, Recommended for Dorran Use.' Dorrans, coming from the world next out in orbit, probably would need some eye protection and he assumed the stuff might work for him too.

He carried these things to a public bath house, deserted at this time of the morning, closed himself in one of the cubicles, and went to work, thankful that Monnans insisted on privacy.

He stripped, then used the small shears from the sewing kit to hack his hair short, evening it up as best he could. Next he went at it with the black hair glisten, working the stuff in from the roots out, checking in the mirror to make sure he covered it all. In addition to blackening, it made his hair stand straight out all around his head, like Kheer's. A startling effect which he found less than pleasing, but no doubt it would help to disguise him. He touched up his eyebrows, giving them a bushy look, but was afraid to use it on his lashes. He considered doing his body hair, but decided it would be too uncomfortable, and anyone who got that close to him could see that the rest was a fake anyway.

After some effort, he got two drops of the retina screen in each eye. The effect on his sight was immediate and gratifying, relaxing a squint he hadn't even known he'd acquired. The small print explained that one application should last for thirty days, which meant that he must be careful to re-apply it in time.

He counted his duats, including the money he stole from Kheer. It shamed him to think of it, much as he had disliked Kheer; maybe someday he could make arrangements to repay it. He had eighty and eight, all told. He slit the waistband of the blue, green and red breeches, slipped in half the duats, then sewed it up again. He dressed, then surveyed himself in the mirror. The young man reflected there looked very different from Tadko Darusko of Elnakt, or so he hoped. The retina screen had turned his eyes a dark brown. The bright clothes made him feel clownish; he lacked the true Monnan dash and flair. But he knew Dacy had been right—bright colors would really be less conspicuous than drab ones. He thought about all the people he had seen on the streets, at the League, at the House of Many Worlds, and decided he would pass. This crude disguise would never stand up to a really close scrutiny by the greens, but it was the best he could do.

The sandals he had worn from the ship were good enough, they looked like standard Monnan footwear. He put on his belt, again hanging his sheathed knife inside, and tucked his pouch inside as well. This made a bulge at his hip, but the smock concealed it well enough, and he thought it would be safer from the likes of Dacy.

One pot of hair glisten he consigned to the trash disintegrator, along with the new clothes he had bought at old Bonu's. It might be safe to wear them again later, but he couldn't be sure. The other pot he saved for touch-ups and this, together with the bulb of retina screen, the sewing kit, and his League badge, went into a bundle which he made of his ship clothes. He included the bits of cloth and the lengths of cordage he had brought from the ship, one never knew when such things might be useful. As for the League badge, he had in effect paid fifty duats for it; it could always be discarded later.

The maps he folded small and tucked into his waistband, and then he was ready to go. He had paid his zina when he entered the bathhouse. Now he poked his head out of the cubicle. The attendant was absorbed in a film on his desk projector. Tadko went past quickly and left by a side door.

On the ground floor of a high and spectacularly shabby building, he came upon a dingy eating-and-drinking establishment. There was no sign, no name. It was only a long, narrow room, one end open to the air, the other disappearing somewhere into the depths. A few people sat at tables, eating plates of squelt. It smelled of bad fish, stale ale, and other unpleasantnesses. Still, it ought to be cheap, and he needed to plan his next move. He took himself into the dim interior, seated himself at an isolated table, and opened his maps.

He wondered yet again if, after all, this running and hiding might be totally unnecessary. What if he went to the college, told them who he was, asked for help until his father returned? Osrin Havard was a senior scholar, after all. There must be those who knew he had married, had a son, and would be willing to help that son. But he had no proof, no documents. He didn't even look as if he were part Monnan. It came right back to that.

No, he must do what he had wanted to do from the first, as soon as he found out where they were. Go to his own people, on Sancy Island. The south coast, Seronico had said.

He studied the map of Monna. City Island was above the equator, in the western hemisphere. Sancy was a long way south, in the eastern hemisphere. Islands were scattered all over this world, but a string of them trended southeast from the city for some distance.... A dish-faced woman in a soiled smock and trousers presented herself at his table, and he looked up.

"Well," she said.

"What's cheap?"

"Mug o' froile, fresh, two zina." She looked sour, as Tadko fished under his smock and laid the money on the table. "Plate o' coppies? Plate o' squelt? Hot bread? Three zina apiece."

"Froile."

She sniffed contemptuously, took his money and departed, returned shortly with a steaming mug which she banged down in front of him, and left.

He needed another name. With the thought came the knowledge that he didn't want another name, he hated the very idea. He *was* Tadko Darusko, of Daruskan, on Elnakt. Another name would mean denial of his deepest identity, of everything that made him who he was. No help for it, however. He would call himself, let's see, Ono Tekall. Ono was a Rhionny word he had heard during his very brief contact; it might even be a swear word, but it made no difference. Tekall was the name of his grandfather's grandfather, and not common on Elnakt. It gave him a queasy feeling somewhere in his belly, but he repeated the name several times, softly, hoping he would get used to it.

He would go to Sancy as directly as possible, traveling as far as his money would take him. When the money ran out, why, he would steal more one way or another. He scowled into his froile, discovering that he loathed Monna, its elegant people, its intrigues and complexities, and everything else about it. Why not steal from them? They weren't his own people. They made him a criminal when he had done no more than arrive on their disgusting hot planet; now he would have to deny his very identity because of them, making himself into a liar as well.

He gripped his mug with both hands, half-tempted to call out his name, shout it aloud, and take the consequences. But that would only be surrender. His frown deepened. He would get to Sancy one way or another, and if he had a new name, he would be a whole new person. People would ask where he came from; he came from...Baratin. It was as good a name as any for a planet. His father was Monnan, maybe he could use that, his parents had separated long ago and his mother had taken him back to her home planet to raise him. That was even the truth. He didn't know his father's name, he had just come back as a tourist, to see the planet on the cheap. He went over it again, hoping he had covered everything. He ran over a sample conversation.

"Where are you from?"

"Baratin."

"Where is Baratin?"

"In the out stars, a long way away."

"What sun?"

"I don't know what you would call it in Monnan. We just call it the sun."

If the question were really uncomfortable, he would simply pretend not to understand. It might be wise not to be too careful in his Monnan speech, to speak brokenly, exaggerate his accent. He nodded sagely, and turned to the map. It didn't show much detail, but the closest island to Sancy, from here, was Padriocosta where the butterlets came from. He would ask about passage there, and ask about Sancy when he reached Padriocosta.

He folded the maps and tucked them in his waistband again, then left the froile place and set out for the passenger docks.

CHAPTER SIX

Some hours later he sat on a sand-strewn walkway not far from the ocean, with a cone of crispbread filled with coppies in one hand, and a really quite tolerable container of ale in the other.

The passenger docks had been even more noisy and confusing than the space port, with the same motley crowd of Monnans, other humans, and aliens. After a cautious period of wandering, watching, and listening, he had joined a collection of tourists around an information booth. It was quite a relief to be in a situation where ignorance was expected and accepted. He had shouted and shoved with the rest until he got the attention of the harried young woman behind the counter. He learned that passage to Padriocosta would cost one hundred and twenty duats, but if he wanted really cheap transport, he might find something at Sandtown, north of the city. The island hoppers went from there; no, she couldn't tell him what they charged, he would have to find out for himself. She did tell him that the trotline fare would be twelve zinae, and she handed him a whole collection of brochures.

He took these to a bench in a relatively quiet corner and looked them over, finding nothing of any real use. They were all lists of resorts; the undersea hostels, the tour boats, the facilities for diving, swimming, fishing. One could go out into the deep ocean and troll for saw-tooth shark, or fish off the lazy beaches of Aramoada for delicata. So said the brochures. A few mentioned winter resorts in the far north or south, and others listed souvenir items the discriminating tourist might want to buy, including, he saw with bitterness, Elnakti fleeces and clothing. There was mention of the deep-ocean races, with betting information. He learned that the trotline was correctly called the Personal Public Transport system.

One thing struck him forcefully as he finished his examination—there was no mention of Sancy island. No resorts were located there, no fine delicacies came from there, no hotels or inns offered themselves for the tourists' attention. Of course it was a long way south and would be cold by Monnan standards, but then so were the polar resorts. He found this disturbing, but there was nothing he could do about it now.

So he had ridden the trotline north, away from the passenger docks, past the guarded harbor where the pleasure boats of the wealthy were moored, glittering with bright paint and polished metal. After that came a long stretch of open beach, empty except for crews working along the high-water line, cleaning up whatever trash was thrown there by the waves. Next came the long wharves of the fishing fleet.

The city was left behind. The steep hills that formed the central spine of the island came down close to the narrow strip of land along the beaches. Here were shabby buildings, small shops constructed of coral block and metal sheeting, rickety piers with one or two boats tied up; finally they reached the end of the line, in Sandtown. A battered metal sign hanging askew on a post just where the trotline halted proclaimed the name. Tadko jumped out; instantly his trotline car rolled back the way it had come.

Beyond the sign an irregular straggle of buildings fronted the beach. Stores and repair sheds, taverns, licensed bettors, warehouses, and minor factories. A line of barges was moored along the shore with heavy cables looped around thick posts sunk deep in the sand. Light dazzled over the vast water. It was wonderful to look toward the horizon without blinking and squinting, and he made up his mind not to be without retina screen again. For a few seconds he almost forgot his worries in the enjoyment of his new vision. Then he passed by the racket of a repair shed and approached the nearest barge.

A young man and woman, carrying a large hamper between them, were having an argument with a wiry old lady who stood on the barge.

"They told us our deck passage fare would include our luggage," the girl said angrily.

"Did they see what you had? Anything that size is cargo, it goes below, and you pay for it, or you'll not come aboard!" The old lady was strident.

The two withdrew for a worried consultation, counting their money together. Tadko put on his best smile, and went closer.

"Passage to Padriocosta—uh—deck passage?"

She shook her head.

"I'm bound north, for Tefto. And you'll not find anyone here going that far. Might find someone going as far as Rowder, try up the line."

He walked up the line, trying each barge in turn. A few seemed deserted; at least no one was on board. Once he had to wait while a thick cylinder was extended from one of the buildings to pour a dark syrupy liquid into a barge hull. The stench was appalling. He waited until the loading was finished, and was relieved to find that this particular barge wasn't going to Rowder.

Several tries later, he was beginning to worry. Weren't any of these people, smelly or not, going as far as Rowder? He consulted his map again. It might be necessary to go to one of the nearer islands, and then on—call it island hopping, indeed.

The next barge was larger than the others. It seemed to have more elaborate and extensive deck fittings; the hull looked freshly painted, and *Tethrinel* was inscribed in curlicued letters on the side.

A man and woman were working at a complicated piece of machinery at the stern, sweating and swearing. Tadko waited again until they straightened up, wiping their faces.

"That sets it," the woman said. "You can go ahead and snug down." She cast a knowing glance at Tadko. "Looking for passage?"

"Rowder. Deck passage. Can I go on from there to Padriocosta?"

"Right enough." She inspected a list posted on the cabin wall. "Thirty-eight and six, that's deck passage and found."

"What's 'found?'"

"Food. Twice a day."

"Right enough." Tadko handed over most of the money in his pouch, thankful for the other forty duats sewed in his waistband.

The woman collected his money, yelled "Taking a fare!" toward the prow of the barge, went into the cabin, and returned with a strip of foil which she handed to him.

"Ticket," she said. "What luggage you got?"

Tadko displayed his bundle of clothing. The woman beamed.

"Right enough, that is. Too many cheapers come down here wanting deck passage and think they can carry on anything from a trotline car to a tankful of glowfish. What's your name?"

"Ono Tekall." It hurt to give the false name, but if she noticed his wince it meant nothing to her.

"Come back at eighteen hundred for boarding, until then we'll be loading cargo." She turned to signal a floater approaching from upbeach.

"What time is it now?"

"Fifteen hundred."

That gave him plenty of time to wait, more than he wanted. He wandered off, passing shops, a tavern, a licensed bettor's office crowded with customers, a repair shop humming with machinery, a huge open warehouse where half-naked people baled an acid-smelling dried weed. Ahead two greens came out of another tavern and strolled toward him, thumbs hooked in their belts, talking together. He was sure these two couldn't be looking for him, but he turned inland past the warehouse, not caring to have them get close.

On a wide stretch of open sand behind the warehouse an awning had been pitched. Under it were five transparent tanks, connected by tubes and pumping equipment; inside of each various creatures squirmed, wiggled, or undulated through the bubbling water. Behind were two large cabinets and a grill; in front a woman of indeterminate age and race perched on a high stool, holding a long-handled net.

Food. He knew he should husband every zina, but it seemed a long time since breakfast at the League. While he hesitated, several people came out a back door of the warehouse and headed for the awning.

"What's for today, Zidien?"

The woman slid down from her stool. "I've got squelt, coppies, walkaway, reedfish, and blats. Five zina, with ale or fizz."

As each made a choice, she scooped out a netful from the appropriate tank, drained it, dropped it into a complex appliance attached to the grill and caught it in the same net as it emerged, presumably well cleaned. Then the netful was dredged in a can of brown powder and the creatures thrown on the grill to hiss and sizzle. Finally each serving was piled in a cone of crispbread and doused with sauce; ale or fizz came from one or the other of the two cabinets. The workers lounged on the sand to consume their meals.

Tadko gave in to the complaints of his stomach and approached the woman.

"Coppies," he said, "and ale."

"No—no hot sauce," he interrupted as she raised her pitcher to finish the process. "Please," he added, for the sake of politeness.

She looked at him and at her pitcher as if unsure of her hearing.

"No hot sauce?"

"No. I'm—uh—from offworld, haven't got used to it yet."

She shrugged and raised her eyes, as if there was no accounting for the strange tastes of foreigners, but handed him his coppies without sauce, along with the container of ale.

He carried them back to the beach road, and found a disused section of walkway from where he could watch the loading of the barge for Rowder without being in the way. Then he sat, munching his food, and waiting.

The afternoon was long and slow, especially compared to the alarms and terrors of the morning. Even now he found himself glancing down the street apprehensively, half expecting someone to appear, recognize, and denounce him, but no one did. The greens he saw earlier were clearly uninterested. When he came back to the beach road, he saw them leaning against an unused barge mooring post, gazing out to sea. An elderly man in ragged breeches slept on the sand nearby, but they ignored him, and after a while they returned to the tavern.

It was easy enough to look at the sea. The waves rolled and tossed, foam flying. Far in the distance he could see the loom of another island. The view was hypnotic, magnificent, and slightly unnerving. Elnakt had its oceans, of course, but they were bitter cold. No Elnakti lived along the shores, or fished in the icy waters, or had even crossed the narrow channel to the southern continent. Not that he knew of, anyway. He tried not to think about the dark deeps below that surface.

He woke with a start, and was horrified. To have fallen asleep at a time like this! A quick look relieved him—the barge was still there—but people were already filing on board. He started toward the mooring, remembered his bundle just in time, grabbed it, and ran, arriving as the last of the other passengers went on board.

The same tall woman took his ticket and handed him a rolled-up mat.

"For sleeping," she explained. "Find yourself a slot, there'll be a stanchion and a rack for the mat."

He took the mat and made his way among the other jostlers, finding a place well inboard, near the cabin wall. There was much coming and going, a few arguments quickly stifled by the tall woman, and presently everyone was sorted out and settled.

"No meal tonight," someone called, and Tadko was glad of those coppies. "Breakfast in the morning."

A horn sounded. "All secure!" The same voice bellowed. The barge rose on its repellers, moved out across the water.

The following days were as peaceful as any he had known on Monna. *Tethrinel* stopped at a myriad of little islands not shown on his map, discharging cargo and passengers, taking on others. Always, another island, or more than one, was visible across the water.

Breakfast was bread, froile, and whatever fruit they picked up on the most recent island. Every afternoon a big net was trailed out behind the barge. When this was full it was raised and allowed to drain, then emptied into a lower section of deck, where several sailors crouched on deck to go through this catch, swiftly tossing inedible creatures back into the water, killing the edible ones and dumping them down a chute that led to the galley.

This was always followed by a descent of kitewings, previously invisible, from all over the sky, clattering and shrieking. The sea would boil for a while as all sorts of teeth and tentacles fought the birds for the leavings, sometimes getting caught themselves.

The passengers considered this a great show, and Tadko soon joined them at the rail, to cheer or insult various members of the tumult.

The edible mixture was cooked up in a kind of chowder and served with more bread for the evening meal. The taste varied from day to day. There were times when he would have given a good deal for meat, almost any kind of meat; a chunk of dried old onca from the winter store would do; but the chowder was sufficient to allay hunger, and so he ate.

He soon discovered that no one was interested in Ono Tekall, or his origins.

"Baratin," they would say. "That's a long way off, right enough?" No one ever admitted that they had never heard of the place.

"Oh yes," he said. "A long way."

"Enjoying your stay on Monna?"

"Oh yes," he lied. "It's a fine world."

That was always the end of that, for there was someone far more fascinating on board. This was a slender, handsome girl who wore a white badge on her shoulder, and a jaunty white cap with a scarlet cord around the brim. She was a starship pilot apprentice, going home to Rowder for vacation. She held court every day, telling an eager audience about her training, the offworld trips she had made, the future she hoped to have, the worlds she hoped to visit.

"I don't want to run just the three suns," she said definitely. "I want to get on the big ships that go to the out stars. Monna's just a tidepool by comparison. The ships don't even land on some of those worlds like they do here; you go into parking orbit, some of the orbits at some of those worlds are stacked as high as from here to Big Moon, and you wait for a shuttle to take you down, and if you aren't scheduled for at least twenty days in advance you can forget it. You have to wear a head comp, too, to give you all the different languages you need."

Tadko listened with curiosity, but without envy. Monna was enough for him; more than enough. Sometimes he wasn't even entirely sure of her meanings, but he didn't call attention to himself by questioning her. One thing was very clear; Elnakt and all his people were truly primitive. That was the only word he could think of, much as he hated it. He thought of the long histories of his people, chanted at the feasts and the holidays. His ancestors had come to Elnakt in five ships, ships so near breaking down that many people died before they made planetfall. They had found the Rhionny there, roaming the long plains of the halm with their onca herds, and had driven them into the mountains, killing them, taking the herds for their own. After that, there was no further contact with the Rhionny to speak of. Spring meant the herds coming out of dormancy, in the caves near the steadings. It meant shearing, then the feasting, then moving out for the summer grazing. Since the trading ships from other worlds had started coming, it also meant carrying packs of cloth and fleeces, whatever was in excess of their own needs, and guiding the herds to arrive at Port Town in midsummer. Then the trading, then the slow return to the steadings. Meat had to be dried or salted for winter, their few crops harvested, turf cut for fuel. In winter, leather and fleeces were tanned, cloth woven, clothes made, harness made or mended. There were the feasts after harvest and in midwinter, and the dances, and the chants.

Thinking of these things one night, he found himself so overwhelmed with homesickness that he huddled on his mat, head on his knees, his throat aching. When the Rhionny came back down from the mountains, everything changed. He wished his ancestors had pursued them into the mountains, wondering why they hadn't. They could have all been killed, long ago. Then he remembered how some of the killing was done, and felt ashamed of these wishes. He was ashamed, too, of having run away, yet he feared what he might find if he ever went back, supposing he ever *could* get back. He rolled over on his mat and lay awake a long time, in a numbed, thoughtless misery.

* * *

One morning he opened his eyes to find no island with plant life in sight. Instead the barge was heading toward a stand of sharp, bare peaks jutting out of the ocean. The surrounding water was a-boil with foam. Waves crashed against the peaks with a constant roar; spray pennoned off the crests.

"Are we going *there*?" he asked a sailor. The man grinned.

"Not much closer. We'll be heaving to soon enough now. Your first trip?"

"Right enough."

"Watch and see what happens."

The sailor went off to the stern, and soon the steady hum of the motors died away. The barge sank down gently to the surface of the water, rising and falling to a long swell, but obviously well away from the turmoil near the sea peaks. Stabilizers were lowered at bow and stern. Berene, the tall woman, came on deck with another sailor, the two of them lugging an enormous coiled shell. With the younger woman helping her to balance the thing, Berene set her lips to the narrow end and blew. At first nothing happened. Then a deep, hoarse wailing sounded from the mouth of the shell. Berene sustained the note for several seconds, then paused. She filled her lungs and blew again. Another pause, then a third blow. They lowered the shell to the deck and waited. Tadko looked around and saw that everyone was waiting. Passengers and any crew not on duty below were lined up along the rails, peering intently out to sea. He joined them, shading his eyes, wondering what he should expect to see.

"There!" It was Idrien, the pilot apprentice, shouting and pointing, and in a moment most of the others had joined her. All around the barge, heads were bobbing out of the water and fins, or wings, were waving. The barge captain was coming on deck, a burly woman with an air of tremendous authority, and a man Tadko had heard called the trader second. They conferred with Berene, who seemed to be third in command, inspected the bobbing heads, and conferred again. Berene stepped to the prow, cupped her hands around her mouth, and produced a series of coughs, croaks, and throat-clearings. Two of the swimmers had come closer, lines were thrown from the deck, and Tadko saw, amazed, that the swimmers were gripping the lines with hands. They pulled themselves up on the lines and replied in similar croaks and barks.

The sailor he spoke to before had returned and joined him at the rail.

"Are they intelligent? Is that really talk?" Tadko asked incredulously.

"Right enough to both, smart as you or me most likely." The young man was enjoying Tadko's astonishment. "Never heard of the Porposin?"

"Never. But do they breathe water? What are they doing here, so close to those rocks?"

"They're staying there, in hollows in the rocks. Swim in and out below the surface, where it's calm. But they breathe air, that's why they go up inside the pinnacles. It's breeding season now and the young ones have to be taught to swim before they go out, but the big ones can go a long way on one breath of air. When the young ones can swim they scatter all over and never come back till next season, that's why we come to trade now."

"How does Berene know how to talk with them? I should think it must be nearly impossible."

"Near enough. She comes from a low island, away south, where Porposin come to the beaches even between breeding seasons, and the fishers work with them. Some of the children, if they start real young, learn the talk. A Talker can set her own wage on the barges, you can go bond on that." His tone was envious, and no wonder.

Tadko watched and listened, marveling. The City was bewildering, infuriating, but human. But the strong ocean smell, the strange heads bobbing in the water, the sound of barking cries and of surf crashing on the pinnacles, the brilliant light glancing off waves—this was alien. He gripped the rail, feeling very small in all this immensity.

"Do they only live around here, or on Berene's island?"

"They live *in* the ocean, everywhere. But they come to breed and raise their young ones in lots of places, island cliff hollows and such, only not many in any one place."

The conversation ended. A sailor brought Berene a mug of hot wine, and she took several long swallows before speaking, a bit hoarsely.

"They want two dozen non-corroding, barb-headed spears with shaft grips, nineteen long knives, thirty-one short knives, and five *ki* of netting." She muttered a calculation. "That's three and a quarter standard rolls, near enough."

"Getting to be sharp bargainers, this group." The trader second pondered a moment. "I've got it, but what have they got?"

"Twenty-eight fire opals, sixteen blue water gems, ten dried flower fish, and sixty prime scrab, live."

"I'll take those off your hands, if you like," the captain put in. "Might sell them ashore, somewhere. Give you five duats."

"Sell them at Rowderport, more likely—House of Many Worlds would pay plenty. Twenty-five."

"I've got the cost of keeping them in staspack until then—House won't take 'em unless they're fresh. Give you seven."

They argued for a while and finally settled on a price for the scrab. Berene finished her wine and held another brief colloquy with the Porposin leaders. They called to their people, who crowded around the barge as nets were lowered. Tadko saw that the fins, or wings, were muscular flaps that extended from "wrist" to "hip," or whatever the Porposin equivalent would be. They oared themselves through the water.

Their goods were piled in the nets, hauled up to the deck and inspected, and the trader's goods were lowered in exchange. The Porposin made their own inspection, expressed, through Berene, their satisfaction, and distributed the goods among themselves. Then they disappeared.

The sailor laughed at Tadko's shout of surprise.

"Down to calm water, a long way down. Then back and up into the pinnacles."

He went to help with the new cargo. The scrab were leggy, humped creatures with huge claws, safely tied up with netting by the Porposin. They were lifted with hooks and lowered below through chutes; the gems, opals, and flower fish, all in skin bags, went into a safe in the cabin under the trader's seal.

Stabilizers were raised, the motors hummed into life, the barge rose and continued its voyage.

CHAPTER SEVEN

Tethrinel was back in the regular routes, island-hopping again. Often they passed other barges, sometimes close enough to hail and exchange information. Occasional wave-jets passed high overhead, and once, in the distance, they saw a deep-ocean liner, driving hard toward the west.

Flocks of kitewings soared overhead, voicing their clattering cries, and now that he knew what to look for, Tadko saw Porposin as they breasted the waves, filled their lungs, then sank into the deeps again.

The nights were pleasant, much cooler here on the water than in the City, and most of the time he slept quietly, worry and homesickness in abeyance, at least. When it rained, a transparent cover was raised at the sides and locked into place above the deck. The flowing water created a silvery dome above the sleepers. On fine nights there was Big Moon overhead, full at the time they left City Island, now waning toward the half. A little crescent, Monninet, waxed above the southern horizon. The stars were hardly visible at night in the City, but out here he could see they were all strange; he was in the wrong hemisphere to look for Yan. Just as well, maybe.

One night a storm blew up out of the south. Waves were hurled to mountainous heights and sheets of water cascaded over the cover. Tadko was nervous for a while. He knew the barge's repeller fields flattened the waves below it, but he wondered about sideways stability. He felt sure he was noticing sudden jerks and lurches, but no one else displayed any concern, and he finally relaxed.

They made several brief stops at small green islands that barely appeared to rise above the waves, unloading grain and cartons of small appliances, picking up a few more passengers.

Then, just before midday on the twenty-sixth of Koried, they arrived at Rowder.

The barge was expected. A regular bazaar had been set up under tents on the beach, and fifteen or twenty people were crowded together on the pier. When Idrien saw them, she shouted and waved her cap, pressing up against the rail. The crowd saw her and responded in kind, the children jumping up and down—some of the smallest were lifted to handy adult shoulders for a better view.

Family and friends, Tadko realized, feeling much more envy than he had had toward her choice of career. She was the first to disembark, and went off with them in a triumphant hubbub. The rest of the passengers straggled off, some heading directly into town, others pausing at the bazaar.

Berene came up to supervise the cargo.

"You're the one going on to Pad?" she asked Tadko.

"Right enough. Where do I buy my ticket?"

"Buy off the barge, same as with us. That'll be *Kelovona*, coming in tomorrow or the next day."

"Where's a cheap place to stay, here?"

She laughed. "You can beach it, if you like. Some of the others will, too. Just don't get into trouble. And find yourself a tipoay tree to sleep under. You won't get so many sand midges."

"Thanks for the advice! I'll remember," he said, turning with some reluctance to leave. It had been a pleasant trip.

He drifted down to the wide golden beach, observing the bazaar from what he hoped was a safe distance. The vendors here were even more aggressive than the ones in Sandtown.

Food, drinks, and a dizzying variety of souvenirs were offered, along with wide hats woven of reeds, scarves like those the locals wore on their heads, tunics in six different colors labeled ROWDER, sandals, and other oddments. One man offered tourist brochures, his deep bass voice usually rising above all the others.

"Information! Free information! See the famous pink and gold grottoes! Bask in the hot pools! Eat at the famous Sea-Floor Inn! Watch the exciting underwater slash-claw fights!"

It was all very interesting, but he had better find out first how far his money would take him.

At one end of the bazaar, an awning had been pitched over a shelved table and a comfortable-looking wicker chair. Here sat a young man in a breech clout, and a shirt and woven hat that could have come from one of the other booths. From the awning hung a printed sign: Barge Information. Schedules. Prices. Barge Protective League. A few people were already making inquiries.

"Pad, forty-three and five," he was saying. "Round trip, eighty-two and ten. Holos, twenty-seven. *Kelovona* comes in tomorrow, seventeen hundred. You want a transfer up to Sargason? Let's see...."

Tadko listened for a while. Various other islands were mentioned, transfer points and schedules, but again no one spoke of Sancy. All the same, he would try to get there. Surely it was just too cold for these Monnans, and he would be with his own people there.

In the meantime, today or tomorrow, he would have to get the money for *Kelovona*; he was two D short, freeze it. No use trying to steal at the beach bazaar. Too public and crowded. Dacy could do it and brag afterward, but Tadko still felt the shame of his theft from Kheer. It was wrong, there was nothing else to say.

Of course, there was the House of Many Worlds. He brightened at the thought. Those scrab from the Porposin were going to its kitchens. He recalled Raul, from the League, saying, "She'll get her meal, anyway." He could entertain in the evenings there and get free meals. Squares? Did you always have to go to their houses to get money for entertaining? He would have to excuse himself, somehow, and make up his mind to steal again. From someone.

Dacy had a nice little slitting knife, very useful for pouches. Tadko tried a few tentative gestures, but concluded there was no use trying that. Like riding an onca, it probably took a lot of practice.

He wandered down the beach. Here and there, plants like giant blades of green grass rolled tightly round each other rose from the sand, growing to three or four times his height, the tips spreading out and drooping over. They didn't give much shade, but even a little was welcome. Quite a few people were leaving their clothes on the beach, under these plants, and going in to swim. It looked cool and appealing, but he didn't care to leave his clothes unattended. At home it would be safe; here, maybe not. He did stretch out under one of the "grass" plants, took off his smock, and closed his eyes.

When he woke, the sun was setting. The bazaar people were closing down, packing up goods and tents to be carried away. Only the food kettles were left. If they filled with rainwater during the night, so much the better; it would save buying from the waterfloat in the morning. The heating units were turned off and covered with waterproof seals.

Tadko stood up to yawn and stretch, batting away some tiny flying mites, scratching at bites on his chest. Sand midges, no doubt. It was at least a little cooler.

Various people were now moving along the beach, toward the part vacated by the bazaar. They began walking across it slowly, looking down at the sand, all with something slightly furtive in manner. Frequently, one would bend over and pick up something.

Certainly! Tadko tied his smock around his waist and joined them, watching sidelong for any sign that they might resent his presence.

They ignored him, as they did each other. He found three zinae, two cracked bread cones, many broken bits of shell and other sea wrack, some badly smashed fruit tarts, what looked like a broken toy of some sort, and a half-filled carton of fizz. He put the zinae in his pouch, brushed sand off the bread cones and ate them, decided he wasn't hungry enough for the tarts, and drank the fizz. It hadn't much flavor left, but it quenched his thirst.

Landward of the beach, a shelf of crumbly rock jutted out, held by thick green turf. Narrow, paved streets wound into the town, bordered by houses and small shops all made of the same pink and gray striated stone, covered with cascades of flowering vines in every color of the spectrum. Buildings and streets, and the beach front itself, were shaded by trees with huge, gnarled black trunks, fish-scale bark, and wide golden leaves. The beach gleaners had disappeared, but several barge passengers were settling down under these trees, one or two people to a tree. Some had even brought rolled pads to spread out on the ground between the massive roots. These must be the tipoays Berene had recommended. He found one unoccupied and inspected it. Bark and leaves both gave off a tart, yet refreshing smell. Too late to do anything about the House of Many Worlds tonight, he was sure.

Now the beach was dark and quiet; Big Moon was waning. The sea offshore was dimly phosphorescent, glowing eerily as the waves tossed. He settled down for the night, grateful for a slow breeze that stirred the leaves. Just beyond the circle of leaves he could hear faint buzzings and hummings, but none of the makers of these sounds landed on him, and he was soon asleep again.

He was wakened by the return of the beach bazaar, and the departure of *Tethrinel*. For a while he lounged there, arms behind his head, leaning back against a convenient root. *Kelovona* would be in this afternoon, departing tomorrow. No use hoping for a lucky find on the beach tonight. It would have to be the House of Many Worlds. What to do? Dance? He was good at it, but shuddered at the idea of performing up on a dais like that, with all those strangers staring. Sickening thought. What was wrong? He had never thought himself a coward, why was this prospect so fearful? He *had* to do this. One of the chants, maybe. He could only do it in Elnakti, but no one had known what those aliens were about, either. A strange human language should be no problem.

Feeling a bit sick to his stomach, he rose and went to investigate the bazaar offerings. Food might help, and he must find out where this House of Many Worlds was located.

He paused by a seafood seller.

"Could you tell me where in town to find the House of Many Worlds?"

"What's wrong?" she shouted. "You want fancy eats, too good for food fresh out of the sea? Just look at these prails!" She held aloft a netful of pink somethings, shook it at him. "Just gutted this morning!"

Tadko swallowed hard and retreated. Someone else was shouting.

"Froile! One zina! Good hot froile! One zina!"

Meager as his pouch was, he just had to have froile. He drank it with much relief; it seemed to settle his stomach a little. He didn't really want food.

"Do all of you come out to the beach every morning?" He asked the froile vendor.

"Only when barges are due in or out. *Kelovona* comes in this afternoon, leaves tomorrow at 0800. Then we close up 'til *Rambirel* comes in, on the 32nd. The resorts are in-island, other side of town, but we get tourists here, too."

"Good idea." Tadko finished his froile and tried the question again. "Can you tell me where in town is the House of Many Worlds?"

"Right enough." Not being a food vendor, this man didn't seem to view the House as competition. He pointed. "Right up Pier Street there, far as the fountain circle, turn right again. Opens 2100."

"Thanks." Tadko left, wondering how to endure the afternoon. *Tethrinel* had departed. He had no timepiece, and didn't want to call attention to himself by frequently asking for the hour. He tried to nap on the sand for a while, but found it impossible. He strolled up the beach, took off his sandals, and waded, trying to get interested in the various items of flotsam left just above the water line, or in the tiny creatures below the surface, scurrying away from his feet.

At last he gave up and walked up along Pier Street, passing the small shops and offices, and located the fountain with the House of Many Worlds beyond it. There were benches in the circle, and a vendor of cold fizz. Here he saw townspeople and a good many tourists, even aliens of types he hadn't seen since the spaceport. The tourists were either better dressed than the beach sleepers, or already equipped with gaudy smocks and reed hats from beach vendors.

Around one corner he even found a public bath, where he spent two of his precious zinae. A good thing, too. He cleaned himself up, washed and dried the clothes he'd been wearing, and re-did his hair with the glisten. He decided to wear his ship clothes for the House, changed, made his bundle as small and neat as possible, and went to wait for the House to open.

Eventually multicolored windows glowed and patrons began to appear. He entered and took one of the little tables up near the dais, wishing he could get rid of the sick feeling, hoping he wouldn't disgrace himself. Gradually the place filled. Near him a group of seven young people, all dressed in silver, settled themselves. Tourists came in, then locals, and finally, to his surprise, richly dressed commercials like those he had seen in the city.

A waiter approached him. "Dinner tonight, grilled scrab with tartleaf, perlau of mixed fruit, savories. Will you order?"

Tadko shook his head. "I—entertain," he said huskily, pointing to the dais.

"Ah," said the waiter, his face carefully blank. "You wish to be served later, then."

Tadko nodded. It sounded revolting.

At last the Master of Ceremonies, a twin of the one in the City, rose to make his announcement. Somehow, Tadko got himself up the steps first and spoke to the man, who turned to the audience.

"Ono Tekall, from a far world, will give us a ritual chant from among his own people." Tadko hadn't said it was a ritual; ah, well.

For one horrible moment he thought he couldn't speak. Then he drew a deep breath and managed to start.

"Five ships there were on a desperate voyage, traveling far from a nameless sun...." It grew easier, his voice strengthening, as he remembered old Kassak, on a many a winter night, teaching them all the chants that were the history of their people.

He thought at first he would bring them all the way to the Landing; then he knew he couldn't, stopped abruptly, bowed, and somehow got himself down the steps and back to his table. He was vaguely aware of rather desultory applause. No one came to "tap" him, but a waiter soon arrived with the meal, including a drink he called "froile fizz." Tadko drank gladly. It was delicious; froile chilled to icy crystals, with sweet spice added. When he quit shaking, he discovered he was hungry after all, and the food was good, too.

He was followed by the silver-clothed young Monnans. While three of them played musical instruments, a complex, dreamy melody, the others gracefully performed an elaborate dance. They received enthusiastic applause, and one of the commercials came to speak with them.

Tadko finished the food and began looking over the other customers. From one of them he would have to steal. Not one of those two stern-faced men in spacecrew uniform. He hoped it hadn't been a mistake to wear his own ship clothes. No one who looked like a tourist, either. He might meet the same person on board *Kelovona*, tomorrow. He frowned worriedly, realizing how hard it could be to distinguish tourists from locals; the latter used barge travel, too. Definitely not an alien. That pale-faced, white-haired young Dorran in dark gray Monnan clothing? He didn't look promising.

The commercials now. Not nearly as many here as at the House in the City, but they would have plenty of squares and certainly wouldn't be traveling by barge. Yes.

If there were other entertainers, he wasn't aware of them. When the Master of Ceremonies announced closing time, he left, trying to get out as quickly as possible without shoving or drawing attention to himself. The fountain circle was lighted now by cloudy globes that hung just above the low buildings, but he found a patch of shadow and waited.

The first commercial to emerge appeared to speak at a mechanism mounted on his wrist. He looked up, and a floater lowered gently into the circle. He called; several others came out and joined him in the floater, which lifted away. Tadko watched, stunned and furious, while the process was repeated. All the chosen prey, escaping. He glanced around. Other customers were departing down the side streets and lanes, but in groups. But there went White-Hair, alone down a quiet alley. Tadko gritted his teeth, crossed the circle, and ran after. The fellow might have a couple of D, anyway.

White-Hair had disappeared. Tadko stopped at a corner, looking around angrily, and was suddenly confronted by a shadowy figure, one hand extended, a knife held out in the other.

"Give!" It said.

"What?"

"Your money, stupid crewboy! Squares! Empty your pouch!" The knife darted forward suggestively.

All the frustration and humiliation he had endured on Monna boiled up in Tadko. He launched himself, knocked the knife away with a blow to the wrist, grabbed the man, and hooked his leg to throw him to the ground. He stood panting, fists clenched.

"Come on!" He urged. "Get up and be knocked down again!"

No response. Tadko sneered. He might not know much about Monna, but he had been a top wrestler at home. He bent over his assailant, warily. Was the fellow shamming? He pulled at a veil that concealed the head...it was White-Hair. He touched the man's throat. No, not dead. But if he was what he seemed to be—Dacy had demonstrated long, narrow pockets that could be suspended inside the breeches. Tadko pulled at White-Hair's waistband. Right enough, two of them. One was empty, the other produced a handful of squares. He tucked them in his own pouch, then looked at the knife. No, he couldn't murder an unconscious man.

He ran back to the fountain circle, slowing to a walk as he came into the light. It was empty, the lights in the House were dark; so were all the shops along Pier Street. He ran back to the beach and ducked under a tipoay tree for a while, watching, hardly daring to think there would he no pursuit, no alarm.

Nothing. Whisper of tipoay leaves, waves slapping gently on the beach, faint snores from a sleeper. He left his shelter and walked away down the beach; away from the town, the pier, and the sleepers. Well isolated beyond a clump of sand grass, he risked leaving his clothes on the beach. He bathed and washed as much as possible of the hair glisten out of his hair. Another change of appearance was desirable, even if it was only partial. He smoothed his hair back as best he could, then spent a wakeful, nervous night under another tipoay tree.

At first light he was on the move. He dressed in his other clothes, then wrapped a stained cloth around his still-damp hair in what he hoped was the local style. With a veil to cover his head, White-Hair had been almost invisible last night, and Tadko hoped he hadn't been too recognizable himself. He checked his haul from White-Hair; only five D, and some off zinae. Pity it wasn't more; White-Hair may have just started his night's activities. But it was enough.

Fearful that White-Hair might have recovered and be looking for him among the departing tourists, he hurried to one of the vendors.

"A scarf and a clothes bag; how much?" he asked. "I'm leaving on *Kelovona*."

The wrong thing to say. He could see her calculating—this young man is in a hurry!

"Half a D, straight up."

"That's stupid!" he raged, in too much of a hurry to indulge in the usual bargaining, and turned away.

"Eight zinae!" She changed her tune instantly, shouting at his retreating back. "Eight zinae for a handsome young man like you! Best quality! Buy from old Millin, you can't do better!"

Probably not, he decided, and it would stop her clamor.

"Right enough. Done. Let's see them."

The bag looked like any other. She offered him a green scarf and he took it, was about to refuse her offer to arrange it properly, then told her to go ahead and flipped her another zina. Best to have it looking right, if he was going to wear it.

He picked up a carton of froile, and hurried to the barge landing.

CHAPTER EIGHT

For several hours *Kelovona* ran down the coast of Rowder: a riot of gold, black, and pale green colors Tadko could not distinguish as plants or anything else. A few villages sheltered in coves, and twice they turned well out to sea to avoid clusters of fishing craft. Then the land tipped up, ending in cliffs and a scatter of wave-rounded boulders. Here the repellers were halted, and they sank to the surface of the water. Tadko was not surprised to see the captain and mate come on deck—there was no trader second—with two young men carrying another big coiled shell.

The Talker on this barge was a strange man. He appeared elderly; his face was a mass of wrinkles, his hair yellowed and thin, his hands were ridged with prominent veins and tendons. Yet his taut, powerful muscles would have done credit to a much younger man. He seemed to have no other duties, but spent the time lounging on deck, wearing only a loin-strap, speaking to no one. Now he opened a jar and began oiling himself thoroughly from scalp to toes. When finished, he stood and put a horn to his lips.

The horn sounded three blasts, echoing over the water. The heads of the Porposin appeared around the barge and he went forward to begin the colloquy. After some conversation he turned to the captain.

"They haven't any trade goods, but they need two and half *ki* of medium weight line."

The captain rubbed his chin thoughtfully, turned to the mate. "I didn't lay in any extra line, could we spare any from stores?"

She nodded.

"Could spare one and a half, maybe a little more. We probably won't need it, we can replace it at Holos or Morneol."

"All right, tell them that, and ask them if they can give us any trade goods on the return trip; I'd like some eye-stones or luck shells."

"Do they get something for nothing?" Tadko murmured.

One of the sailors with the shell made a sawing gesture with his hand.

"We'll get it back one way or another," he said.

"Sea people are different. We like to keep on their good sides." That was an old lady, one of a pair traveling home from a visit to their families on Rowder.

The old Talker had finished his discussion.

"They'll accept that." His voice was hoarse, vocal cords roughened from years of producing the difficult Porposin speech. "They say there'll be no eye-stones this year, raspers got in and ruined the three-year crop. Luck shells are nearly mature, they should have plenty when you come back."

The coil of line was brought up and lowered on a hook. The old man had been edging toward the rail, and now he caught the captain's eye. The captain seemed to hesitate, then shrugged and nodded. The old man sprang over the rail and dove, his body slicing the water without a splash. He reappeared after a moment, waved, and then was swimming toward the cliffs with the Porposin. The repellers began to hum and the barge was rising.

"Will we leave him here?" Tadko exclaimed in astonishment.

"He'll stay there, with the Porposin, until we make our return trip," said one of the sailors. "Stay with them permanently, if he could. Old Raf is more than half Porposin, himself."

Tadko's eyes widened. "Really?"

The sailor only laughed. The other passengers were laughing too, even the old ladies, but one of the young men took pity on him.

"No, not really, that's impossible," he said. "But it happens to some Talkers, after a while. They get so they're happier with the Porposin than with their own people; the language gets to be easier than their own, and all they want to do is be in the water. You saw him oiling himself, that will protect his skin for quite a while. But of course they can only be with them at breeding time, the rest of the year they're out at sea, and no human can stay in the water like that. No human can go as long on a single breath, either. So old Raf probably has enough squares laid away somewhere that he could go to the City and live like a commercial if he wanted to, but he rides the barges in spring to be with the sea people. The smart ones retire before the craving takes hold of them, but some don't." He added with a grin, "He may even have a wife, there in the cliffs."

"Young man, that's a terrible slander!" The two old ladies were actually scolding in unison. "Such things never happen!"

"Of course, grandmothers, I apologize. One really shouldn't say such things." The young man's tone was respectful, but his face as he turned away bore a faint grin, reflected in the expressions of several others.

Tadko found the idea more saddening than amusing. Rowder was left behind now, and the barge was alone, the last rays of Seleme glittering over the waves. He looked out at the darkening water, and wondered aloud.

"Do they ever—well—forget they're human, and try to follow the sea people—way out there?"

The others' looks grew as somber as his own, as they followed his gaze out to sea.

"Sometimes." That was one of the girls. "Sometimes."

During the night he was vaguely aware of a stop at a small island, and the rumble of cargo being unloaded from below. In the morning he discovered that the old ladies had left as well, and been replaced by a young couple with a small toddler. The little girl was buckled into a harness attached to a line, the other end of the line being secured to the stanchion where her parents spread their mats. With this to keep her from falling overboard, she wandered freely around the deck. She found Tadko's foreign appearance quite fascinating, and often stopped—at a safe distance—to eye him solemnly.

The only other passengers were the half dozen young people who had boarded along with him at Rowder. They were even taller and more graceful than most Monnans, with long, smooth muscles under their tunics and loose breeches. They, too, were interested in the foreigner, and for the first time he faced potentially awkward questioning.

"What is your name? Where are you from? Where is that? What is your home world like? How did you happen to come to Monna?"

"Ono Tekall, from Baratin. It's a long way off. It's a cold world, compared to Monna. I was born here when my parents were visiting, and I thought I'd like to come back and see what it was like." No mention of his father being Monnan, he had decided this might be wiser. Now he tried to deflect the questioning. "Where are you from, on Monna, and where are you bound?"

There were shrugs, and that sawing gesture. The young man who told him about the Talkers seemed to have appointed himself spokesman.

"We were all visiting our people on Rowder, but we're going back to our jobs on Morneol, that's all."

"Visit the fabulous undersea gardens of Morneol," said another in a bored voice.

"Why, aren't they really fabulous?"

Looks of consternation flashed across the young faces. After all, this foreigner might be a future customer!

"Oh, right enough, of course they are, well worth seeing; it's just that we work there all the time, diving to tend the gardens, and keeping watch on the tourist cells when they're underwater. You ought to see them, yourself. Might you be stopping on Morneol? We could tell you all about it."

"I'd like to stop, but I'm going on directly to Pad."

A fortunate remark. Tadko's origins and motives were forgotten.

"Oh, you're on your way to the carnival, then! You're in luck, you'll get there just as it starts."

"I will? I hadn't known about this carnival, I've just been island hopping. What is it like?"

All of them talked at once, words tumbling out in a stream.

"It's the biggest thing in this hemisphere, *everybody* will be coming to the carnival! You're really in luck, wish *I* could afford to go some time—my parents took me once—there'll be the swimming and diving championships, and the slideboard sail races, and the paddleboat races, and the end of the Milian Oceans' Run, around both poles. On land there are contests too, running and racing and wrestling—anyone can enter for those, but for the water events you have to be sponsored by one of the commercial houses. Oh, and the waterbatics. And there's dancing in the evening, and free food on all the beaches. They'll bake quannits this big on the shore—" The tallest young man stretched out his arms. "And there'll be buckets of sauce, and barrels of vegetable pickle, and platters of crispbread. Everyone gets a free glass of ale, too, although if you want more of that you have to pay for it, but all the rest is free, all you want. The tour boats will line up at sea, and they have viewing stands all along the south shore."

It sounded like great fun, especially the free food. Tadko experienced a pang of deep regret that he was not, in fact, a footloose traveler, free to wander wherever he wished. But he would have to steal the money to go on, and manage to avoid being stolen from, as well.

He ventured a question he had never dared ask before.

"I would like to go on from Pad to Sancy Island, after the carnival, of course. Will I be able to get barge transport?"

Now the looks were bewildered.

"Why ever would you want to go to Sancy? There's nothing there."

"It's an island, there must be *something* there."

"Right enough, but there's nothing much. It's cold and barren, no mountains, not many trees even, nothing to do or see."

One of the girls shook her head.

"I've never even heard of any resorts there, so where would you stay?"

"The north coast of Sancy is fifteen degrees south of Pad, and it really makes a difference." The tall young man sounded genuinely concerned. "Nothing there except the kelp processors."

"Remember I come from a cold world, I think I would enjoy seeing a cold part of Monna. It probably won't seem that cold to me."

"There is that. Still, if you want cold, you would do better to go to one of the resort islands. There are mountains, and sports, and Mount Proin, on Corcrypht, is snow-capped all year round."

Tadko was left dissatisfied. They still hadn't answered his question as to whether he could get transport to Sancy from Pad, but he thought it would be safer not to press. After Morneol perhaps he would ask one of the sailors; surely they would know.

He did learn a great deal about Morneol in the next few days. He heard of the Rainbow Garden, the Crimson Garden, the Golden Garden. All these "flowers" were a strange plant-animal combination, and one of the tasks of the divers was to feed them with bits of fish and seaweed, to make them display their colors before the tourists.

He heard, too, that a great many tourists would be waiting at Morneol to go on to Pad for the carnival. Many would arrive by wave-jet or shuttle—there were landing plats on Pad—still others would come by tour boat and live on the boats during the festivities, but all the barges in the region would be carrying eager loads as well.

So they came to Morneol, soon after dawn on a rainy day, moving for two hours across a deep lagoon surrounded by a narrow circle of island. Tadko stood at the rail with the others, watching the shore through the veil of water that ran down over the deck cover.

The young couple had been quiet and bashful during the rest of the trip; suddenly they became loquacious. They were fishers from Holos, who had saved their money and were now taking their first voyage off their home island. They hoped the accommodations would be pleasant; they hoped they had enough squares; they hoped they would be able to see everything *important*; they hoped their little Prelissa wouldn't be scared by all the crowds. Tadko was amused and not a little gratified to discover that they regarded him with some awe—he had been to the City! He found himself describing it with more enthusiasm than he really felt, and more of an air of knowledgeability than his experience really warranted.

Then they were arriving at Morneolport. The deck crew came up, the barge was turned and eased up carefully, stern first, to the dock. Lines were thrown and there was a bustle of departure. The mate beckoned to Tadko.

"You're going on direct to Pad?"

"Yes."

"Right enough, but you'll have to go offboard for a while, say three hours, we'll be loading. You can leave your bag here, tie it up good to the stanchion and it'll go right up when we raise deck. Better get something to eat ashore, too. Then come on back, you can make sure of your place before the crowd arrives."

"Will there be a crowd?"

She grinned broadly.

"You can go bond on that! There'll be lots of people who've been touring Morneol going on now to the carnival. We only make one more stop, that's Tallenport, then direct from there to Pad. Leave any later than this, by barge anyhow, and they'd arrive too late for the opening fireworks."

"Thanks, I'll make sure I'm on time."

Having no timepiece, he thought it best to hang around the docking area, keeping an eye on the loading. There were plenty of shops for browsing, even here; round white buildings with fluted scarlet roofs like tall pointed hats, the "brims" extending a long way out to shelter customers from the frequent rains. He came across a display of Luck Shells, and understood why the captain wanted them. They were small, thick, polished ovals, one side a translucent pink shading to gold at the edges, the other mottled in silver, greens and blues; no two were exactly alike. Each was fitted with a loop, to be hung around the neck on a chain or attached to belt, pouch, or wristband. They were cool, very pleasant to touch, and five duats each. He realized he had seen them on many people, especially sailors.

Another shop offered living souvenirs. There were brilliantly multicolored fish, clawed creatures in fantastically convoluted shells, or miniature specimens of the "flowers," with instructions as to their care and feeding. Many of these aquaria were guaranteed to be self-contained and self-cleaning, fully sealed, and generally safe to take off world. All were unbreakable. Tadko wasn't sure he believed it, but clearly a lot of tourists did. Yet another place featured cages of tiny green birds, warbling cheerfully. They were the first birds he had seen on Monna, except for the kitewings that hovered around all the shores and followed the barges, and he found them enchanting. Elnakt had no birds at all.

He thought it would be wonderful to come back here someday as a real tourist, see the gardens, grottos, and other attractions whose luminous signs hung seductively in the air, buy a couple of Luck Shells and perhaps a little singing bird, and generally enjoy himself. Some day. Maybe.

As it was, he had to keep a sharp eye out as the loading progressed on the barge. Mindful of the mate's advice, he followed his nose to a section devoted to food stands. Squelt was the cheapest here as in the City, so he bought it, and was agreeably surprised to find it much tastier than the product of the park cart. Dacy must have been right about the scrapings. Then he threw caution to the winds and spent six zinae for half a dozen fruit tarts, rolled in crystallized sugar. They were delicious.

Comfortably filled, he whiled away the rest of the time watching the dock activity. Barges and tour boats crowded the water as far as he could see. Signs at the mooring posts advertised either cheap travel to the carnival or luxury travel, by barges or tour boats, respectively.

At last he saw the loaders depart and the decks lowered, and returned to his barge. A gaggle of people was already waiting behind a restraining cord, with a couple of burly sailors on guard. They recognized him and waved him on board, where he went straight to his mat and checked on his bag, figuring it would be best to make sure his claim was well established before the others started looking.

From his place before the steering cabin, he heard them coming on board.

"Easy, easy, no rushing, plenty of room," the captain was booming.

"This is primitive traveling, but it will leave us more squares for the carnival, that's the important thing." The voice was penetrating, high, and distinctly condescending.

Tadko went rigid. He knew that voice! Then he dropped to his mat, pulled up his knees, put his head down and his arms around his head. In this position he listened to the shuffle of feet, the discussions and arguments, the thump of dropped luggage, creaks and bumps as racks were pulled down and mats unrolled. Had he imagined the voice? He tried to pick it out again, but could not distinguish it above the general hubbub. Cautiously he shifted until he was able to peer out between his arms, and searched among the passengers. He found three young Eilonsaders. They were dressed in decent Monnan style instead of the absurdities some of them affected in the City, but there was no question—one of them was Kheer. Tadko's first impulse was to run to the rail, jump over, and try to swim back to shore, but he forced himself to sit still. Everyone would see and wonder why, the barge captain might feel obliged to make inquires, and the chances of his being allowed to disappear quietly were nil. What ghastly set of circumstances had brought Kheer to this barge, on this day? Why, everyone was going to the carnival, of course. They probably came out to Morneol by wave jet or passenger shuttle, saw the local sights, and now were going on to Pad. It wasn't even that surprising for him to be on this particular barge. Later departures might not get there in time for the opening fireworks, according to what the mate had said. The tour boats could leave later and still arrive in time, but he and his cronies had chosen to travel cheaply for this last leg of their tour. Tadko almost groaned aloud. How many days to Pad? Five or six at least, even though they would be moving fast now, making only one stop.

He wondered if he could evade Kheer's notice, even on the barge. There must be thirty or more passengers now, which would mean not much moving around except to go to the heads; at least, not if this captain kept the kind of order that obtained on the first barge he rode.

His clothes were different, he carried a proper bag instead of a grimy bundle, his eyes were darkened. He had washed out his hair and continued to wear the green head scarf purchased on Rowder, and for this he was thankful. A hair style too much like his own might have attracted Kheer's attention. He sat, trying to decide.

The barge moved on. They hadn't slowed to garner a meal from the sea, but before sunset bowls of chowder were brought up from below and passed around. Each one had a thick slice of bread on top, and this was followed by mugs of froile. Tadko continued to crouch over, head bent, holding the bowl of chowder up in front of him and spooning it into his mouth with his arm held akimbo as a shield.

With the meal the other passengers became merry. There was much talk about the carnival. One man, a broad-shouldered, somewhat coarse-faced fellow raised his mug like a wine glass and spoke grandly.

"If we were all to be together, I would bet with you all; as it is, I make a prophecy—House Ornibeck to win the Oceans' Run, the deep diving championships, and the swimming triad."

"You'll not win many squares if you bet like that," came a sardonic voice from the other side of the deck. "Never is it that certain before the trials. I pick Crale for the deep diving."

"Concoras for me," a bright-faced girl sang out. "In the Oceans' Run and the paddle boat races."

"Crales are too miminy," the coarse-faced man objected. "Their apprentices spend all their time at their work. Concoras are too cheap to buy first class equipment, if it doesn't produce a profit they won't touch it."

"We should introduce ourselves," a plump woman put in, "If we are going to travel together. My name is Zarit Laynithen, this is my husband Uvis, my son Arlin. If we are going to bet we might want to keep in touch after we arrive at Pad, place some wagers among ourselves."

She glanced at her husband with a sly smile, which he returned.

"A fine thought!" said the coarse-faced man. "I am Gradoro Virn. When we arrive we will exchange our addresses, and place our wagers."

Now they were all introducing themselves, and yes, he heard Kheer announcing himself in that lofty, supercilious voice. Tadko stretched out on his mat and turned his face away, feigning sleep. He heard the round of introductions coming closer.

"Parl Ken," said someone close to him, repeated it more loudly, sniffed, and added, "dull fellow. Seems to be asleep."

He was mildly curious about this person, the name did not sound Monnan, but not nearly enough to turn and look. He lay as quietly as possible, arm over his head. He would have introduced himself as Ono Tekall, certainly Kheer would not know the name; would he have known the accent? In any case, his chances of remaining unrecognized seemed poor, not with this cheery pre-carnival camaraderie beginning to pervade the passenger group. No other choice, though, beyond jumping into the ocean.

His muscles began to feel cramped; he moved a little to ease them. He wanted to sleep but feared that during sleep he might turn over and expose his face to the others. He dozed for a while in spite of his worries, woke again. He shifted his arm carefully, and opened his eyes. Darkness. He listened intently. Silence. Quiet breathing, a few barely audible snores.

Slowly, making no noise, he sat up and looked over the barge. Sure enough, everyone was deep asleep. He relaxed, leaned back against the cabin wall, looked out to sea, and saw the dark loom of an island close by in the southeast. That would be Tallen, they should be in Tallenport in the morning.

He was not really aware of making the decision. He would leave the barge tonight, swim to Tallen, and cross the island to Tallenport. There he would find another barge, and go on.

There was no light on deck, except for tiny spots along the rails. Riding lights at bow and stern illuminated the water before and behind, and a dim glow came from the high windows of the circular cabin. They would be coming from the instrument panels, since the cabin itself was kept dark, not to interfere with the outside view. There would be two, possibly three on watch, but they would be looking far out to sea, not to the deck directly below them.

He removed his head scarf, sandals, and pouch, put them in his bag, and closed it securely. He slipped the handles over his belt, pushed the bag around to his back. The heads for deck passenger use were on each side toward the stern. He rose in a half crouch, keeping close to the wall as far as possible, and made his way back.

Instead of going into the head, he went to the rail alongside, inhaled several deep breaths, swung himself over and leaped out as far as he could.

A sear of cold as he dropped through the edge of the repeller field, then it was thrusting him down, down, into glinting black water, trailing a cloud of phosphorescence behind. Down, down—he flailed arms and legs with the beginning of panic, felt a surge of relief as he started to rise again. Up, up...he broke the surface at last, managed to keep still while he gasped for breath and filled his lungs again.

For a little while he hung there, treading water, orienting himself. He found the stern light of the barge, dwindling away to the east; the hum of the repeller fields had not ceased, there was no outcry—no one had yet noticed that they were short a passenger.

The night was enormous and dark. The sea went on forever, reflecting the stars with a dull gleam. Big Moon was below the horizon. Swift-moving Monninet was just past full, but no larger than the palm of his hand; it gave little light. The only sound came from the lapping waves, not even a kitewing clattered overhead. In the distance some creature of the sea breached, a black outline against the stars, then sank below again. With a chill that had nothing to do with the tepid water, he turned toward the loom of Tallen, laid himself out, and swam.

He began to understand that he had made a fatal mistake.

Swimming in the shallow sinks along the Ice River was wholly different from swimming in the ocean. Calm as it had looked from the deck of the barge, this water was rough to an inexperienced swimmer. Sometimes he was borne up on a crest; sometimes he was carried down and dunked, the wave slapping him in the face. Every few strokes he got another swallow of salt water. His bag hampered him, interfering with his swimming movements; when he pushed it around to the front, it weighed him down. For a while he paused to rest, treading water again, trying not to admit to himself that the island looked as far away as ever—farther. He tried pacing himself, swimming twenty strokes, resting for a count of twenty, swimming for another twenty, but the rests grew longer, the swimming shorter. His limbs felt like stone, dragging through the water, almost too heavy to lift.

Then, between him and the shore, heads appeared above the water; dark `wings' rose and fell. Porposin! Might they help? He tried to call out, choked and sank.

Then a large, firm hand was gripping each arm, lifting him out of the water. One of the dark-furred sea people swam on each side of him, holding him up, carrying him toward the island at an impossible speed.

They came to a stop some distance from the beach, holding him up, touching his face gently with their long-nailed, furred fingers, speaking in their croaking, coughing voices. At first he didn't understand. Then he felt sandy bottom, and realized they had arrived. He staggered up and out of the water, fell on his knees, and spent a long time vomiting, mostly sea water. After that he crawled on a little farther and rolled over on his back.

When he managed to sit up, he saw them watching him from the water's edge, and he returned the scrutiny. Larger even than the tall Monnans. Heads that sloped directly into torsos shaped like V's, with the strong hands at the ends of the V. A narrowing into something like a waist, then a rounding into something like human hips, a final tapering of tail, dividing into broad horizontal flukes at the base. They were covered in dark smooth fur. When he saw them in the water, he thought their features looked quite human, with heavier jaws and longer noses; now he could only see the glowing dark eyes. They wore harnesses of straps, with sheathed knives and other equipment attached. One had a mane of heavier hair on head and shoulders; the other, a more rounded abdomen. He thought they must be male and female; no, he corrected himself, man and woman. He raised his hand and waved.

"I'm all right now. I thank you very much, I know you saved my life." He hoped they would understand his gratitude, if not his actual words.

Perhaps they did, for each raised a hand in response, stretching out the triangular bands of heavy muscle that had given the impression of wings, or fins, in the ocean. Then they were hitching themselves toward deeper water, awkward outside their proper element. They found the depth they required, and disappeared.

Now he understood the trade that wasn't always trade, and the remarks of the islanders on the barge. "We get it back one way or another." "We like to keep on their good sides."

He nodded and silently wished them well, then turned and crawled father up the beach, through grass, a few shrubs, and into the shadow of trees before he collapsed in sleep.

CHAPTER NINE

Water. More than anything else, he had to have water. Aching all over, he struggled to his feet and stood blinking and swaying. Far to his right rose the peaks that formed the central mountain spine of Tallen, not high, but sharp and precipitous. Pennons of smoke trailed from their summits. Off to his left was the sea. Somewhere ahead there should be a stony ridge pushing up through the sand. He had glimpsed it last night, and if his experience on other islands held true, that ridge ought to be a source of fresh water. He headed in what he hoped was the right direction.

He pushed through a stand of plants like shoulder high white feathers growing in the dark soil. Creatures that looked half-lizard, half-fish perched on the crests, chirping at him in tiny squeaky voices. Something else skittered away from beneath his feet. He told himself that according to the geographies he had studied, there were no dangerous animals on the islands of Monna, but he felt his heart speed up just the same. Now the feathers gave way to larger plants, soaring dark trunks covered with gray fuzz and bearing great green crests of leaves. Below them were smaller shrubs, vines, and clusters of fleshy growths; finally he heard the sound of running water just ahead.

It was a ledge of porous volcanic rock, with lush small flowers rooted in every crevice. Water trickled from a dozen openings, running into a pool at the base, then overflowing to cascade toward the beach. He sprawled on his belly and plunged his whole head into the pool, then drank, drank, paused for a moment to draw breath, and drank again. Sighing with relief, he sat up and leaned back against the damp rock. A glare of light, painful even though filtered through overhanging vines, told him he needed more retina screen. He unhitched his bag from his belt and rummaged for the bulb. The bag was waterproof; only a little dampness had seeped through the closure. He found the bulb and applied the screen, then considered the jar of black hair glisten, deciding that it would be impossible to apply without a mirror, and he would be staying in the forest anyway. He put on his sandals, for the sandy soil was already hot underfoot.

Now for food. The nearest was the beach, and he knew, now, what to look for. He told himself it was no worse than the hoppers and summer crawlers that they all ate on the trail at home, if only things here didn't have that perpetual ocean flavor.

Cooking and saucing made all the difference, but he didn't think he had better risk a fire. He followed the stream down to the water's edge.

Out at sea three floaters were maneuvering, moving slowly, close to the surface. He paused to watch. In the distance he could see two others; now one of the nearby craft broke formation and headed toward the beach. He turned to run, then stopped dead, all his new-found energy draining away.

They had to be searching for him. He should have guessed a tourist couldn't just vanish in mid-ocean without any notice taken. He looked again, longingly, at the forest. If he had only stayed out of sight, they might have assumed he was drowned, but a real tourist wouldn't run away from rescuers. It might even be a crime to jump off a barge—

best to say he had fallen. He picked up his bag and stood waiting, pulling his shoulders back, trying to muster a look of eager enthusiasm.

The floater hummed in and lowered to the beach; a ramp was let down from a door in the side and two young people sprang down. At least they weren't greens. They wore calf-length dark blue pants, lighter blue tunics with white shoulder straps, and round brimless caps bearing a silver badge in the form of a coiled shell. They regarded Tadko with a kind of austere detachment.

"You're Ono Tekall, off *Kelovona* last night?" The young woman inquired.

"Yes, that's right." He attempted a pleased smile. "I'm glad you found me."

"Routine," said the young woman. "We're from the Oceanic Patrol, Tallen base. Get aboard. Moderio, give him a hand."

Tadko was grateful for Moderio's help. His legs were suddenly wobbly, whether from hunger or nervousness he couldn't be sure. Someone with two silver shells on his cap was waiting for them inside the floater, and the young woman sketched an easy salute.

"It's Tekall, all right, we can message *Kelovona* and let them know."

Tadko was ushered to a cabin, snug and comfortable enough, given a flask of fresh water, and left. A little later the young man, Moderio, came in.

"On our way to Westowere now, that's our base," he said. "You'll have to see the Commander, of course. Did you swim ashore?"

"No. After I fell I called to the barge, but I guess they didn't hear me. Then I tried to swim ashore, but I wasn't going to make it, but two Porposin helped me to the beach."

The young man whistled.

"You were in luck. Not many are likely to be in the north side waters, this time of year. Most of them have gathered at the south side cliffs, by now. Anyway, we'll be making port by midday. You need anything in the meantime? Want something to eat?"

"Yes, thanks." Whatever happened later, he'd be foolish to turn down a free meal.

Moderio brought him a platter of cold pickled fish and vegetables with plenty of crispbread on the side; he finished it all, and sat, working on the story he would have to tell this commander. After a bit he considered his appearance, and found a mirror. Too late to reapply hair glisten, probably. He neatened himself up as well as he could, tied the green scarf around his head, and hoped for the best.

The commander was a stern-faced woman of middle years, her bronzing hair cut short and confined by silver clips. Over her pants and tunic she wore a knee-length coat of darker blue, severe in cut, with some improbable-looking sea creature in gold on the shoulder straps. She looked at Tadko coldly; then the corners of her mouth lifted in a caricature of a smile.

"I hope, Siro, that you are suffering no ill effects from your unfortunate experience."

Tadko blinked. Whatever he had expected, it certainly wasn't this.

"Uh, no, not at all, thank you, Sira."

"I trust there was no negligence on the part of the barge crew that might have contributed to your—accident?"

"Oh no, not at all. Sira."

"The safety regulations were explained to all passengers?"

"Oh yes, Sira."

"There was no overcrowding of the deck accommodations?"

"Oh no, not at all, Sira." He hadn't sweated so much since he first arrived on Monna.

"Well, I was very sleepy, you see, Sira, it was very late at night, and I went back to the—er—head, and I thought I saw Porposin out in the water, and I must have leaned over too far, and it seemed to happen so quickly—I don't swim very well, you see, and by the time I got back to the surface the barge was already a long way off —I called, but they didn't hear me." He had to pause and draw breath.

"I have here the report from *Kelovona*. According to this, you were acting rather strangely all afternoon, and in fact were already half-asleep when the sunset meal was served."

"Uh, well—"

The commander's mouth quirked again, slightly.

"You had gone offboard on Morneol? No doubt you had some refreshment there?"

So that's what she was thinking! All he'd had to drink on Morneol was a carton of cold fizz, but he hung his head, contriving to look both guilty and repentant.

"Uh, well—"

"Something local and exotic, no doubt; was it a Hurricane or a Fire Spout, or possibly both?"

"Uh, I'm afraid I don't remember, Sira."

"No doubt. I understand you were rescued and brought to shore by two Porposin who happened to be in those waters."

"Yes, that's right, Sira."

"You were extremely fortunate. You understand, our friends of the sea are very good about helping humans in difficulty, but we can't expect them to be there at all times, or to look after those who are simply careless. Especially at this time of year, they have their own concerns, and while they do trade with us, we must be careful not to impose. They come to bear their young and teach them to swim, you know."

"Oh yes, Sira. I'll be very careful in the future—I really will. This has been—an experience I won't forget. I'll be very careful."

The commander turned.

"Comper, see if there are any charges outstanding against Tekall, Ono, of Baratin."

Tadko tried not to hold his breath. Would they discover that neither Ono Tekall nor Baratin actually existed? But the crewman addressed as "Comper" spoke into his mouthpiece, listened, and presently reported.

"No outstanding charges."

"Very well." The commander turned back to Tadko. "Let this be your first, and we hope your last, warning, and of course, Siro, we do hope you enjoy the rest of your stay on Monna."

She gestured dismissal. Moderio tapped Tadko on the shoulder, then led him out of the commander's presence. Tadko discovered he was shaking all over, and having trouble getting his breath. Moderio helped him to a bench in a side room.

"Here, sit for half a jo," he said. "The commander does that to people, especially if you're not used to her. Lucky you're a tourist—she was being polite."

"If that's polite I'd hate to see her angry," Tadko said feelingly.

Moderio's rueful smile suggested personal experience, but he changed the subject.

"Where were you bound, on *Kelovona*?"

"To Pad, for the carnival."

"Oh, that's hard lines. You'll miss a lot, now. You'll not find any off island transport, here. There's a passenger flyer to and from Tallenport, goes every morning, but you missed the trip today."

"What about all those boats we saw, coming in?"

"Just local fishers. There's nothing much here at Westowere except us, at the base, and Fishtown, across the bay. You can probably find someone there to let you stretch for the night, and the ferry will be going soon. Two zinae for the crossing."

Tadko made his thanks, and left. A bumpy ferry ride took him across the bay to Fishtown, a village of a couple hundred inhabitants, no larger than Port Town on Elnakt during the trading season. In contrast to Westowere, made of rectangular buildings in a glittering white synthetic, buildings in Fishtown were fashioned of a local stone, striated in pink and ochre. Green vines covered most of the structures; the odor of their waxy white flowers, mingled with the strong smell of fish, was not entirely pleasant.

Tadko found the flyer plat on the inland side of the town. Two battered flyers sat on the field, and an elderly man dozed in what Tadko took to be an office at the side. He knocked on the door frame to wake the man up.

"How much is the fare to Tallenport, one way?"

"Five D. Leave at seven hundred, pay as you board."

It seemed an outrageous sum. Tadko would have tried to bargain, but something in the man's manner forbade it.

"I'll think about it," he said, preparing to turn away, then turning back. "Do you have a tourist map of Tallen? Showing resorts and such?"

"Ahh, hm. Should have some somewhere here— " The man rummaged on shelves at the back of his office, finally turned up a folder which he handed to Tadko. "Here you are. Courtesy of Tallen Reliable Transport. We don't do any tourist runs, ourselves, though—all tours go out of the hotel complex, west side of Tallenport."

Tadko made a careful circuit of the village, walking up and down every sandy street and finding six zinae in the sand. He was stared at everywhere he went. People working in gardens, in shops, and along the beach all paused to look at the offworlder, and many didn't hesitate to ask questions.

"Who are you? Where do you come from? What are you doing here?"

Fortunately they were satisfied with the information that he was a tourist, had fallen off a barge on his way to Pad, and was now planning to go on to Tallenport. Their reaction suggested that such carelessness was only to be expected of tourists, who seldom came to Fishtown in any case.

In the afternoon he walked down the beach until he found a secluded spot, sat down, and opened his maps. Even with the six zinae he had found, he didn't have enough money to pay that outrageous fare to Tallenport, and he could see that trying to steal would be a very bad idea, here. It was too small, and the Oceanic Patrol base was too close. He would have to follow his original plan and walk up the island to Tallenport, hoping the man with the flyers wouldn't mention his failure to show up. It was strange. Despite his first fears, he had felt safe on the barges, somehow cut off from the complications of everyday life on land. Perhaps it was only that out on the sea one could look to a far horizon, like at home on the halm. On the islands he felt cramped, constrained, hemmed-in, as if his options were being steadily reduced, and danger was coming closer all the time. He sighed. Nothing to do but run as far as possible while he still could.

He examined the maps again. Westowere, reasonably enough, was at the extreme west end of Tallen. He could follow the coast south for a little way, skirting Fishtown, then around to the east. Guiding himself would be no problem; as long as he then kept the mountains on his left and the ocean on his right, he would be walking toward Tallenport. Most of the population seemed to live along the coast, except for tourist spots in some of the thermal areas. The map should help him avoid these. As for food, he hoped wild fruit was as plentiful here as it had been on other islands—loads of it had provided much of the passengers' diet.

The heat was intense, here on Tallen, and the air steamy. He decided to start his journey at nightfall, when the air was cooler, and, he hoped, no one would notice which direction he went. He stripped to his breechclout; after all many of the local fisher-folk wore little more. Far out at sea the fishing boats rested, apparently unmoving, on the water. Kitewings soared high in the air as they had along the coast of every island he had seen, occasionally dipping down around the fishing boats. Another kind of bird was flying here—backs shimmering with green and silver, they floated on long, slender wings just above the wave crests, crying mournfully—ah-ooohhh. Ah-ooohhh. He leaned against a hummock of sand, half-asleep, until Seleme began to slant down in the west.

Then he donned his clothes, tucked the maps in his belt, and went back into town. He paused at a small food shop, and bought a carton of dried squelt and a stack of crispbreads. Next he visited a tavern, or the nearest thing to it that Fishtown possessed. The floor was the sandy beach; there was a back wall where the cooking equipment stood, a scatter of tables and chairs, and an open framework around three sides. Slatted screens were rolled up to the roof, and netting; presumably these could be lowered against rain or flying insects.

Half a dozen patrons were already there, eating. Tadko beckoned to the single waiter, a solidly built, bare-chested man with a large towel tied on over his breeches.

"How much for a meal?"

"Full meal and a drink, six zinae."

"Sounds right enough." Tadko seated himself. "Do you have a Hurricane, or a Fire Spout, to drink?"

The waiter gave a sniff that seemed to indicate disapproval.

"You'll not get any o' them fancy tourist mixtures, here. Can give you a Tallen Lively, or a Fisherman's Smack."

"Make it Fisherman's Smack, then."

When the food and drink arrived, Tadko laid his squares on the table, took a long, moody swallow of Fisherman's Smack, and brooded on his ill-luck. Fifty duats for a League membership, and the only good he had of it was a night's lodging and a morning meal. Forty-three and five for a ticket to Pad, and he had come as far as Tallen so it wasn't completely wasted, but still it was bad luck. Would he ever get to Sancy? Best not to think about it, just keep going. He beckoned to the waiter again.

"What's the date?"

"Thirty-seven Koried."

"Thanks." Forty-six more days, until his father came back from Eilonsad. Yet it seemed years since he left the City. Best not to think about it.

He attacked the meal, reminding himself that it might be a long time before he had another. There was a hot spiced chowder, a bowl of mixed fruit, and the usual crispbread. He was tempted to order another Fisherman's Smack. The brew was dark, slightly bitter, but pleasantly heady. Common sense prevailed; it would be a thoroughly foolish way to start a walk in the dark.

He sat in the tavern until well after dark; then he walked out of the town, and made his preparations. He hung his knife from his belt; one never knew. The packages of squelt and bread went into his bag, although it was a tight squeeze. He looped the straps of the bag over his shoulders; a cord tied across his chest held it in place.

Then he started walking, following the beach, but staying close enough inland to walk along the outer line of trees. He wouldn't be visible from out to sea, but there was enough light so that he could see to walk. At dawn he would go into the forest, and continue walking as far as he could, before he absolutely had to rest.

CHAPTER TEN

In summer, Elnakti rode everywhere; in winter, they went nowhere. Add to that the lazy days spent lounging on the deck of a barge, and it wasn't long before Tadko's legs were aching. He trudged on.

He had no way of judging the time. Now that he was part way down in the southern hemisphere, some familiar constellations were coming into view, but they were upside down, and the day of Monna was longer than the day of Elnakt. Here he could only be sure, by the slow movement of those stars, that time *was* passing.

He was plodding along in a half dream when a sharp question came at him from the dark of the woods. He stopped dead.

"Why!?" It demanded. "Why!? Why!?" A pause, and then again "Why!? Why!? Why!?"

He stood rigid, hardly breathing, through several more repetitions, finally decided it must be some creature of the night, and went on. The question followed him at intervals, until he was too far away to hear. Other than that, he heard very little. The rustle of vegetation, tapping sounds, occasional chirps, squeaks, and whistles which might have been birds or insects, all sounding very faint and far away. For long periods, the night was silent. He kept going.

When the eastern sky began to gray, he turned under the trees. He was very tired, his legs and feet were growing numb, but he forced himself to continue until it was full light. The forest outskirts were not as solid and forbidding as they looked in the darkness. Straggly bushes formed most of the undergrowth, with leaves like lengths of ribbon in blue, green, and dark red. There were more of the gray fuzz-covered trunks with their vast shady crowns, and slender, supple trees that grew to a great height, with shaggy green bark and clusters of yellow-green foliage at the crests. A little furry thing clinging to one of them suddenly opened a big mouth and poured out a stream of melody—Tadko found it completely enchanting. Just the same he also found himself wondering if the furry thing might be good to eat. He was hungry as well as weary. Life on the barges had also accustomed him to eating regularly.

Water came first. According to the map, there were any number of small streams running from the mountains or bubbling out of porous volcanic rock to the sea. He had waded through the outlets of several of them during the night. Now he slanted inland, hoping to find one of them at a point well away from the salt water.

It took longer than he expected, but he found it at last, a cluster of springs filling a deep rocky pool. Smaller trees grew thick around it, and the vegetation beyond was denser. He drank gratefully, ate some of his bread and dried squelt, then pushed his way along the ground, under the heavy bushes, and slept.

When he woke, he was almost too stiff and sore to move. Slowly, painfully, gritting his teeth to stifle groans and curses, he pushed himself out from under the bushes and managed to stand up. His legs ached all the way up to his waist. Silently but fervently, he cursed Kheer, who was responsible for his being here. Otherwise he would be almost at Padriocosta by now. He drank some water, ate a little bread, settled his bag in place across his back, and headed inland. By the angle of the light he thought it was past midday; he hadn't intended to sleep so long. He decided he had better walk through the forest in daylight now—easier to find his way. He followed a gentle rise of ground, planning to get farther inland, some way up the lower mountain slopes, before he went east. It would mean less likelihood of running into people.

He watched carefully as he moved along, eyes and ears alert for any sign of human beings, and also for signs of edible fruit.

Once he saw an oval, segmented thing, as long as his arm and half as wide, trundling slowly over the ground. Each segment bore a tiny pair of legs; there was no distinguishable head. It flowed along and left nearly bare soil in its wake. Small plants and fungi, fallen leaves, twigs, and plant bits, all were absorbed by its passing. He wondered about having the thing flow over him while he slept; then he noticed two little shelled animals the creature had passed over. They appeared tumbled, but unhurt. They struggled briefly, righted themselves, and hustled off. The thing must be strictly vegetarian.

The woods grew lusher. The ground was covered with red moss, tiny flowering plants, ferns of many types. The tree varieties increased, and air plants seemed to attach themselves to every branch, trailing long narrow leaves to the ground or producing great bursts of bloom, white, lavender, pale blue, pale yellow, silvery. The air was humid, and warmer than near the ocean. He saw more of the little furry things, climbing in the trees or scampering away over the ground as he passed. The salt-mineral tang that seemed to hang everywhere on Monna had disappeared. Here there was the smell of damp earth, and a nose-twitching mixture of flowery sweetness and decayed vegetation. It was very quiet, just as it had been during the night. Sometimes he heard the singing of the furry things. A few tiny squeaks and buzzes came from the underbrush, similar to, but different from, those heard in the darkness; that was all.

Walking soon worked out the stiffness in his legs. In other circumstances, he might even have enjoyed himself.

Five days later, Tadko came out of the forest and looked east along grassy, partly wooded slopes on the outskirts of the mountains.

He wore only his breech cloth and sandals. His dried squelt had spoiled quickly, in spite of the assurances of the shopkeeper who sold them; since then he had foraged. He had eaten lizards, insects, some conical shell fish he found growing in a pool, and even one of the segmented ovals. The differences in these alien creatures had made cleaning them difficult, especially the segmented oval. What were those dirty-yellow nubbins at the junctures of leg and body? Or the white strings that radiated from a bundle of gray fiber? He thought it best to avoid all such things, carefully dissected them out, and concentrated on what he hoped, at least, was muscle tissue. He wanted meat badly. Once he had steeled himself against the appeal of their singing, and hurled a stone to bring down one of the small furries. The result was disastrous. It had given him a terrible bellyache, and after he emptied his belly he spent the rest of the night with dry heaves. He thought cooking it might have made a difference, but he still hesitated to risk a fire.

Water was no problem. There were streams, springs, and pools everywhere. He found less fruit than he had hoped, but enough so that he could ration his bread. Twice he found toa trees, but very little of the fruit was ripe. He harvested a few, and ate them with great pleasure. Pejol bushes were fairly common, and much of the fruit was ripe, even rotting. These had been served several times on the barges. The white flesh was mealy, and he had considered it rather insipid; these tasted much better. An empty belly improves the flavor, as they said at home. He still had enough bread to last a good many days.

He had developed a cough, and a dull ache in his chest, the result, he supposed, of sleeping on the damp ground. Finding a dry spot in this humid country seemed impossible.

Often he had heard floaters, but from the sound they were high in the air; he didn't think any were looking for him.

Now he peered out at the terrain he would have to travel. The grass was long and there were some taller shrubs. He thought it would be enough cover. In any case his skin was blotched with many stains from plants and food animals. Bathing in the pools had not removed them, soap would be necessary, and now he decided that the stains would act as camouflage. To add to the effect, he paused, took out his hair glisten, and tried it on his skin. It didn't work. He considered throwing it away, then put it back in his pack.

Now he prowled out along the mountainside.

Tadko soon discovered he was not crossing one continuous slope. The land rose up and down, up and down, an endless series of sharp rises with tiny valleys at their feet, usually with a stream flowing through. It was much harder going than the forest, and by midday he was tired. He turned away from the mountain, hoping to find easier going lower down. It struck him that at this rate he would be struggling across Tallen until his father came home.

He coughed, as usual trying to stifle it as much as possible. He had seen no signs of people and perhaps there was little danger of his being heard, but still it worried him.

He reached a tilted, narrow plateau that slanted toward the east, and followed it. He had traveled for some time when he realized the ground was growing warm under his feet. He went on, cautiously. Up ahead he saw a spire of steam, rising through the lush green of the grass. He approached it, curious. Some of the tourist brochures he had seen told of this phenomenon. There was no crater or pool where it originated, it simply rose from the soil. He went a bit too close and jumped back with a gasp—a droplet fell on his shoulder, and it was scalding hot.

Out along the plateau he saw other steam spires, and although the plant life was as thick and moist as ever, his sandals grew warm from the heat of the soil.

At sunset, he found a spot under a tree, pulled a lot of the long grass, and spread it on the ground. It dried in no time, and he slept very comfortably.

In the morning he ate some of the pejols he had brought with him, and some bread, and went on. The soil grew warmer; the vegetation began to thin; eventually the ground was bare, and sounded slightly hollow under foot. He walked as lightly as possible, setting each foot with care, testing each step for solidity before trusting it with his full weight. He came suddenly to the lip of a bare depression. A smell of sulfur had been increasing as he moved, and now it came strong from the depression.

Down in the center was a pile of greasy looking gray bubbles. As he watched, he saw that the largest was very slowly expanding. He stood fascinated, while it gradually enlarged, then burst with a "plock!" and sagged into a little crater. Now he saw that others were growing too, very, very slowly. He watched while another burst, and another. Now a new bubble was growing, in the crater formed by the first...he came to himself with a start, unsure of how long he had stood here, watching the bubbles. There was something hypnotic about the things; he must move on.

He found his way back, still cautious, to solid ground, covered with plants. The sulphur smell still hung in the air, but he thought if he stayed in areas where the grass grew thick, he would be safe. He had to go a long way around the place of the bubbles.

He came to a stream of hot water flowing east, and followed it. As it flowed it grew cooler. He began to see small fish and shellfish in the water and along the banks. He came to a big colony of the cone-shaped shellfish with their neat oval caps, sitting on the bottom of the stream, the caps opening and shutting as they fed. He decided this might be a chance for a real hot meal. He pulled up half a dozen of the largest, broke them out of their shells, and cleaned them. Then he carried them back upstream to where the water ran boiling hot, strung them on a cord, tied the cord to a branch, and lowered the things into the boiling water. He didn't know how long to cook them, but let them boil until they began to smell appetizing, then pulled them out and laid them to cool on some leaves. He admitted that the usual Monnan hot sauce would have improved them, but nevertheless, with some bread and fruit, they made an excellent meal.

He drank from the stream farther down, where it had cooled, and continued along its banks for some time. When it turned south, he left it and kept going east.

The next morning he consulted his map, afraid that he might be nearing a tourist area, but it gave him little help. He had no idea just where he was, or which of the smoking mountains shown on the map was the one looming above him now. Nothing to do but move on, as cautiously as possible, and keep his eyes open. Later the plateau sloped upward. Tadko followed the slope, climbing through long grass, a stand of bushes with thick blue leaves, spiky plants that gave off a strong acid smell when crushed under foot, slim trees with coiling trunks.

He found that from this ridge he could see a long distance on either side, and determined to follow it as far as possible. It rose enough to give him a view of the coast, now rising into the cliffs mentioned by Moderio.

He lay down for a while to catch his breath and look over the land. A road came from the west, along the edge of the cliffs, and disappeared eastward. While he watched, a vehicle sped along it in the same direction. Overhead six or seven floaters came in from west and south, all heading east. Two more came in from the north, over the peaks behind him. He wondered at the great attraction of Tallenport. According to the map it was a large city, but no one on the barges had ever spoken of it as a tourist center.

He stood up and moved on, careful to stay under cover.

Some time later he paused, listening intently. From somewhere in the distance, off to his right, came faint noises that suggested human activity. He crouched below the level of the tall grass and prowled across the ridge, toward the southern edge. He dropped to his hands and knees, then flattened himself out, parting the grass stems before his face.

A big resort occupied the lower, less precipitous part of the slope. There was a long semicircle of white dwellings with the hat-shaped roofs he had seen on Morneol, a cluster of larger buildings, several pools, one of them steaming, extensive park and garden areas. Across the road, contained in a hollow between lower hills, a wide lake bubbled. The shores were a mass of lacy white filigree from mineral deposits.

Several floaters and other vehicles were ranged along the road, and a crowd of humans and non-humans was lining up at a rail overlooking the lake. Others came hurrying out of the white dwellings to join them.

The center of the lake boiled more fiercely. Steam rolled out. The water surged up with a roar, growing and spreading. It seemed the whole lake was erupting, up and up and up, still roaring. The base was hidden by clouds of steam. Many viewers moved back hastily. Distant as he was, Tadko's ears were hammered by the sound. He felt the earth tremble below him. The column grew until he feared it must surely topple over and drown the whole resort. Then after an interval impossible to measure, he realized it was sinking again. Down and down and down, until there was only the bubbling surface of the lake. He let out his breath, surprised to find he had been holding it, and hitched himself away from the edge.

Now at last he had a landmark. This had to be the geyser Voice of Thunder, at Thunder Lodge, in the Sequana valley. The satisfaction of knowing his location was diminished by the realization that he hadn't come very far. Not nearly as far as he hoped. Too much up and down. He told himself he must push harder.

The valley north of the ridge was as empty as any others Tadko had seen: a descent down a brush-covered slope to a narrow stream, fed by brooklets from above, then a rise on the other side to another, higher ridge. The vegetation was green, blue-green, blue, silver with patches of dark red or yellow. The peaks were clothed to their summits, except for occasional long scars left by recent lava flows. Rarely now, he heard the melody of the singing animals. Once a kitewing soared over, but it was out of its proper place; it circled, clattering, and headed out to sea again.

The air was heavy with scents, sweet, pungent, at some times ethereal, at others rotten. Steams rose in several spots, and he gave them a wide berth. From time to time a breeze brought the odor of sulphur again. He was now so accustomed to it that his nose did not even wrinkle, but he kept a sharp lookout for possible sources, mud pools and the like. His cough was worse, and he suspected the sulphur was causing it.

East along the valley side, a climb to a pass where the ridges joined, down the other side into the next valley, and east. He found a segmented oval and some recognizable fruit, and at dusk he prepared another meal. He chose a spot by a steaming pool and hot spring. The soil was warm, but he judged it not dangerous. Cooking the oval gave it no more flavor than it possessed raw, but it was easier to chew. He slept nearby, pressing his chest against a warm flat rock.

He woke to a painful internal convulsion that left him coughing violently. On his hands and knees, bending over his rock, he coughed and coughed and finally brought up mouthfuls of gray, foul-tasting phlegm. He had to rest a while before he could manage to eat and drink, gather his energies, and set off again.

He had hoped that being able to sleep through the night, and to sleep dry, would clear up his cough. Nothing would be so likely to give him away as coughing, and he had no idea how far the sound would carry. So far he had managed to stifle it fairly well, but this morning he was sure he heard an echo from across the valley.

Later, he regained some optimism. He was still tired, but no one came to investigate, and he did no more coughing. His chest felt a little easier, as if he had rid it of some constriction.

Now he avoided the top of the ridge, trying to stay just below it on the north side. The emptiness of these valleys still amazed him, when he remembered the crowding and bustle of the City. He recalled a line from one of the geographies his mother tried to make him learn—"Population on the smaller volcanic islands is largely concentrated around the coasts." He read it, but until now, it wasn't real.

Clouds had been piling up all morning. Now, with no preliminary sprinkles, the rain flooded down. Tadko tried to continue, but in the torrent it was hard to see and even to breathe. He crouched under a clump of ribbon leaf bushes, head down, the jacket of his ship suit pulled around his shoulders. Then the wind blew, the clouds scattered, and the rain ended as suddenly as it began, leaving everything soaked.

Late in the afternoon, he topped another rise and discovered two small houses in the valley below. For a moment, he hardly realized what they were. The resort had been expected; ordinary habitations were not. There was a little lake, not boiling or steaming, with boats drawn up on shore. Gardens surrounded the houses. There were a few outbuildings, and some squarish ponds he believed were for raising fish and shellfish. A wide landing plat for floaters was built on the side of one hill. Trees of the type he had seen in the lower forest, with rough green bark and topped by high-held leaf clusters, shaded everything.

It looked unbelievably pleasant and peaceful, and more than anything else he wished he could go down there and ask for help. He tried to think of a suitable story.

"I'm walking through Tallen for pleasure, but I've developed this cough and I need something to cure it...." Absurd. he thought of how he must look, hair wild and dirty, dirty breechcloth and sandals, stained dirty skin. He had bathed in streams, warm and cool, scrubbing as best he could with sand, but the result left much to be desired....

Out of the question. But it looked very quiet down there, and no floaters were parked on the plat. There should be plenty of food in the garden, and something better than insects and segmented ovals in the ponds.

He made some preparations. A stiff length of branch and a slender, supple one were both trimmed and stripped. He whittled the ends to fit, bent the smaller in a loop at one end of the larger, set the notches together, and tied it firmly in place. Next he poked holes around the edge of a cloth and tied it to the loop. This ought to make an adequate fish-scoop, and his green head scarf was big enough to carry a fair amount of melons and such.

He went down the hill watching alertly for any sign of life. At the base, he circled, staying under cover, until he reached a spot where the wild-growing bush came near the end of one pond. He waited while Seleme sank slowly, and just at dusk threw a rock into the pond.

A splash, followed instantly by a raucous demand of "Why!? Why!? Why!?" Tadko's heart nearly bounced through his ribs. He tensed back ready for flight, but nothing more happened. No one rushed out of a house to investigate the disturbance. No lights came on in the gathering twilight, and the whole scene gave a distinct impression of absence. He made up his mind and walked out boldly to begin foraging.

The cries of "Why!?" continued, and at last he saw the creature, on a high perch near the pond. A scaly body, clawed limbs, something like a glider's wings flapping as it danced up and down on the perch, a round head with huge, round eyes.

He scooped up a good net full of fish, almost falling in during the process—the ponds were deeper than he expected—but the fish were crowded, easy to catch. Bubbles rose from below, and he thought these pools must be built like the tanks used by the beach vendors. He collected melons, toa fruit, a bundle of crisp vegetable stalks, and some pods commonly served as a pickle. Someone had mentioned them as being very good raw, as well. The Why creature eventually gave up and fell silent; perhaps it had come to the conclusion that anyone who moved about so openly must be legitimate.

He loaded up with as much as he thought he could comfortably carry, then faded back into the forest and headed for the ridge.

Just in time. Overhead came the humming of a floater, and when he peered out he saw it descend to the landing plat by the houses. Tadko pushed on, up and then east to the other end of the valley. Better keep going as far as he could. Big Moon was nearing the full, the woods were sufficiently open to make traveling at night not too difficult, and he was now used to the terrain. He moved as fast as he could without making any noise.

Two more floaters came in to land, but still there was no outcry, nor did the Why start up again—presumably it was used to the people who lived there. Someday he must find out *why* anyone would want such a thing around. Wouldn't it keep you awake half the night? It hadn't looked like something he would want as a pet.

He was a little worried for fear there might be other Whys in the trees here, to cry out and give the alarm that someone was passing, but the night was silent as usual. The pet Why must have been brought in from the lower forest.

He reached the pass between valleys, and went a short way down the other side, before he thought it was safe to stop. He had meant to go even farther, but he came to a boiling pool among warm flat rocks, and he was so tired. He cleaned the fish and part of the vegetables, boiled them, finished off with toa fruit, nibbled on some bread, and reluctantly threw the rest of it away. It had lasted much longer than the squelt, but was now mildewed.

Again he stretched out on a smooth rock to sleep. He wasn't sure why, but lately he had felt cold rather than overheated, and the warmth was soothing. His chest had begun to ache again, and he thought the heat would be helpful.

In the morning he had another coughing spasm. It took a long time to bring up the phlegm that seemed to be causing his problem, and when it was over, he was tired out. He had crouched over, head close to the ground, hoping to smother the sound, but he was glad he left the valley with the houses before he settled for the night.

He made a good enough meal, with cooked fish and vegetables. The rest of the vegetables and the fruit he could carry with him. He wished he could dry some of the fish, but this meant building a fire. Too risky. He lay on his warm rock for a while, then forced himself to get up and move.

This valley was higher, with a wider, flatter floor, than any others he had passed.

The flat was covered with a bright yellow, low growing plant. All around grew the usual bush, with steams rising everywhere; the sulphur odor was intense. Off to his right he saw a real waterfall, larger than the little cascades that trickled down most hills and ridges. This one carried a fair head of water, tumbling over a rocky ledge and splashing into a pool. The central stream was the size of a small river. Foam flew and water sprayed, to catch rainbows in the sun. The noise of water and a sound of buzzing insects gave the place a sleepy feeling.

Tadko was tempted to take a day off, and spend it here, just snoozing. Find a spot that was sunny, yet sheltered well enough to keep him from sight of passing floaters. Instead he hitched his bag on his shoulders and got going. The western slope was rocky and steep. He climbed down, then started walking the flat. It was easier going, and he stayed close enough to the trees to duck under, if necessary.

He sat for a while at midday to eat. Traveling the flat was not entirely pleasant. The yellow plants, tiny leafy things, possessed a slightly carrion smell to add to the sulphur. The buzzing sounded nearer, although he hadn't seen whatever made it; together with the breathless heat, it made the sleepiness hard to fight.

So, up and on again.

Sometime later he came to a halt. He had been walking in his sleep and was much farther out on the flat than he wanted to be. What woke him? Had the ground shaken, just a little? He stood perfectly still for a moment, then turned, took one cautious step, set his right foot down, slowly let his weight come to rest upon it, slowly brought his left foot forward. Schluck! His right foot sank up to the ankle in muck. A horrible stench exploded around him. He pulled up his right foot with another schluck and his left foot sank in, producing another blast of stench.

Suddenly the distant buzzing was a nearby roar and a cloud of tiny red flies descended on him, clinging, biting, stinging, going for his eyes, his nose, his mouth, clustering all over his body. He yelled, staggering, beating at his head and face, ran schluck-schluck for the trees, dragging his feet out of the muck and stumbling as he went, but the flies stayed with him. Still beating at himself, moaning, he ran through the trees blindly, stumbled into a scalding pool, leaped out with a shriek, beat away the flies just enough to locate the waterfall and head for it, the stinging on his scalded legs increasing his agony. He reached the pool below the fall, and threw himself in. Oh blessed cold water! He struggled through the turbulence and pushed into the gap at the back of the fall, between the water and the rocky ledge, then poked up his head to try for a breath.

Cold wet spray on his face, nothing more. He hung there for a long time, clinging to the rock, afraid to venture out lest the flies should be waiting for him. He ducked his head frequently, the cold water easing the stinging bites all over his face and neck. Not until he began to feel thoroughly chilled did he push out through the fall; the buzzing sound was far away again: they had given up. Tadko dragged himself out on the bank and sat gasping.

He was covered with angry bites. His feet, and his legs from the knee down, were bright scarlet. He saw no blistering, or sloughing of skin, so perhaps the water hadn't been as hot as in some other pools, or he hadn't been in long enough to scald deeply. Even so, the pain was severe. He moaned, and lowered his legs into the water.

He half expected to see a black-and-silver floater of the Oceanic Patrol coming in over the ridge. Certainly, if anyone had been within earshot of all that tumult they would come to find out what had happened. But no one came, and again he wondered at the emptiness of the island interior.

The afternoon wore on, and he felt hungry again. His scarf with its load of food was somewhere out there in the muck. Quite possibly it wasn't even too far from solid ground, but right now he couldn't even think of trying to retrieve it. Impossible to hunt for fruit with his feet in this condition. He found some little green shellfish attached to the sides of the pool, and ate them, digging them out with a fingernail.

In the morning his head ached, his chest ached, his cough was worse than ever, and he was shivering with cold. Hardly surprising, since he spent the night sleeping with his legs in the water. He pulled them out for inspection. The skin was wrinkled and puckered from long immersion, but the scarlet had faded to a dull red, and the pain was gone. He wanted food badly. Once more he thought of the scarf full of food lost in the muck, but felt no inclination to look for it. With his feet fairly well healed he could forage, as usual. His bag was still on his back, still tied by a loop of cord across his chest. In his misery the day before he had almost forgotten it.

Feeling a bit lightheaded, he searched the pool and ate some more of the green shellfish. There were other fish, bony looking things, swimming in the water, but he had also lost the fish-scoop that he made the day before. Or was it two days? He couldn't be sure. He drank from his cupped hands, wrapped his feet in wet cloth before donning his sandals, and set off.

This time he stayed well above the flat. He walked until his feet started to hurt, then sat down by a trickle of cool water and removed his sandals to soak them. Again he fell asleep sitting, to wake in an awkward sprawl, chilled and miserable. It was already dark, but he put on his ship clothes for a little warmth, and went on.

After that, he no longer made many conscious decisions. He woke or slept as exhaustion required, losing track of the days. He wore both sets of clothes when he was cold, stripped when fever came. He wanted water and fruit more than anything, unable to stomach the ovals and other things he had eaten along the way. When houses with gardens became more common along his route, he raided them. It was easier than foraging. Most were deserted during the day, with the owners returning at dusk or shortly thereafter. All of them kept Whys, often more than one, but he learned to ignore the creatures.

One afternoon he peered down from a wooded pass at the biggest layout he had seen yet. Many buildings, one like a palace, really extensive gardens. Melon vines blue in the sunlight, with glimpses of red-orange through the foliage. Rows of fruit trees, more melons on trellises, row after row of vegetable plants in green and green-yellow. Everything was neat as a toy model, with wide grassy walks laid out between sections. Whys were perched everywhere, enough so he thought he had better try to keep them from sounding off, even if no one was home. There were shrubs he could use as cover until he got in among the melon vines. A couple of crisp, juicy melons would go well.

He looked on through burning eyes, breath wheezing in his chest, knowing he couldn't go on much farther. He would have to give himself up at one of the houses, ask for help, and take the consequences. He lay down to rest until sunset, hopeless, oppressed by an appalling loneliness. Easier, and much quicker, to have drowned in the ocean, and in the long run it would have made no difference.

It wasn't the thought of death itself that filled him with such despair. He had faced it many times at home. If he had died in the midwinter hunger, or in an early fall or late spring blizzard, or attacked by a slaen on the trail—well, such things happened. His people would have mourned him and sung the prayers for the gone-ahead. Buried him properly, if his body was found. It was the thought of dying here alone, on a strange world, with no one of his kin ever to know what had happened, that made his throat ache with a pain which had nothing to do with illness.

His mind wandered again, and he fell into a restless half-sleep.

Later he moved down through the shrubbery. His legs shook and he had to stop often to catch his breath, but he made it into the melon patch without stirring up the Whys. The vines were waist high, the bright orange melons ripening on sheets laid on the ground below. The scent was deliciously sweet, and the huge leaves brushed moist and cool against his skin....

"What's this? A vagrant! A trespasser! Here, get him out of here—let's have a look at him!"

CHAPTER ELEVEN

Tadko was seized by the ankles, dragged out from under the melon vines, and hauled roughly upright between two burly young men. He half hung there, bewildered, wondering what had happened, and where all these people came from.

One of them caught his whole attention. An elderly woman, she wore a wide sleeved, long blue robe embroidered in silver. Across her chest was a baldric vertically striped in violet, cerise, and black; from it depended a slender carved black rod. A cap of silver filigree confined her yellowing hair, silver rings adorned her fingers. Her face was lined and predatory, her expression had such ferocious authority it made the commander at Westowere seem mild. She poked the end of her rod under his chin, raising his head.

"An offworlder! Filthy, too. All right you, who are you, where do you come from, what are you doing here?"

"O—Ono Tekall," he mumbled. "From Baratin."

She turned to a young woman who stood nearby.

"Comper, call the central plenum and get Entry Records—Ono Tekall or Tekall, Ono, from Baratin."

The young woman's smock and breeches were striped in the same colors as the older one's baldric. She carried a small instrument at her belt. Now she raised it, spoke into it softly, tapped herself behind the left ear, waited a moment.

"No entry record for any such person," she reported.

"All right, it's a false name. Check on anyone entering from Baratin."

Another brief pause.

"No entry recorded from Baratin at any time...wait, there are cross references coming...no planet or sun called Baratin noted in these records. Here's another...minor infraction. Tekall, Ono, of Baratin, drunkenness. Fell off barge *Kelovona* on night of thirty-six Koried, picked up by Oceanic Patrol, Westowere, warned and dismissed."

"Didn't even check Entry Records!" the old lady exploded angrily. "Ah, well, I suppose they can't bother for every fool tourist who gets into trouble. Here you!" She prodded him again. "Let's have your real name, and no lies this time. And your planet of origin, wherever that is."

Now would be the time for a clever evasion, but he was too tired and sick to think. He had run as far as he could, and they finally had him boxed in. With a feeling of genuine relief he wheezed, "Tadko Darusko—Daruskan—Elnakt."

"Elnakt?" She peered at him. "My life, he is Elnakti! Comper, call the Sancy nexus for a Tadko Darusko, find out what he's doing wandering around off Sancy."

"No Tadko Darusko listed on the refugee records," the young woman reported. "No such person listed with the original arrivals."

"So!" The old lady turned on him. "An illegal entry, I'll go bond! All right, check entry records on *him*."

A pause, then the younger woman began her report. "Darusko, Tadko, of Elnakt. No entry permit recorded. Illegal entry assumed, on or about two to four Koried. Attempted to obtain membership in Students and Apprentices Protective League, eleven Koried. Petty theft, thirty duats, seven zinae from league member, Kheer U Rhenearr, same day. Fled, presumably to avoid arrest, same day. Report by Gelmin Seronico, house warder."

Tadko was sufficiently conscious to curse both Kheer and Seronico, wishing now that he'd had a chance to kill them both. But the old lady was turning on him again.

"All right you, when did you come in? Who brought you?"

"Don't—don't know. Don't—remember." He must at least try not to mention *Werauer.*

A young man strode up. Harsh-faced, arrogant, he too was dressed in robe and baldric, but without the rod. He slapped Tadko across the face.

"Tell us, you stupid savage! Who was it? Who brought you in?"

"Oh stop wasting your time, Edhrin," the old lady said impatiently. "Can't you see he barely speaks Monnan? Ugh! Get away from him, he's sick! Call Doctor Anwiler."

The slap had started a coughing spasm. Tadko was lowered to the ground to cough and retch, trying to empty his lungs of increasing amounts of foul-smelling phlegm.

"Take him inside until the doctor comes," the old lady said brusquely when he was quiet.

They lifted him again, carried him inside a building, laid him on the floor among dim shapes of tools and machinery, and left him there. He tried to rise, failed, pushed his bag back to prop up his head, and closed his eyes.

After a while he heard more voices. He was poked and prodded some more but not ungently, felt a sting of cold on one shoulder.

"As I suspected," said a calm, slow voice. "He's got bubble lung. It's what they're all getting, on Sancy."

"Bubble lung?" It was the old lady, sounding incredulous. "That's a children's disease! And it doesn't act like that! Besides, everyone is immunized for it."

"Everyone in the three suns, or nearly everybody, and anyway most of us have all our immunities and susceptibilities pretty well mixed by now. Visitors are checked on their home worlds and given whatever immunizations they need before they come here. These Elnakti have been too isolated...I don't know why no one thought to check into it when they came here. Too much confusion, I suppose."

"But he isn't a danger to anyone else? He can't give it to anyone here?"

"No, no danger of that."

"I'll go bond he came in on a Wintollen ship! Old Farrus was dead against me about handling these refugees. I would have seen to it they went to Dorra. We can put enough pressure on the Dorrans for that! Useless savages! What's more they'd be better off on a cold world." She ranted on for some time, but simmered down at last.

"Well, what do you want done with him? Send him to Sancy? Simplest thing to do."

"*We* don't do any runs to Sancy, and I'm not likely to pay his fare on Ornibeck Transport, am I? You might as well call the Civic Orderlies. Use him for mine fodder."

"They'd not thank you for someone in this condition. Unless it's treated he'll die before long, and no work to be had out of him in the mean time. Still, bad as it looks, it's simple to clear up. Send him to the company infirmary and he'll be ready to work in a couple of days."

"I'm not likely to cure his ills for the benefit of House Garline, either."

"Well, then put him to work for yourself, Concora. Can't you always use packers? Keep him on base stipend and found, notify entry records of capture and assignment, and you'll have a bargain rate worker."

"Hmm. Oh very well, have it your way. Right enough, we might as well use him ourselves. Comper, call for an infirmary carrier."

His face was slapped again, lightly.

"Wake up, young man. Come on, open your eyes, that stim should be working now. Open your eyes."

Tadko managed to obey. The doctor was a stern-faced, beaky-nosed man in the same striped livery as the young comper.

"Can you understand me?" he asked.

"Yes," Tadko wheezed.

"I hope you're grateful, you won't be going to the mines. You'll be working for House Concora. Work hard, follow the rules, don't get into trouble or try to run away. If you do, the House won't protect you. You understand all this?"

"Yes."

He discovered that it was possible to breathe, freely. The sensation was so pleasurable he lay for quite a while, doing just that. Then he stared at a gray ceiling. Memory returned, and he knew he must be in the company infirmary. He stretched, testing the capacities of arms and legs, then sat up to have a look.

It was a cavernous building, smelling of medicine and sickness, lined with row upon row of high beds; each one had a table and a tall gleaming cylinder alongside. A few men and women in gray uniforms moved among them. Ventilators whirred. There were occasional moans, and a background murmur of low voices.

He turned, felt a tug at his chest, and found a flexible band around his rib cage. A bundle of colored wires connected it with the cylinder. He felt the band gingerly, then examined the cylinder. The thing was quite incomprehensible. Coils of wire and tubing, openings of various sizes with some sort of instrumentation protruding, everything in bright colors or shining metal, readout screens, lights that pulsed or shone steadily. A blue light was blinking on top of his cylinder, and now two of the attendants approached his bed.

"Feeling better?" the woman asked.

"Right enough."

She pressed buttons on the cylinder, examined the readouts.

"Ninety-six point three. I'd say he was ready for discharge, wouldn't you?"

The man looked at a few other dials and readouts. "Want to wait until he's one hundred percent?"

"Not likely. Charity case. He'll do well enough, he's going to one of the packeries." She pulled a sheet from the cylinder. "All right, what's your name, Darusko? You can dress and leave. Hand this to the coordinator as you go out, and he'll tell you where to go from there." She removed his chest band, tucked it into the cylinder.

He took the foil strip. "Which way is out?"

"Down to the end, past this line of beds, then to your right. First door, that's the coordinator."

Tadko nodded. Their chilly manner discouraged an expression of thanks.

They left. He found his bag on a shelf under the bed and dressed slowly. Before slipping his pouch over his belt, he checked the contents—it was empty. His knife was gone, too. At first he was almost paralyzed with rage. Thieves! Dacy, a professional, was more honorable. Charity case indeed, when someone here had stolen his last few duats! He glared balefully around the huge room, fighting the urge to yell and attack the nearest attendant, then gulped several times, somehow swallowing his fury. The Concora doctor had told him not to get into trouble, and he could guess that accusing anyone here of robbing him would be counted trouble making. It could even have happened on the way here, in the what did they call it—the infirmary carrier. He breathed deeply, calming himself, set his face grimly, picked up the rest of his possessions, and headed for the door.

Inside he backed up, catching his breath, while it slid shut behind him. The coordinator was a green, sitting behind a desk in a confusion of comp outlets, screens, and other equipment.

"Calm down," he said sharply. "You won't be hurt. You're Darusko?"

"Uh—yes." Hopeless to try to run anymore.

"Sit down." The man gestured at a chair at one corner of his desk. "Right hand in there."

"There" was a white tube fixed to the desk, part of the maze of connections. Tadko sat as ordered, slid his hand into the tube. Something gripped his wrist snugly; a prick, and his hand began to grow numb. He cried out involuntarily, tried to pull away and failed.

"Calm down," the green repeated. "You won't be hurt, that's for your ident and tracer. You have your discharge slip? Let's have it."

Tadko handed over the foil strip, and the green turned, busied himself with his screens. Tadko relaxed a little and looked around the small room, still apprehensive, but curious. A sign on the wall said, "CONCORA LIAISON. UTHAK FRENSEN, CIVIC ORDERLY." So now he knew a green was a civic orderly, a bit of information that did him no good at all.

As Frensen worked, a printout strip slid from a slot. A small cylinder on a loop of cord popped out of another orifice. A "ping" sounded above the white tube, and the wrist grip withdrew.

Frensen turned back to Tadko. "From Elnakt, hmm. Do you understand what's going to happen here?"

"No." Sullenly. "They said I would work for Concora's."

"Yes, but not as a free worker. You'll work as a prisoner, to pay off the money you stole plus a fine for illegal entry. You're very lucky Concoras were willing to take you in as a worker, otherwise you would have gone straight to the mines. Do you understand the work cycles on Monna?"

"Yes." That he had picked up from talk on the barges. "Eleven days per cycle, eight days work, three free days."

"All right. Now look at the palm of your right hand."

Tadko did so. His hand was still numb, but a row of numbers gleamed in the center of his palm; when he touched them, he felt a hard place underneath. He looked back at Frensen, who nodded.

"Your ident number has been registered with Civic Control, and the patch contains a tracer." He picked up the printout. "Now this is the schedule you'll follow. You have been assigned to barrack number three, to work at the number seven packery. The work cycle starts tomorrow, the nineteenth of Talior, so you will check into the barrack tonight. Now these are the rules. Your palm ident will admit you to the barrack. Your bunk assignment is—" He picked up the small cylinder. "—first floor, number thirty-seven. You'll be given two meals a day at the barrack, a midday meal will be served at the packery on work days. While you are in the *barrack don't touch any of the other workers for any reason*. There are stun circuits in the ceiling that will knock you out, so learn to keep your distance. If you or anyone else are sick or injured there's a signal by the door for the infirmary, but don't misuse it; you've had your recent stay at the charity of the Concoras, but any more use of the med department will be deducted from your pay. That will be fifteen zinae per day, totaling four duats per cycle. Half will be deducted until you have paid off the money for U Rhenearr, plus a fine of five hundred and fifty duats for illegal entry.

From quitting time on eight day, to twenty-six hundred on eleven day, your time is your own; stay at the barrack or do what you like, wander the town, but if you get into any trouble you'll be flogged and your fine increased—remember the tracer! Whether you run or get into trouble we'll have no problem tracking you down, so you might as well know it's no use trying. Now is that all clear?"

"Yes."

"All right, this is your locker key, that'll be alongside your bunk—notice the number on the end—one thirty-seven." He gave the cylinder on its loop of cord to Tadko. "Turn right as you leave, barrack three is straight down toward the docks. Dismissed."

Tadko plodded down the street, bag dangling over his arm, holding his right hand in his left, flexing it as the numbness began to wear off. The buildings lining both sides of the street were high and packed close together, but bare and featureless, with none of the color and gleam of the city. Most had only numbers, but one bore a name—HOUSE CONCORA CONTRACT MANAGEMENT. This street was also deserted, although down the cross streets he could see people and vehicles moving. Once a floater passed, slowly, overhead. He hoped he'd be able to find this barrack three.

At a corner he came upon an eat shop, called, for no reason he could discern, THE BEACHED BARGE. It was only a large square room, as plain as the building whose ground level it occupied. Bare walls, a scatter of tables and chairs, bar along one side, double doors at the back where the waiters came and went. Hardly in a class with the Houses Of Many Worlds. Still it looked clean and decent; the odors of food and drink were appetizing. He stood for a few moments looking in, thinking of his empty pouch, and then moved on.

Some blocks later he found barrack three. The sign was luminous and spread across the entire front. His lip twisted. No chance that any prisoner would miss it. The wide door had no handle. He looked it over, puzzled, then knocked. An oval plate by the door began to glow and a disembodied voice said, "Your ident." He placed his palm against the plate and the door slid aside.

This place was lined with rows and rows of bunks, too brightly lit by strip lights in the ceiling. It smelled of human bodies with an overlay of disinfectant. His nose wrinkled. The nearest bunks were ninety-nine and one hundred, so he set out to find his own. There was no bedding, only a think gray mat, pierced with many tiny holes, on each bunk. The lockers were attached to bunks, ceiling, and floor, as if to make very certain they could not be moved. Beside many of them, pairs of gray boots sat on the floor. He passed a few men sleeping, naked or wearing only breechcloths, but all had their locker keys on cords around their necks. It was hot, yet he heard no ventilators.

Along one row he discovered an elaborate decoration on the floor. A huge, irregular spiral had been drawn, filling the space between the rows. The spiral was divided into sections, and each section contained several little pictures, done in red, green, yellow, black, white or blue. There were buildings of many sorts, barges, boats, floaters, and even spaceships; what looked like sections of City street; islands, mountains, people doing many things, some of them obscene; animals, a few Porposin, and a great many others that he couldn't make out. Some were rendered with great skill and some with childish crudity. A few were bright as if recently repainted. He shook his head, wondering why prisoners should want to decorate the floor.

Shortly after, he found out. Four men were grouped around another of the spirals, one on each of the adjoining bunks, one sitting on the floor at each end. He stopped, mindful of the rule about getting close, and saw they were using it to play a game. They were far too intent to notice Tadko. The man nearest him was kneeling, bent over. Now he scooped up a pair of dice, shook them vigorously in his cupped hands, cast them, inspected the result.

"Seven, blue," he said, and gestured at the man on he bunk at his right. "Move me, will you?"

This man was old, his body scarred, his face lined. He shifted position, wincing a little, found one of the markers and moved it, leaned over to look at the last section.

"No blue here," he said. "Have to stay where you were." He moved the piece back to its original position.

"Squat on it!" the younger man exclaimed angrily. "My luck's been off all this cycle!"

"The luck comes and goes, no matter who throws," the old man chanted in a half-singsong.

"Want me to throw for you then?" The younger man's tone was nasty.

"No! Let's have them." The old man put his hand on the floor, and the other flipped him the dice. He shifted again uncomfortably and got himself settled on his belly, arms dangling down, to throw the dice properly.

"Eleven, black," he announced. "I know that one. Vrodir, I'm over there on the outer coil, move me, will you?"

Vrodir was on the other end of the spiral. He moved the old man's marker, caught the dice for himself, leaned back, and became aware of Tadko. The others noticed his changed expression and turned to look.

"Just arrived?" Vrodir asked.

"Yes."

"Care to sit in?" The fourth man, younger than the others, gestured at the spiral. "We got room."

"Not now, but thanks. Uh, is there anywhere here where someone could make a comlink call?"

"Cost you fifteen D," the first man said promptly, and held us his right hand to display the number in his palm, "Just show your ident to the pickup panel and they'll give you your call and deduct from your pay, no trouble to you. It's over in the dining room." He pointed toward the rear of the bunk room.

It seemed like a lot. In the City such calls were free, as far as he knew.

"How much for a call to the City?"

They looked at each other, obviously quite taken aback.

"Thirty D?" Vrodir suggested. "Maybe more. Maybe a lot more." His mouth curved, mockingly. "Why, you got someone important in the City, you going to call and then you'll be leaving us?"

"No, just curious." It might be true, he had thought it was going to be true, but now he was no longer so sure. "Where can I get a drink of water?"

"That way, in the tank." The old man pointed, and they turned back to their game.

He went back down the aisle and around so as not to walk through their game, then in the direction indicated.

The Tank lived up to its name, large and echoing, all finished in a rough gray tile. Pipes coiled over the ceiling, dripping here and there; drains were spaced at intervals on the floor. There was a row of drinking fountains along one wall, with a few spigots where a cup could be filled, if you had a cup. Shower stalls, waste stalls, a garbage disposal, a row of clothes cleaners. Several of the latter were marked Out of Order.

He found mirrors above a line of washbowls and stared at himself with shock. He had seen his skin burn almost Monnan dark under the sun although it had a blotchy, patchy look no real Monnan would ever possess. Now he realized his hair was bleached white. It felt dry and brittle to his touch. No wonder that old lady hardly recognized him as Elnakti. A fine disguise, Tadko thought sadly, and it did him no good at all.

He drank from one of the fountains, returned to the bunk room and finally located his own, relieved to find it was a lower. He opened the locker, put his bag inside, took off his smock and breeches and put them in too, closed it. He stood for a while holding the locker key in his hand, then hung it around his neck as the others did. He shivered when the cord touched his skin, although he couldn't have said why. After that he stretched out on the bunk. A call to his father? No, better not, even if it didn't cost so much. Osrin Havard seemed a hazy, unreal person now, someone from a tale told long ago. There would be other plans to make, later.

He might have dozed, or just lain there thinking of nothing, but some time later a gong sounded. He sat up, remembering signals at the League, wondering about food. They must have fed him at the infirmary, somehow, but he couldn't recall.

A dozen or more men, including the gamers, were gathering in the dining room. This was separated from the bunk area by no more than a wide space of floor. Five long parallel tables ended at the opposite wall, with a pair of small doors just above each. Then others seated themselves side by side at one table, and Tadko found a place at the end. Even the chairs ran in grooves to keep the diners a correct distance apart.

Once they were all seated, the small doors opened and trays of food slid down the table, one to a person. Squelt, fairly bland vegetable pickle, crispbread, a tepid, slightly flavored drink that bore a distant resemblance to cold fizz. Tadko found it well enough, compared to some of the things he'd had recently, and ate with good appetite. Many of the others grumbled while they ate, but it had a flat, perfunctory sound, as of a complaint they felt obliged to make, but knew was useless.

Partway through the meal, rain began to fall in the bunk area. Streams of greenish liquid poured from orifices all over the ceiling, down through the bunks with their porous mats, thundered on the floor, and flowed away toward the tank and its drains, smelling powerfully of the same disinfectant. A few vagrant trickles ran into the dining room instead, although a floor drain between the rooms caught most of it. His nose wrinkled, again.

"Do they do that every night?" He asked the man next to him.

"Once per cycle, supper time on eleven day. Fewest people likely to be around. It's not so good for the lungs." He gestured toward the ceiling. "They do this part tomorrow morning, when we've all left for work."

Tadko wondered if he was likely to get bubble lung again, if the stuff was bad for the lungs, and why they used it at all, but he said nothing. He even thought the food had acquired a taste, but told himself it was surely his imagination, and made himself finish.

When all of them were through, the trays were slid back inside the doors to disappear somewhere below and the men returned to the bunk room. Tadko noticed the com links on one wall, but they meant nothing to him now.

He watched a game for a while, until his bunk was completely dry, then lay down to sleep.

CHAPTER TWELVE

Another gong in the morning, and he woke to find a lanky Monnan form sliding down from the bunk overhead.

This person looked at Tadko with a melancholy expression. "Just arrived?"

"Last night."

"I'm Zhak. You?"

"Tadko." The other gave no surname, so Tadko didn't either. This Zhak had a longer, bonier face than most Monnans he had seen; a diamond shape was tattooed or scarred on each cheek, and a line of them ran across his chest. Tadko was curious, but asked no questions. A tourist on the barges could be expected to ask about everything he saw and heard, but here it was probably safer to keep still.

"Come on, get up," Zhak said irritably. "This is a work day, don't you know?"

"Uh, that's right, sorry." Tadko jumped up and went for his locker.

"What are you doing?"

"Getting my clothes."

Zhak grunted, gesturing impatiently. "Just wear your clout, it's all you need. Too hot in the Packery for anything else. Come on."

Tadko joined a long line of men, filing into the tank and then the dining room. They walked with dreary decorum, obviously well accustomed to "keeping their distance." There was little talk, but much hawking and spitting, coughing and belching, and assorted abdominal noises.

Zhak did look back once.

"You got boots?"

"No."

"If they put you on lower level, you'll need 'em. It's damp. You'll get foot rot."

"Where do I get them?"

"Buy 'em from the company, twenty-six and twelve, deduct from your pay."

Tadko said nothing, but hoped he wouldn't be assigned to lower level. In any case he would refuse to buy boots from the company. No matter what.

Breakfast was much like supper, with the addition of mugs of froile, too bitter, but decently strong and hot. Then they filed back through the bunk room to the outside entrance. They passed one man still lying on his bunk. He was hugging himself, his body jerking spasmodically, his eyes wide open and staring in different directions.

"What's wrong with him?" Tadko asked, shocked.

The others hardly glanced at the man.

"Flyouts," someone said indifferently. "He's off on another world, and a bad one, looks like. Nothing anyone can do."

They passed on.

Outside into a steaming rain. Here the ranks closed up, splashing and jostling along at a half run. Across the street, women and girls were pouring out of another building. Ramps descended from the upper floors, carrying more of them; when he glanced back, he saw the same thing at his own barrack. Some joined Tadko's group, trotting along in the same direction; others went off down the side streets they passed. He could hardly believe the company would have work for all of them.

He said to Zhak, "What would happen if we all ran off at random, or just sat down and did nothing?"

Zhak jerked a thumb skyward. Tadko looked up, and saw a small floater, painted in Concora colors, hovering overhead.

"Lot of those, watching the whole city," Zhak said. "Stun circuits. You want to try it?"

"No." He thought of something else. "Why is it so hot here? Someone told me it was mid-winter."

"Who told you that?"

"Someone I met in the City."

Zhak laughed. "No wonder. That's up in the northern hemisphere! You're down in the south now, it's mid-summer and besides it's always hotter here. You're an offworlder, hah? Should've learned something before you landed."

His tone was contemptuous. Tadko would have liked to turn and slam Zhak to the ground, tall as he was, but thought about the stun circuits and refrained.

Then they arrived at the Packery, and he understood why they had so many workers. It was at least fifteen stories high and appeared to cover a whole city block, or more. They entered one of the many doors, all the others holding up their ident numbers as they did so, and Tadko was left with the scheduler.

"Your name?"

"Tadko Darusko."

"Ever worked here before?"

"No."

She fussed with her screens. "Palm here."

He displayed his palm, with his number, to the correct screen. She produced a shiny card, handed it to him.

"You're assigned to lower level. Take the ramp down, over there. Report to the floor super."

Tadko felt his shoulders slump. It would have to be lower level. Maybe it wasn't as bad as Zhak thought. He *would not* buy boots from the company.

He rode down into a clanging cavern, the ceiling hidden by tangles of machinery, other machines filling all the floor space. It smelled of metal and oil, the iodine reek of ocean, sweat, and other, less definable things.

He guessed that the man at the desk surrounded by comp screens was the floor super, and presented his card. Like the woman above, this man wore ordinary Monnan garb with a patch in Concora colors on the left shoulder. His gaze was tired and cynical. He accepted the card, fed it into a slot, worked with his controls, finally spoke into a mesh at one side.

"Neradis, they've sent us another live body and you have priority. Want to come and see him?"

After a moment a woman came out of the maze of machinery. She was past middle age, lean and stringy-muscled, dressed—or undressed—like the women prisoners in clout, boots, and breastband. The super nodded at Tadko.

"Darusko, Tadko. From Elnakt. Illegal entry. Petty theft. Probable status, unskilled. Assigned barrack three. I know you need someone else on your line, you want to try him?"

Hands on hips, she surveyed Tadko like a trader finding faults on an overage onca. "This your first layup? Elnakt, eh—had any experience with machinery at all?"

"No."

She turned on the super. "All right, Cly, if I'm taking on a fresh caught sprat, how much training time am I allowed?"

"One cycle, same as for anyone, You know the rules, Neradis."

She threw her hands high, let them drop. "My life, it's one thing with people who've been here before, shove them on line and go ahead, but a first timer from offworld—you go to the company meetings, can't you get it across that some of these types don't know *anything*?"

Cly's weary look deepened.

"You know better than that, Neradis. Higher ups don't care any more for me than they do for you. It's just push, push, and if the poor scrabblers down on the floor don't like it, they can go take a dive. You want to try him for a cycle, if he doesn't shape up I can move him so it won't affect your quota. Best I can do."

"And let someone else get the benefit of his first cycle." She considered briefly, then nodded. "All right, I'll see what he can do. What's your name? Tadko? Come along."

He followed, simmering with resentment. They talked as if he wasn't there!

"I speak Monnan quite well," he ventured in a tone he tried to keep neutral.

"That's good, it'll make it easier." She looked at him curiously. "How'd you manage to get into trouble? Why aren't you on Sancy, with the rest of your people?"

"I landed late, and I was just trying to get there. They caught me."

"Bad lines." She did not add any words of encouragement.

They passed through the maze, with people on every side settling into place, stretching, preparing for the day's work.

"This is my station." Neradis came to a stop, produced a towel from somewhere, and handed it to him. "Here, dry yourself off, your hair is still dripping."

While he worked on that, she asked "Don't you have boots?"

"No."

"You'll need them down here, you'll get foot rot eventually. Ask in the office, up on first floor."

"No," he said. "Isn't there anyplace else to get them, or a cheaper place?"

"Not anywhere in Tallenport, as far as I know or second-hand either. Concoras don't like it." As he finished toweling, she added, "You'll need a towel too, for wet days."

"Where—oh yes, I can guess. Up in the office, on first floor. *No!*" He yelled the word before he could stop himself, then cringed a little, waiting for a stun circuit. Neradis only shrugged.

"Wait and see," she said.

She poked her head into an alcove next to her own station.

"Yoseka, you'll all have to move up one, Adwig will be in section eight; Tadko here has to be next to me, he's new."

The young woman picked up her towel and stepped out, stooping to get under the tangle overhead. Neradis guided Tadko in, and arranged him to face her. To his left was a pillar, about as big around as his arms could reach. A little water fountain projected from it just above his head. Neradis did something that brought this down to shoulder height.

"Drink as much as you can, you'll need it," she said. "At least they don't stint us on that." She pulled open a panel below, revealing an open space. "Your food will be delivered in here, it comes up from below." She pointed to where the upper end of the pillar disappeared above. "It goes up to all the floors through these pillars, most of it, anyway, so you'll hear the rattle when they start. The door pops open by itself when yours arrives, so be sure to take it out right away, or you'll lose it."

Below the meal delivery panel, a round plate was set flat against the pillar. Neradis snapped it out, then pushed it up again.

"You can sit here to eat."

"What if I have to—uh—you know."

She pointed back along the line. "Way back there, plenty of stalls. But you'd better learn to wait until meal time, because it slows up the line, and I have a quota to make."

She showed him the work he would have to do. From Yoseka, on his left, a stack of seven frames, each loaded with six sealed aquaria in foam cells, would slide into the form in front of him. He had to pull a lever that dropped an eighth frame on top, pull another to drop the six aquaria in place, then kick a foot release that sent the whole stack on to Neradis, who sealed it and sent it on to Shipping. She had barely finished explaining when a whistle blew, and the noise suddenly increased.

"Rest your weight on your left foot," she said hastily, and slid back into her own station.

He waited nervously until the first stack appeared, pulled, pulled, kicked, and watched it go on to Neradis. Her arms flew, her body swayed back and forth, sheets of tough film shot up and snugged around the stack followed by strapping, she kicked and it went off down a center conveyor.

Yoseka called, "Hoy!"

Neradis glanced over and yelled, "Move! Don't gawk!"

He had another stack, with yet another pushing alongside. Panting, he pulled, pulled, kicked, pulled, pulled, kicked, finally settled into something approaching a rhythm, not without stops and starts and breaks when he absolutely *had* to shift his weight off his left leg. When the whistle blew again he was hardly aware, and stood blinking, fumbling at levers that no longer moved, until Neradis yelled, "Get your food before you lose it!"

He turned and grabbed the tray just in time, then stood holding it while he drank a lot of water. He hadn't managed a mouthful while he worked. Neradis had noticed that, too.

"Try to get a drink every so often," she told him. "It's hard to work it into the rhythm, but you need it, you'll get dizzy."

He looked at the levers, at the kick release, and asked, "Can't they fix it so it all works together, so people wouldn't have to do this?"

"If they don't, it's because it's cheaper this way," she snapped. "Eat up, they don't give us much time."

He ate up, drank a lot of water, paid a quick visit to the back, and returned to his station just in time. Pull, pull, kick. Pull, pull, kick. Pull, pull, kick. The levers grew heavier and heavier, so did his arms.

When the whistles sounded for the end of the work day, he leaned against his pillar, too exhausted to move right away. Sighs and groans came from all around. Neradis dropped her arms and slumped where she stood, eyes closed, breathing deeply. Across the aisle in the next line, a man pulled down his pillar seat and sank onto it, stretching his legs, bending over to hang arms and head between his knees. Many, Tadko included, stooped to their water fountains.

Neradis straightened up, although her face still sagged with weariness. She produced another towel, quickly wiped herself down, took a smock and breeches from where they had hung at the back of her pillar, and dressed. She added the usual belt and pouch, patted her hair down, and took a look at the faintly reflective pillar as if to make sure her appearance was properly respectable.

Now there was a general movement toward the exits; Tadko tried out his arms and legs to make sure they would function, and joined it. They moved slowly, in silence.

He noticed the floor. In most Monnan buildings this would be made of a smooth, synthetic material; here it seemed to have been sliced out of the island bedrock. It was rough-surfaced and damp. Moisture collected in low spots and crevices, and stung where it splashed his feet. He thought drearily that he might have to buy those boots after all.

Outside the rain was bucketing down again—or still. It battered on their naked shoulders, soaked hair and clouts, sluiced off the day's sweat as efficiently as any shower, and flowed into the drains set along both sides of the street. Back in the barrack, he took his turn with the others at a row of hot air vents along one wall of the tank, drying himself off before the evening meal.

When they lined up to go into the dining room, Tadko saw the empty bunk where the man "on flyouts" had been.

"What happened? He asked, pointing.

"Oh, Moricky?" Someone said. "When he didn't show up for work, they'd send a company stropper to check up. Would've taken him away, in that shape. Dunno how much longer he'd last, any route."

Tadko considered this while they sat down to wait for their dinner.

"If he dies, what will they do with his body?"

"Send it to the dead boiler."

"The what?"

"The burner for the dead, Spratso." The speaker, a hard-faced youth with a cocky manner, looked around the table. "Anybody know if he had any family? Company would send 'em his oil, if they paid for it."

"He got sent here from somewhere east, the Boreo Islands, I think." That was a scar-faced man from Moricky's section of barrack. "Wouldn't think he'd have anyone to pay shipping. They have to let next of kin know, but that's all."

From his mother's lessons Tadko had learned something of the Monnan method for disposal of the dead.

"How do they—well—turn them into oil?" he asked.

Zhak waved a hand dismissively. "Dunno exactly how it works but it's with hydrogen, out of the ocean, you know. Turn the corpse into oil, then if you do it right, you burn the oil in a memory lamp, on anniversaries and all."

"My family has a lamp, goes way back to my great-great grandfather," someone said proudly.

Disgusting, Tadko thought, as he ate. Petty criminal, thief probably, proud of the family corpse lamp! On Elnakt, the dead were buried decently, with proper rites.

Aloud he said, "What do they do with the oil if his family don't send for it?"

"Just add it to the general pool. Use it for in the council chambers, and the judges' halls, and all, for the ceremonies."

Zhak laughed. "Company might even have to hire someone to replace him—they say they're really pushing for quota in Packery Four."

There were snickers and grimaces from around the table.

"Company'll not like that," said the cocky youth. "Have to pay a free worker citizens' standard. More like, they'll just push it all on to the poor workees, like us. Eat up," he added. "Time's almost up."

The next morning he ached all over again, especially his left leg where he had had to balance all the work day, and his shoulders, from holding his arms up. The other men laughed at his groans of misery, but it was a rueful laughter—they had been through it, too.

"You can get something for pain up in the office," Zhak told him. "A duat per tab, deduct from your pay, as many as you want. Or you can tough it out if you're smart. Take too many and you can't stop. You can work, right enough, but you'll never pay out."

Tadko nodded. "I'll tough it out."

When he arrived at work, he was astonished to find Neradis waiting for him with a pair of gray boots.

"Here," she said, handing them to him. "If they fit, they're yours."

He began, "I don't want to pay—" but she interrupted brusquely.

"No charge for these, my son's long outgrown them, your feet're probably small enough."

Meekly, he tried them. A bit large, but more than adequate for standing all day at his station. When he attempted, clumsily, to thank her, she waved him to silence.

"You might as well use them, and there's no use training you in and then having you get foot rot, after all, I have a quota to make."

He settled himself to work, reaching for his levers, grimacing in pain as he lifted his arms. Would she let him keep the boots if the quota wasn't made? If they sent him elsewhere it might be better than this. It might be much worse, too; best to try to stay with Neradis until he knew a lot more about this place.

On Eightday, Cly Varnen, the floor super, came by Neradis's line during the midday meal.

"What about Darusko?" he asked. "Is he shaping up, or do you want me to move him?"

Neradis considered, "He'll do," she said finally. "Might as well leave him."

"Right enough, I'll record it then, Darusko, Tadko, permanent on line fifty, Luxane, Neradis, line supervisor.

Tadko was too tired to resent their impersonal manner, too tired even to decide whether he was glad or sorry to be staying with Neradis. He finished his food and stood up, ready to work again.

The last hours were the hardest of all. When it was over, he could scarcely believe that the next three days would be free. Some people went haring out of their stations as if suddenly charged with tremendous energy; others, like Tadko, moved slowly, sleepily. Neradis, as usual, took time to dress, and make herself look respectable.

"Why are some of them going off so fast?" he asked, hoping the question was acceptable, and that she wasn't in too much of a hurry to answer.

"Some live close enough so they have time to visit their families, or friends, over the free days," she explained. "A few idiots just can't wait to collect their squares, what little they get, and head down to Rotten Pier to spend it. If you're smart and you want to get down to Sancy, eventually, stay away from there."

The name had occurred in snippets of conversation he'd overheard during the last cycle.

"What's at Rotten Pier?"

"Oh, fancy boys and girls, bad food and worse liquor, gambling, flyouts, and worse. Everything cheap as beach pebbles, too. I'll give you some advice—leave part of your pay in what they call a Company Account. You won't get any interest, but you'll save a little extra in case you need any deductions, and if you *don't* need them, you can draw it out for something you want. Nothing wrong with lifting a mug or two, or getting a decent meal, of course. Which barrack did you say you were in?"

"Number Three."

"The Beached Barge isn't far from there, try it. Decent food and drink, and a fair price, too."

"I'll remember."

Out on the floor a line of little desks, with comp connections, had been lowered from above. Workers filed past, showing their idents to the screens, picking up their money as it dropped into the cups below. Tadko stared at the two black squares in his hand. He had known he would get no more, but seeing it there in his palm made a real difference. He turned to Neradis, behind him.

"I think I'll leave it in a Company Account, the way you said."

She was startled. "All of it? I *said* there's nothing wrong with lifting a mug or two."

"All of it. How do I do it?"

At her instruction, he dropped the squares back into the cup, pressed the right key, showed his ident to the screen again, and watched them disappear.

The first free day he slept, waking for meals, then sleeping again.

The second day he went out to wander the streets. Tallenport was the biggest place he had seen since he left the City, even possessing a trotline system, but it was drab. Blocks and blocks of packeries, warehouses, barracks, and offices. A couple of apprentice houses, pleasanter than the prisoner barracks—these had wide verandas in front, and through the long windows he could see tables, comfortable chairs, viewscreens with young people in Concora colors lounging or studying. Loungers on the verandas looked with disdain at Tadko in his clout and sandals, and he didn't linger. He knew he ought to wear proper dress to keep from being recognized as a prisoner, but none of the other prisoners did—possibly none of them *had* proper clothes—and they were the ones he had to live with. He understood, now, why Neradis dressed so carefully before she left the packery. He thought she wasn't a prisoner, not exactly, anyway, but also thought it safer not to inquire.

He found a district of smaller shops and eateries, low-priced but decent looking, and felt some regret for the duats left in the Company Account, but told himself he had better begin as he meant to go on.

There were one or two places that advertised "Repairs and Exchanges—Purchase of Oddments," like Unser's in the City, with a similar mixture of goods. He wished he had something left that might bring him a few more duats. His other clothes would bring a few zinae, but not enough to do him much good. He wondered if they would buy his League badge, but decided to wait until he learned a little more about the rules. If he still had his knife, now—he still felt a dull anger when he remembered that theft.

Down some streets he could see a long vista of houses and other buildings climbing the hills around the harbor, and once he turned a corner to find a broad avenue very much like one in the City.

Lights, transparent panels in many colors, windows displaying jewelry, elaborate clothing, exotic toys and ornaments. There was a Herenna's store in silver and pale green, and some distance down the street, a House of Many Worlds. He wondered about entertaining there, for a free and excellent meal, but then he realized how the people were looking at him. Commercial castes, all of them, gorgeously dressed, house colors in their hair or on their shoulders, they stared with expressions that were little short of loathing. Down at the next corner, a green was moving in his direction.

Tadko turned and ran, expecting a stun circuit any moment, wanting to cry out that he had only come there by accident and he hadn't *done* anything. He headed toward the harbor as the safest direction, turning as many corners as he dared without losing his way. When he had to stop to catch his breath, he ducked into the door alcove of an empty shop and looked out for any pursuit. Nothing and no one appeared; he decided they had only wanted to scare him away.

They simply didn't care to have a mere prisoner cluttering up their high caste district. He hated them, every one. This idea had never struck him before, but now he examined it and found it highly satisfying. The commercials had been no more to him than exotic fauna of Monna. Now he knew he despised them, from the old Concora woman who sent him here, on down. Having come to that conclusion, he trudged back to barrack number three and the evening meal.

The third free day, he joined Zhak and some others in one of the Voyage games. Rumard had a look of part Eilonsad parentage. Loy was short for a Monnan, with spindly, slightly crooked limbs. Homistho was—different. Heavy boned and heavy featured, pale skin that grew a haze of short dark hair; he even had hair on his face. Tadko's hand went up to his own chin when he saw that, but he snatched it down, afraid of embarrassing Homistho.

He tried not to look at the man, while the four of them, with an air of conveying great mysteries, explained the game. It had been invented many generations ago by some unknown prisoner, and was always drawn and painted by hand, using whatever paints or inks the players could scrounge or buy cheaply. You started in the center circle and worked your way out along the spiral to the finish. Two dice were used, the first with facets numbered one through twelve, the second with six facets colored black, white, red, blue, yellow and green. These were made commercially as replacement parts for an entirely different game, but there was always someone willing to spend a few zinae for a set; the buyer—in this case Homistho—owned them, of course. Most sections along the spiral contained pictures in five different colors; a few had all six, others had only four, the proportion worked out by a formula Tadko made no effort to remember. You moved according to number of section and color of picture; if there was no picture of the required color, you lost a turn.

As for the pictures, many were standard, like the spaceship in black halfway along; if you landed there you could finish in one more turn. Others were up to the imagination of the artists. Various pictures or printed messages sent you forward or backward for various distances, or to specific destinations. The playing pieces were anything at all. Shells, stones, broken bits of metal or plastic, dried fruit pits, a cracked belt buckle. The stakes were low, they told him. Just a zina or two, no more than you would want to risk, not like down at Rotten Pier where they tried to gut you every game.

They were taken aback when Tadko explained he had left *all* his money in a Company Account, and intended to do so every cycle. They looked at each other.

"Cheaper, cheaper," Homistho grumbled, his voice as rough as his appearance. "You think you'll get ahead of the Company, doing that. You won't. You'll be laid up for twice, three times your sked, if you're lucky. You can go bond on it."

Tadko looked at the man's dull eyes, his face set in lines of permanent bitterness, and felt a tightness somewhere inside. It could be true—which to believe, Homistho or Neradis?

"You may be right, but I guess I'll try it, for a while, anyway."

Homistho gave a distinctly Monnan shrug, and said no more.

After a lengthy discussion, they agreed to let him play without hazarding any stakes. He could take his turn and play, laying no bets and receiving no payments. Rumard assured him that he would lose half the fun of it—there would be no point.

But when he insisted, they shrugged and gave in.

So he played Voyage. For a playing piece, he discarded the jar of hair glisten he had carried so far, and used the cap. He found that the game was intensely important to these men, more important, perhaps even more real, than the work they did day after day. They argued over which was a better destination, the Blue Palace or the Red Tower, or the Island of Women, discussing the pleasures to be had at each place as if they were actually available, groaning over an arrival at the White Packery, or a yellow squiggle intended to represent a squelt processing plant, praying, as they approached it, to avoid the Mine in the White Waste. This would send you back to the start again.

Tadko thought he could never become involved in the game to this extent—but it passed the time.

The next morning, back to work. Neradis surprised him again; she brought a basket of toa fruit, from a tree in her own yard, and passed out one to each person on her line, to eat at midday. Her manner was as brusque as ever— "After all, they aren't that rare, they'd only go to waste"—but he decided to try hard to stay on Neradis's line.

The light in the packery bothered him that day, and when he came back to the barrack it was even worse. He blinked and squinted for sometime before recalling the retina screen, still in his bag in the locker. He used it with some reluctance. When the bulb was empty he would have to buy more, and he had promised himself not to spend any money if it wasn't absolutely necessary. He decided, eventually, that retina screen *was* necessary. Without it, there was the danger of making mistakes at work and he couldn't take the risk.

On seven day, before they left work, he nerved himself to ask Neradis a question.

"I need to know the cost of a round-trip ticket to the City. A fast way, not barge travel. Do you know where I can find out?"

She looked at him with concern, and said softly, "You're not going to try to run, are you? Don't do it. You'll not get off-island, I promise you."

"No honestly, I swear it. I swear by—by those of the Five Ships, who came to Elnakt." He thought impatiently that such an oath would mean nothing to a Monnan, but his looks and manner must have convinced her.

"I'll find out, but don't speak of it to anyone else."

The next day, after the others had left, she murmured, "Three hundred and fifty D, current fares by wave jet, and we've not discussed it, ever."

He nodded, and left.

CHAPTER THIRTEEN

The next day was free, but he had no interest in exploring the town. After the morning meal, he joined Zhak and the others at the Voyage game.

The betting was complex, and he was glad to be excluded. It had nothing to do with when, or even whether, you finished. One time Rumard threw a score of twelve, green, more than enough to take him to the end of the spiral; he counted five and out, went back to the beginning, and counted seven, green to start over. They bet on whether or not they would land on certain squares or colors, or whether or not they would avoid others, or sometimes how many turns it would take them to travel a certain distance. Zhak had a ploy of betting with one man that he would land on a certain spot and with another that he would miss. This required a nice calculation of odds; the rules didn't permit it very often, and the others seldom tried it.

During the afternoon, Loy threw a score that took him to a green circle, decorated with tiny stick figures in more or less athletic poses.

"Right enough!" He exclaimed happily. "I made the carnival at Pad! Squat, wish I'd bet on it."

The others congratulated him. "Lucky catch!"

"Want to try for an event while you're there?" Zhak suggested.

"Might as well," Loy pondered, frowning a little. "I'll try for the deep-diving championship," he announced. "Bet a zina. Anyone else want in?"

"You want to bet, or you want to pick your prize if you win? You can get an extra turn." Rumard was intensely interested in moves that might give him an extra turn. Speed around the course was most important to him.

Loy considered the question as if his future career depended on the outcome.

"Guess I'll pick my prize," he decided. "Everybody roll."

"Tadko, you roll for this too," Zhak ordered. "Since it's not a money bet."

All five rolled their twelve-sided dies, cast, and inspected the result.

"High roll!" Loy announced. "I win! I'll take another turn, right enough." He cupped both dice in his hands and shook them vigorously, first down near the floor, then up by his left ear, finally cast them. The result was obviously pleasing.

"Eight yellow, that takes me to a trotline car, and that gives me five more sections and my choice of spots. Guess I'll pick...black, that's the House of Many Worlds. Try entertaining there next turn."

Tadko was thinking of a barge, out on the open water under the sky, and half a dozen eager young voices, telling him about the carnival—the real carnival—at Padriocosta. He felt a surprising pang of homesickness, and wondered again how these men could become so caught up in a mere game, talking as if Loy had really gone to the carnival, and taken part in one of the contests, and traveled on from there. He waited until play resumed, then ventured tentatively, "About the carnival, the real carnival, I mean—" He paused, hoping it wasn't a serious breach of manners to mention the real thing. But they were willing enough to switch from one to the other.

"What about the real one? Were you there?" Zhak's voice was eager.

"No, but I wondered—who won the ocean's run? I heard people talking about it before I—before."

In a moment, the game was forgotten.

"Gerdiana Quiproyen, for House Ornibeck," Rumard proclaimed. "Call her the Wave-Scorcher! Went past the westcliffs on Pembol so close you could have jumped down on the deck of her soloship."

"She's one of their deep-ship pilot apprentices, isn't she?" Loy asked.

"No, she's out of apprenticeship now, going as fifth officer on Ornibeck Mariner. She's really good! Came in a close second last year, and every year she's entered before that, she was second or third."

"Where does the race go?" Tadko asked. "Do they run the whole thing in carnival time?"

"Oh no, the soloships aren't that fast. They start back on the first of Milian from the north coast of Pad, run up the longitude to the pole, down again the other side to the pole again, then up the longitude to the south coast of Pad, that's where most of the events are held. Of course the route isn't straight, there are some islands in the way and that's the trick of it—cutting close to shorten the route. If you run aground you're disqualified."

Zhak illustrated with wide sweeps of his arms. "And they try to finish during Carnival. The leaders always do."

"She set a new record, a hundred and fifty days," Loy put in excitedly. "Best overall time for any deep-ocean run in what—twenty-five years, wasn't it?"

"Right enough." Even the usually taciturn Homistho joined in. "Ornibeck took the deep-diving championship, too—Jarol Slannery, from their wave-jet maintenance department. He set a new record, too, any of you remember how many fathoms it was?"

"Really deep, really dangerous," Rumard said. "Don't remember just how deep, but enough to bring him close to sinking it—they wondered if he was coming up."

Tadko smiled. "Someone I met on a barge will be happy about that, or was happy—is the carnival over, now?"

"Just ended, last cycle, twenty-ninth of Talior," Loy said.

"Did anyone from Concora's win anything?"

The enthusiasm vanished. All four were silent.

"A sprat named Cresmio, some tattered-smock relative of the House, took one of the sprint swims," Homistho rumbled at last. "Won, but no record."

"House went on as if he'd dome something big," Rumard said disgustedly. "Played 'The Final Triumph' through all the buildings, and even passed around little cups of Silver Rain, for us all to drink his health."

"At least they said it was Silver Rain," Loy added. "Would we know? It's imported, costs about fifty D a dram, so you can guess."

Tadko laughed. "How did it taste, whatever it was?"

"Might not have been too bad, if they'd given us more than a little midgin to taste." Zhak held up his thumb and forefinger, barely apart, to indicate the quantity. "But they said they were passing it out to all the contract workers all over Monna, and that's a lot of people, so Loy's got it, right enough."

"Squat on the Concoras," Homistho muttered, half under his breath. "Sink them all. Who's turn is it? Play."

He brought the jacket of his ship suit to work with which to dry himself in the mornings, but Neradis continued to nag him about getting a towel. He did not refuse flatly, but he didn't go up to the company store, either.

One day as they left, Adwig, the man at the end of Neradis's line, fell in beside him. He was stocky, middle-aged and weary faced, with long scarred stripes across his back.

"Need a towel?" he said, his voice low.

Tadko nodded.

"What barrack you in?"

"Number three."

"You're on Harbor Way then. Make south past the sick tank till you come to Cross Seven, turn left, keep going till you come to Rotten Pier. Look for Narn Didthow's. Two, three zinae if you bear down."

"Why didn't she—" Tadko jerked a thumb in the direction of Neradis, some distance ahead.

"She's career housey, can't steer you off the Company. Couldn't have given you those boots, only Company's not likely to have anything small enough. How long you been on Monna?"

"Uh, six, seven cycles, I think."

"Don't go anywhere but Narn Didthow's. Safer."

Tadko nodded again. Adwig offered no further conversation and Tadko joined his group outside, splashing away to Barrack Three.

At the end of the cycle he collected his pay, and the following morning set off for Rotten Pier. It was a long way; he refused to spend even a zina on the trotline fare. When he turned on to Cross Seven, he noticed that the buildings here lacked the sterile, self-satisfied look of those on Harbor Way. They were lower; the walls bore dark rough streaks as if eroded by rain. The shop fronts in the lower levels were often empty, and those occupied were mostly taverns, eatshops, licensed bettors, and "Repair and Replacement—Purchase of Oddments," all of them smelling of cheap drink, rancid squelt, and other, equally unpleasant matters. Scrawny children dashed about, pausing briefly to give him that "Oh, an offworlder" stare, then ignored him.

When the morning rain cleared, street vendors came out, offering sniffs and gulps that promised a great flight. They also offered cheap jewelry, timepieces, sweets and snacks in a bewildering variety, gambling systems guaranteed to make you rich enough to buy out your contract, or coupons for bargain rates at the fancy houses or the taverns.

Most of the customers swaggering along were clearly prisoners from the barracks, wearing only their clouts and sandals, locker keys swinging around their necks. They bargained eagerly for almost anything offered, pushing into the taverns and shouting for ale, or hurrying away with what they called their "flight tickets."

The area locals were either shabbily dressed or too gaudy. Coils of glitter rope circled their torsos or hung from belts, swinging around their long legs. All had a hard-eyed, tight-mouthed look totally unlike the raffish cheer of Seawrack Bay, in the City. Tadko thought he wouldn't trust any of them.

He saw one-story buildings made of slats on a frame, or coral chunks irregularly set in a gray, oozing matrix, or tenting propped up on spars with cookshelf set underneath. Some appeared ready to fall into the street, and were propped up with beams. Bottles and miscellaneous trash littered the streets and walkways. Little round-bodied, sand-colored animals prowled and rooted in the garbage, squatting on thick hind legs to feed themselves with unnervingly human-looking forepaws, or stuffing side pouches and scuttling away on all fours. Sometimes they looked around, hissing, but for the most part they seemed to ignore the humans, and were ignored in turn.

He paused at a corner. The building across the street was in a little better repair than some of the others, still bearing a thin layer of dirty green paint. But doors and windows gaped into darkness. Two men lounged on the steps in front. They were hairy as Homistho and their blotchy dark skins had probably started out equally pale. Their bared teeth behind insolent grins were a silent challenge to every passerby. Tadko quailed a bit inwardly, but knew what to do. He thrust back his shoulders, twisted his face into a scowl, hooked his thumbs into the sides of his breech clout and stalked past stiff-legged, looking straight ahead. They muttered together as he went by, but did nothing. He kept up the pose, his scowl deepening as he passed on.

More taverns, awnings with men and women sprawled on the sand below, staring into nothing as Moricky had done, presumably taking their flights.

Sturdier buildings, with closed doors, barred windows, and small, discreet signs. "Ask for The Athlete." "The Dancers Will Entertain, Your Choice." "For Comfort and Relief, the Oceans' Fancy." Tadko knew what they meant, more or less, and gave them a wide berth, although most had several people hanging about outside, waiting their turns. He reflected sourly that for a new arrival from offworld, a stint as a barrack prisoner did have its uses.

Down the side streets he could see the gambling halls, brightly painted structures that looked out of place in this section with their color, shine, and luminous signs. The Star Tower, Luck's Volcano, The Fountain of Fortune, and others vied for patronage.

A desultory breeze blew, first from one quarter, then another, stirring up little whirlpools of trash, bringing sickly sweet odors from the fancy houses, the smell of stale cooking oil, rotting garbage, overloaded waste stalls, plus an occasional clean whiff of sea and salt air, and once a delicious fragrance of fresh cooked fish and bread. Tadko's stomach growled in response, and he followed his nose.

This tavern was quiet and dim. On a raised dais at one end sat a sad-faced youth in garments striped black and white. From a multi-stringed instrument held in his lap he twanged out the dreariest, most mournful tune Tadko had ever heard, and he sang,

> Far, far away is the lonely isle.
> When will I see the lonely isle?
> Does anyone wait for me?
> Ooooh, the lonely isle, long gone.

Tadko thought he had never heard such sadness in his life. The audience, mostly young men and women from the barracks, were silent. Many had their arms around each other. A few wept openly. The place was clean, the food smelled good, but Tadko fought down a wave of anguished homesickness, and fled.

He noticed a surprising number of commercials, unmistakable in their costly clothing, rosettes of house colors glinting in hair frosted with rainbow hues. He wondered if they were truly safe here; but a couple of floaters hovered overhead and he decided they were probably safer than anyone else.

One of them, young, haughtily graceful, jostled against another coming in the opposite direction and bowed himself away with many elaborate gestures of apology. The gestures were oddly familiar, and suddenly Tadko knew—the young man was a snaffler!

He opened his mouth to cry out, then shut it again and moved on. His conscience twinged somewhat, but he ignored it. Let them look out for themselves! They could afford it.

Now the walkway came to an end. Before him a wide expanse of black sand stretched down to the sea and away on either side. To his right it curved round and rose into a cliff; flocks of birds circled above it, and he heard again that cry of ah-oooh, ah-oooh. To his left, past a long row of beach-front shops and taverns, stood a single large building. Nearly the size of the barrack, it bore a single luminous sign stretched all the way across the front—NARN DIDTHOW. He turned left, wondering how far out to sea that sign must be visible, especially at night.

As Neradis had warned him, the small shops, most of them set up directly on the sand and decidedly flimsy in appearance, offered flyouts, smokes, tired-looking young men and women, drinks, food, pocket peepers and other portable porn equipment, cheap fishing gear, and novelties. Hair frosting of various colors was the stock in one place. Others had no signs, only curtains of beads strung across the front, or a very small printed notice: *Discretion.*

Extending from the beach out into the water was, he supposed, the Rotten Pier. It looked more like a collection of them, five lines of crumbling stone connected at the ends by a cross pier. Even from here he could see the holes and dilapidation. A sixth pier had collapsed completely, leaving a row of irregular blocks standing up from the water. The end of the cross pier had gone down with it.

People sat around the ends of these piers dangling fishing lines in the water; some fished right through holes in the pier. Farther along the beach, many sprawled on the sand, asleep or unconscious. A good many were swimming; shouts and laughter carried up the beach.

Tadko repressed a shudder. One dip in the ocean had been enough for him.

So into Narn Didthow's. This appeared to sell everything anyone could ever think of buying at second, third, or fourth hand, in various stages of repair or disrepair, much of it jumbled together in no particular order. He finally managed to find a towel in a heap of them. It was fairly large, a faded gray color, somewhat worn and stained in one or two places, but he thought it would do. Better than his jacket, anyway.

The clerk looked him over and suggested contemptuously, "Half a D."

Tadko replied with equal contempt, "For this thing? Not worth a zina." There was more than one thing one could learn, he reflected, from the conversation of his fellow prisoners.

The clerk tried to bargain with him; Tadko responded by insisting stubbornly, "It's not worth a zina."

The clerk sneered, "Why d'you want it then? Could you make it two zinae, your high bornness?"

"Done!" Tadko grinned and tossed them over.

The clerk, a skinny youth about Tadko's age from the look of him, opened his mouth, closed it, then appeared to be trying to work this out. Had he truly offered a final bargain?

While he puzzled over it Tadko strolled off, feeling much less confident than he tried to look, half expecting a shout and pursuit behind him. Nothing happened, and he left the store without difficulty. Possibly the youth preferred to keep quiet about mistakes of this type.

The towel smelled musty. Tadko tucked it under his arm, hoping it wouldn't disintegrate when washed.

There were vendors with bubbling tanks and cookshelves under awnings, like the one on the beach in Sandtown. A few bore signs offering, "Cook your catch here! Cheap!"

He watched while two young women brought nets squirming with sea creatures to be cooked. One held her net well away from her body; half a dozen scaly legs tipped with vicious claws waved through the meshes; bits of the netting were already torn.

She dumped the full net into a tank with a whistle of relief.

The vendor looked askance.

"You like those raspers?"

"Good meat once you get rid of all the rest of it," she said. "Chop off the claws when it boils up, and I'll do the rest."

"Right enough." He turned to the other. "What've you got?"

"Prails." She spread her net to display a pile of limp pink forms, some still moving feebly. "You got hot sauce?"

"Hot enough to fry your tongue, right enough."

Tadko watched from a distance while the food was briefly cooked and served on large, shiny plates. When his customers had finished and left, the vendor used tongs to dip the plates in yet another boiling tank, then set them on a rack to dry.

Far along the curve of the beach was a stand of the feather trees he had seen in the forest, and occasionally a couple or two would head off in that direction.

"What's out there?" Tadko asked a passing shell crafter, his stock-in-trade suspended from hooks all over his smock and breeches.

"Nothing." The man leered. "Privacy is what, where they'll not be disturbed. Look there!" He added, pointing. "Fight! Want to bet on it? Go up to Gull's Pocket Peepers, they do betting, too."

Tadko started to explain that he didn't bet, then thought better of it. But he did go over to watch the group of young men now sitting down in a circle on the sand. They left a clear space in the center, where two men stood glaring at each other.

Someone called, "Now!" And the fight began.

It didn't last long. Fists flying, they pummeled each other, kicked, gouged, and even tried to bite. Then one hooked the other behind the knee and kicked him in the groin as he fell. The fallen man doubled up, clutching himself and moaning, while the victor yelled, "Right enough! I get my D back, you furshing droghead! And watch those dice!"

He stalked away through the circle of watchers, sucking at the knuckles of one hand. The others began to disperse, except for the kicked man who was helped to sit up, still moaning, by two others.

Tadko passed by, thankful he knew none of them, and more determined than ever to avoid betting.

He was growing hungry. It was still some time before sunset, but most of the fishers and netters were bringing their catches in. Some went to the Cook Your Catch vendors. Others knelt on the beach, did their own cleaning, added sauce from bottles they carried with them, and ate it raw. The leavings or unwanted items were simply tossed down at the water's edge. A flock of kitewings appeared, apparently from nowhere as always, to dive, squabble and clatter over this bounty. They were clearly accustomed to being fed; small groups of them settled on the sand to watch the humans, ready to pounce as soon as scraps were thrown.

It was so hot. He could feel the heat of the sand through his soles. His eyes and skin were beginning to feel prickly, and his business here was done. Back to the barrack? Safer, Adwig had told him.

Off to his right one vendor had put up a huge awning, big enough to shelter a good many customers as well as his equipment. Tadko thought he might as well spend a few more zinae. He felt slightly guilty, but at least he hoped this would be better than barrack food.

It was. He joined a good many others for ale and a mixture of blats and shelled-out pipelets in the usual cone. He felt hesitant about talking to strangers here, but one young woman looked him up and down curiously. She wore smock and breeches, but around her neck dangled the telltale locker key of a prisoner.

"Where in space you from?" She asked abruptly.

"Elnakt."

"Never heard of it."

He shrugged and sawed his hand, indicating that he didn't care, one way or another.

"Offworld." He pointed to where another fight was taking place. "What do they fight about?"

"Mostly over the game. Game, any kind of argument. How long you been in?"

"Three cycles."

"You know, then. No fight, no touch, no nothing in barrack. Come out here for both."

"Huh," Tadko said. "How long you been in?"

"A year. Two more to go for the squatting Concoras."

"Does everyone work prisoners on Monna?"

She shook her head. "Only Concoras. They make all the souvenir stuff, and most of it has to be cheap."

Interested, Tadko described the aquaria they packed in Number Seven.

"Right enough, they're all over. Concoras make all the souvenirs sold on Monna, on and offworld. Clothes, even. Sandals, pouches, belts; shell, coral and stone jewelry; luck shells when they can get them. Holopicture sets, toys, seascapes, volcanoes—"

"Volcanoes!" he exclaimed. "What are they like?"

"Imitations of old Purple Peak, there." She pointed north, to where the clouded summit of the great volcano seemed to hover in the sky. "It's in a crystallite cylinder. There are controls to make it erupt, lava or sparks, and they're absorbed into the base until you set it off again."

"Are they made here?"

"No. Someplace else, where they can get the materials cheap. Concoras wouldn't let 'em touch old Purple Peak, itself."

"Why do you say luck shells, when they can get them? Those aren't cheap."

"Sea people will only trade with bargees, and bargees keep most for themselves." She snickered. "Concoras would like to do something about that, but sea houses have more say. They really do bring good luck, you know," she added earnestly.

Tadko wished he'd been able to bring his own luck piece from home, the left eartuft of a black onca, to hang from his belt.

* * *

Far out at sea appeared a thing like a silver tower on a black platform, growing incredibly large as it moved slowly along to pass the cliffs.

"What's that?" He asked.

"Cargo deep-ship. Going in to Tallen Prime Port. More work for us workees, more squares for the squatting Concoras."

The floating city, now displaying a whole superstructure of towers and squat cylinders on the long black hull, gradually moved out of sight beyond the cliffs. Dark shapes followed it, dipping and soaring in the air.

"Ploters," the young woman said. "They never come in to land."

He had noticed that on each cheek this woman had a crescent tattooed, and he was reminded of Zhak.

"Someone in the same barrack with me has diamond shapes," he said. "Does it mean something?"

She scowled and rubbed the tattoos irritably. "He's from Tamatey, then. I'm Perinhome. Dead-in-the-water islands with dead-in-the-water customs. Someday, when I have the squares, I'll get rid of them."

She continued to scowl and Tadko was silent, feeling rebuffed and annoyed. How was he to know? True, Zhak never referred to his tattoos. Nor had anyone else, at least not within Tadko's hearing, and now he decided he would never ask.

He continued to sit, wondering about walking back to the barrack. It was a long walk. It would be pleasant to sleep on the beach, but it might not be safe. Not far away the trotline from up the street curved around, on a raised track to keep it above the sandy beach, and came to an end, the signal kiosk forming its final bumper. He had already spent some extra on food, in spite of his vow. Easier to make such vows than keep them.

While he debated with himself, the beaded curtains on one of the nameless places parted, jingling, and a couple of commercials appeared. Their badly rumpled clothing was the gaudiest he had seen yet. Man and woman, their age was indeterminate, their hair hung awry about their faces. The man kept trying, without success, to brush his away.

Giggling unpleasantly, they staggered down the beach, somehow supporting each other. They reached the base of the trotline kiosk and leaned against it, proceeding to fumble with their wrist comps. No floater appeared. They shouted at the comps and each other in slurred voices. They looked up and waved as if coaxing their floater down. Then they seemed to give up. After a quieter consultation, the man dug several zinae out of his pouch. Moving with great care, he climbed the few steps and got them into the trotline slot. Then he slid down the steps and collapsed on the sand. The woman stood for a moment, looking puzzled, than dropped down beside him.

Someone whistled and said in a low voice, "High flyouts. Clear offworld and out to the stars. Be a long time coming down."

"Should we do anything?" Tadko asked.

"Not likely. Let 'em take their chances. They don't come home, someone from their house will come for them. Locate their flyer, easy enough, then them." A snicker. "Take 'em off to a drench tank, I'll go bond."

At home on Elnakt you always went to help people. But this was different. They brought it on themselves, he thought angrily.

Then the trotline car they had summoned appeared and rolled up to a stop. Neither moved. Tadko hesitated only an instant, then ran up to the car and jerked the door open before it could roll back. He looked back at the other ordinaries, and the prisoners, scattered on the beach. All were grinning and waving their hands enthusiastically, even the young woman with tattoos who had been so offended. The commercial couple were still unconscious. He jumped in, said, "Barrack Three, Harbor Way," and sat back as the ride began.

CHAPTER FOURTEEN

Now Tadko understood the men who limped in at the end of the free days with assorted bruises and contusions, bashed knuckles, split lips, or swollen-shut eyes. They treated themselves in the tank with cloth pads soaked in cold water, or whatever nostrums they could afford to buy. He had seen women too, plainly the survivors of fights, limping along toward their work in the mornings. Next day during a lull in the Voyage game, he described the fight he had seen.

"I thought the company and the greens didn't allow fighting?"

Rumard snickered.

"Long as you don't do it on company time, or company property."

"And long as you don't get hurt bad enough, or hurt someone else bad enough, so you can't work, or have to go to the sick tank," Loy added. "End up there too often and it's up north for you. Even if they don't do that, it's double your fine every time, and flogging."

"Remember that big man, Balt, that used to be here?" Zhak asked. "Came from some place way over east. He liked to fight just for nothing."

The others nodded. "Go down to the pier on free days, and pick fights." Loy said. "He was sleek enough at first, didn't hurt anyone too bad, but then they started going to the sick tank with broken hands and teeth and even worse, and they flogged him a couple of times, and then he was gone. Probably north."

"The others only got fined," Zhak finished.

Tadko thought it hardly seemed fair, if this Balt had deliberately picked the fights, but he supposed the company wouldn't be concerned with "fair," only with getting more work and more fines. Or did they get them?

"Who really gets the fines?"

"Half to the Commercial Council, half to Concoras. Same thing, here on Tallen." Rumard spoke with just a touch of contempt at such ignorance.

Tadko ignored the tone. He was trying to work it out in his mind, and finally concluded that half of the money presumably paid to him was in fact never paid at all, but kept by the Concoras; but then where did it come from in the first place? Didn't the greens get, or want, their share? Whatever the situation, he was being cheated, he was certain of it.

"Squat on the Concoras," he muttered, glowering at the game design, adding in his own language, "onca futters. Freeze their cluts off."

The others grinned, understanding the intention if not the actual words. All except Homistho, who never smiled.

"Nothing you can do." His hoarse voice had a perpetually angry sound. "Watch your marker and stay out of fights."

This was good advice, but not easy to follow. Game markers had to be picked up between each session on the work days, because of the traffic in the aisles. Each man had to remember where his marker had been and replace it when the game resumed.

The opportunity to "forget," or to accuse someone else of forgetting, was constant. Then would come a sudden forward tension of the body, hands and teeth clenched, a string of half-smothered curses, and finally a few deep breaths and subsidence. A wonder there were not more fights. Even though Tadko had no money involved, he was learning to hold his own in these arguments, to exhibit the proper degree of anger when accused, and to watch the others for floating markers, as they were called. There were other ways of cheating and some games were a continual shouting match, but this group was quieter; the disputes were usually brief, and not too frequent.

So the time passed. He took his towel to work, wondering about Neradis's reaction, but she only gave him a sidelong glance and a magnetic clip with which to hang it up. A few days later the heavy rains ended, giving way to light showers that passed through the city once or twice a day, but seldom lasted long. He swore a good deal about the weather change; he hardly needed his new towel, but was told by Yoseka that he would need that towel, next year. Next year! And the year after that! That night he sprang up from the game to pace round and round the barrack, panting, trying not to run out and away down the street, tracer or not. No one paid any attention, and when he sat to play again they handed him his marker without any comment. He was grateful, but after the lights were out he lay awake for a long time on his bunk, trying not to sob, aching for the great open plain, cold winds, the light of his own sun and the faces of his own people. He would ask his father to send him home—if he ever reached his father—no, don't think about it. Think about work. Remember the money is adding up, slowly, but a little more each cycle. Flyouts were said to give you cheerful, pleasant voyages and afterward you didn't care about anything. But they cost money, and you might end up like Moricky. Bad voyages were really bad.

A few nights later he definitely gave up the idea of flyouts. Someone overdosed, right there in the barrack. The screams were loud enough to wake everyone; Tadko sat up, and Zhak slid down to go and investigate. There were cries of "Get water!" the sound of running feet, a thud that Tadko could feel through the floor, and silence. Zhak returned immediately, and a murmuring traveled from bunk to bunk.

"Flyouts really bad," Zhak said. "Fell off an upper, cracked his head. They're signaling the sick tank, for a wagon."

"Is he as bad as Moricky?"

"Oh, lots worse. They'll just finish him off, like they did Moricky."

"Here comes the wagon," someone called. "Feet on the floor and line up, you workees."

There were grumbles and curses as the men stood up in the dim nighttime illumination, each one taking his place before his locker, hands behind back, shoulders against the locker, feet slightly apart. Tadko imitated the others, shuffling wearily into place as the bright lights came on. He heard the door opening, voices in conversation, and wondered why they all had to stand up like this. Then he saw a green at the other end of the aisle. The man came along slowly, giving each prisoner a careful look, occasionally raising someone's eyelid for a closer examination of the eyes. The stun circuits must be off, Tadko thought sleepily, or maybe these greens were immune. He was relieved when the man passed without touching him and glad to fall back on his bunk when the doors closed and the lights dimmed.

The deaths of two men, strangers though they were, both frightened Tadko and calmed him. If he meant to see Elnakt again, no matter when, he must not go that route. And after all, it wasn't as if he were a real criminal, like the others. What he did, he was forced into. It would be a terrible mistake to let himself be drawn into a criminal way of life. He was a leader, a Mosor of Daruskan, taught to guide his people in right customs and right ways.

He made himself rise briskly in the morning and do his work cheerfully. He ate the food that was given him, telling himself there were lean times on Elnakt when he, and all the others, would have been glad of such food. He let himself be drawn fully into the ambiance of the Voyage game; it was honest, and harmless—and it passed the time. Only, he still refused to play for money.

When the effect of his retina screen wore off, he tried for a couple of days to do without, but the light, indoors or out, hurt too badly. Reluctantly, he used the last drops in the bulb. The stuff had cost him three and seven back in the City, he would just have to allow for the expense.

One Sevenday, as they prepared to leave work, Neradis beckoned to him.

"You're doing well," she said. "Do you have any proper clothes?"

"Yes, why?"

"You might bring them tomorrow. Come and spend the free days at my house, get out of the barrack for a while."

He stared at her. There was plenty of talk in the barrack about career houseys, as they were called, both men and women, willing to pay a healthy young prisoner for sex. It was said you could even buy your way out doing this. It was said that if you had the money in hand before they caught you, they asked no questions. Still, Neradis—she seemed decent enough, and he had come to respect her—but not that much.

She looked puzzled at his hesitancy, then her face twisted with a mixture of amusement and disgust.

"I've no designs on you, you can go bond on that. At my age, hah! My son is home for a visit, you can meet him, eat something besides barrack food. Do you good."

He managed an apologetic smile. "I will, and thank you very much."

That night he took out the bright clothes he had bought so long ago in the City and cleaned them in the tank, to take to work.

Next morning, just a moment after the machinery started, it stopped. Bells rang, followed by an announcement— "All workers to the front section."

He heard Neradis and the others muttering under their breath. All along the aisle people were filing out to the open section in front, line supervisors ahead of the rest. Against one wall was a huge holoscreen; this was the first time Tadko had seen it lit up. It swirled with rosette patterns in violet, cerise and black, the Concora colors. The patterns faded, and a voice proclaimed, "Vikteborin Esco Concora, of the House." A man appeared on the screen, nearly twice life size. He was robed in scarlet and silver, with Concora rosettes scattered at neckline, sleeves, and hem. Over his left shoulder was the wide Concora baldric, bearing a black rod. His sandals were golden, his earclips scarlet, his hair was frosted with magenta, his hands were covered with gemmed rings. Now he raised them theatrically.

"My fellow workers!" He intoned. "And I call you this with pride, for we are, indeed, all workers together for the support of House Concora and its people. It saddens me to have to tell you Herenna Commercial Houses have announced plans to open a series of low to middle range clothing establishments, including," he paused and lowered his voice, "a line of souvenir items for visitors to Monna. As you well know, House Concora has always striven to be fair in competition with other houses, fair to its workers at every level, and to produce quality merchandise at reasonable prices. Will the House survive this attack? We cannot say, but you have our promise that we will do our best." Voice raised again. "But if we are to survive, we must *all* do our best. All of us, my fellow workers, must work harder than ever to meet this unwarranted attack. We must strive for speed, accuracy, and improved production in all that we do. We must dedicate ourselves to our work, wherever we work, day by day. I trust you, my fellow workers, to do your part to secure your own future, and the future of Our House, Concora." He bowed deeply. "My fellow workers, I thank you."

The screen went dark. The workers filed back to their places. Nobody said anything, which surprised Tadko. Only Neradis snapped, just before the machines stared up again, "All right, move it! We've already lost some time."

After work, bound for Neradis's home in the trotline car and properly dressed, Tadko asked, "Is the House really in danger, the way he said?"

She snorted. "When you see the Concoras riding the trotline and eating squelt, then you can worry. No, they just want to hustle us to speed up. God of the Galaxy, I hope they won't be raising the quota, it's bad enough now." She sighed heavily. "Two more years, and I'll be retiring, with full benefits. Hope I make it."

"Why wouldn't you?"

"The speed up. They do it especially to workers like me, near retiring. If we can't make quota we get discharged, no pension and no benefits. It's cheaper for them. And my husband, Ingol, died on the job ten years ago, so they had to give me his pension, that's Monnan law. They don't like that."

"But aren't you a career—a citizen employee?"

"True."

"But why do you work for them, then?"

She looked at him astonished.

"Why, younker, there's hardly any place to work on Tallen *besides* Concoras—not if you've only got basic education and want a decent wage." She sighed again. "Ingol and I used to think we might set ourselves up in an independent, maybe a restaurant or something, but it never worked out. Anyway, it's been worse since this Vikteborin took over at the top. He's a real rasper, you can go bond."

He thought that in some ways, she wasn't much better off than a prisoner, but he said nothing.

"Is it really true that Concoras get half my pay?"

"No, not really. They pay you, and give half your designated wage to the rehabilitation section of the Civic Orderlies Board. But here on Tallen they control most things, that's true. Cheer up," she added. "It's a lot worse on some of the out stars, I've heard. On some they crowd rapists, murderers, violent assaulters, all together with petty thieves and everyone; you could get killed, or worse, by your fellow prisoners. And they don't work—you have to admit it keeps you occupied. Or they go in and change the cells of your mind, so you think the way they want you to. Or you get frozen."

"You mean to death? For anything?"

"No, no, it's called cryo something. Freeze you for as long as your sentence is, then thaw you out."

Tadko thought of the noise of the packery, the heat and stench, the glaring lights, the deadening routine of work and barrack life that made flyouts seem a welcome relief.

"I think I might rather be frozen," he said.

"No you don't," she told him. "They're not so careful about doing it, and you could end up with a missing arm, or leg, or other parts. And if it's a long sentence, then you're all wrong in time."

The part about the time would be unpleasant. As for the missing pieces, he suspected that was what Monnans were told.

They rolled a long way from the center of the city with its blocks of packeries, apprentice and prisoner barracks, administrative towers, warehouses, and all the rest, rising as they moved on a gradual slope. They passed an attractive park, with tall white-trunked trees bearing clusters of green or pale blue foliage, and small green birds, like those he had seen for sale on Morneol, darting from branch to branch. A good many people lounged on the blue-green grass; children played running games, and he noticed a few food carts along the walkways.

"Are those commercials?" He asked, gesturing.

"No, no, Just ordinaries, like me. Commercials go out to Diamond Cove, or Purple Peak Resort, places like that. No ordinaries allowed unless they're servants, and no tourists, either."

"Even though they make their money off the tourists?"

"Right enough. Tourists bring in money, but they aren't class."

Neradis's home was a tiny plank-built house with a tile roof, one of many dotted up and down a ridge of steep slopes north of the city. Each one had a small fenced garden and at least one fruit tree. As they entered her gate, Tadko heard a strident cry of, "Why! Why! Why!" He jumped as if stung and fell to his hands and knees. Neradis was bending over him, fussing worriedly.

"Are you all right? What happened?"

He got his breath back, pulled himself to his feet, brushed himself off, and looked around. There was the creature prancing up and down on a perch under the toa tree, not far away.

"Are you all right?" she repeated.

"Right enough. I was startled. Does everyone keep those—whatever they are—on their property? What for?"

"Oh, if you have any kind of garden, or fruit, you keep them to eat pests. Any kind of bugs or slugs. They even scare away missets, although they aren't carnivorous. Was that what startled you?" Her lip twitched slightly as if she were trying not to smile.

"Well, yes. What do you call them, anyway?"

"Whys." She held up her left arm and the creature came to perch, so he could see it clearly. Long legs with clawed feet, leathery wings also equipped with claws at the ends, a wicked looking beak and beady yellow eyes.

"Oby isn't beautiful or musical," she explained, "but I couldn't keep up the garden without him, and we eat a lot out of the garden." She flipped her hand, and the Why flew back to his perch. "Come on in, my son should have food ready."

They entered a small room with a low, padded couch along one wall, three chairs along another, a small round table in the center.

To the left of the door was a shallow alcove, painted white, the color of mourning. A gracefully shaped white flask stood upon a metal trivet, also white, under a white table that bore a white ceramic lamp. It was a flattish lamp with a wick, not unlike the lamps they used at home to burn onca fat. Above, on the wall, hung a holopic of a man about Neradis's age. His face was lined, his hair yellowed, but he had a look of cheerful friendliness. Above his picture hung a whole series of much smaller ones. Ancestors, maybe.

Neradis bowed slightly, touching the fingertips of her right hand to her forehead. Tadko dithered, wondering if he ought to do the same, but she nodded at the portrait and moved on into the room.

"My husband, Ingol," she explained.

A young man came in though the door opposite, a large apron over his tunic and breeches, and a long-handled spoon in one hand. "This is our guest?"

"Right enough. Tadko Darusko, from Elnakt." She beamed at the young man and announced, "This is my son, Donnil," as proudly as if she had said, "This is the Master of the World."

Donnil was taller than his mother, wide-shouldered but lanky, with an engaging grin and pleasantly homely features. He laid the fist holding the spoon against his left shoulder and bowed.

"Welcome to our house."

"Thank you!" This time Tadko did manage to imitate the gesture.

"Donnil earned an apprenticeship with House Ornibeck," Neradis said, as if that explained his courtesy. "He's fifth level now, studying wave jet and floater design. Is dinner ready?" She added.

"Ready and waiting."

The three of them squeezed around a table in a small kitchen equipped with cook-shelves, coolers, and the like, a little more elaborate than Dacy Wile's furnishings, but not much more. Donnil served a mixture of squelt, sliced vegetables, and hot sauce, with crispbread on the side.

Squelt or no, it tasted better than anything Tadko had eaten in—well, in a long time. He scooped the food in as fast as he could eat, realizing suddenly that this might not be good manners. He glanced at the others, discovered that they were eating as voraciously as he—especially Neradis—and returned to his own share. Second helpings were passed around and devoured with equal enthusiasm.

At last Neradis pushed her plate away.

"You always were the best cook in the family," she told Donnil.

Afterwards, they went to sit on a bench outside the house. Donnil poured three mugs of cold fizz, and handed them out. Neradis took a long swallow, sighed, and leaned back against the rough planking of the house. She gestured with her mug at Tadko.

"Now tell us how you got yourself into this tangle," she ordered. "You seem like a decent enough sprat. Why illegal entry and theft, of all things?"

There was much talk in the barrack about places people had been, things they had seen, good taverns and willing girls and boys, islands where the greens were inclined to be slack, whispered rumors about the work, the supers, and so on. But almost nothing personal. No one spoke of what he or anyone else had done to end up here. Even Dacy's talk, Tadko now realized, had that curious impersonality. Dacy, according to him, had lived in the City all his life, yet he never mentioned family, friends, or past history. It might be lack of trust when they hadn't known you for a long time. Or maybe these things were only discussed outside the barrack.

In any case, Tadko was willing enough to describe his experiences to a pair of unusually-sympathetic ears.

"You really shouldn't have stolen that money," Neradis told him severely, "although I can see that young man was enough to drive his own mother to drowning. Of course you have to pay the money back. But it is hard lines about the illegal entry."

"You could have asked for a hearing, at the League," Donnil added. "Didn't they tell you about that?"

"No. But if I had asked for a hearing, are you sure it would have been all right?"

"Well, no," Donnil admitted. "It would depend on how much influence this Seronico had with the Board, I suppose."

"Then I'm glad I didn't try. Why do they create such a dust-up about illegal entry, anyway?"

"It goes back a good many generations," Neradis said. "There was a time when we had outright criminals dropping in from everywhere. Thought they could move out to the smaller islands, and beach it, and live easy. Stick knives in the locals who didn't like it, be off to another island before the law could dock in. So now they keep a tight watch on landing and permits. Some still get in, but even then they're easier to track if they cause trouble. I should think they would have made an exception for someone like you," she added, "but I don't really know."

"Running might have been the best thing after all," Donnil said. "Hard lines you didn't get all the way to Sancy. And what happened then?"

Tadko continued his narration. They accepted his theft from White Hair, on Rowder, with equanimity. The man was a thief himself, after all. They were envious of, and amazed by, his rescue by the Porposin.

"I'd give a lot to see a Porp up close," Donnil said.

"Haven't you, ever?"

Both shook their heads.

"Only at a distance, out at sea," Neradis told him. "There's caves in the rock, and a colony that comes to breed on the southwest shore of Tallen, of course. Some people go out along the Rim Road to watch for them, but you don't see much, sometimes one or two diving out at sea. If you hit it just right you might see the whole colony coming in, but not many guess right on that."

"The sea Houses, Crale and Doyarvin, don't allow real tourism anywhere near a Porposin colony, even off season," Donnil explained. "A few years ago Concoras wanted to put out a doll, furry, that looked like a Porp. Sea Houses really showed their power." He laughed out loud. "What a storm! Water spouts all around the world, and councilors nearly coming to blows."

"Oh, Donnil, it wasn't that bad." His mother said. "Although it was about then the old lady retired, let this beach scour of a Vikteborin take over. She's still The Concora, though, and no one had better forget it."

"But how did you end up here?" Donnil asked.

Tadko explained, and went on to describe his trek through the center of the island. They were by turns amazed, sympathetic, and sometimes shocked.

"You ate a—" Neradis began with a near shriek, then dropped her voice to a near whisper. "You ate a Singer? Why, that's against the law! They're protected! And raw! Ugh!"

Donnil was laughing again. "Oh, Mother, he couldn't have known. But don't tell anyone else! How did it taste?"

"Not bad. But it gave me an awful bellyache."

"Served you right," Neradis said. "What else did you eat?"

"Some flat things." Tadko described them.

"Those are platteys, they're scavengers. Ugh! I'm surprised they didn't make you sick."

"How did those taste?" Donnil wanted to know.

"Like nothing much at all. What do you call some conical things, with caps, that grow in the water?"

"Perlaus. Those are good, some of the inland places raise them."

Tadko finished with a brief description of what he called the Stinking Valley, his sickness, garden raiding, and his capture.

"Anyway, I woke up in the sick tank—the infirmary—and here I am."

Neradis was frowning, puzzled. "But Tadko, I don't understand. You said your father would be back on the eighth of Perian, and we're long past that now, this is the third of Dusiem. Why haven't you called—oh, I forgot, they charge the ocean full at the barrack, that's to discourage people. But why don't you call from here?"

Tadko looked away, out over the city.

"Thanks very much, but I've decided not to."

"Why not?"

"I meant to, all along. But since I got to the packery here, I changed my mind." He sighed. "When I first came to Monna, I wondered: Would he remember my mother and me, or want to have anything to do with me? I wondered, but I suppose it wasn't real. Now it is. For all I know he long since married a woman of his own people, raised a family of proper Monnan children.

"I don't have any proof of who I am, and I certainly don't look part Monnan. I could be an embarrassment, calling and claiming to be his son."

"Why, that's bogswash!" Neradis exclaimed, then waved a hand impatiently at his outraged glance. "Oh, I suppose I respect your nice sensibilities and all, but if he's your father he has an obligation to help you, and you have a right to ask for help. That's the beginning and end of it. We can check the time so you won't be calling in the middle of the City night, and you can call from here."

"*No*," Tadko insisted. "I do thank you, but I've made up my mind."

"Bogswash," she repeated, then threw up her hands in defeat. "Well then, what do you want to do? Anything?"

Tadko drew a deep breath. "I'll save my money until I can afford a trip back to the City, by wave-jet. I will go to his home, and tell him who I am. I'll be able to tell by his reaction whether I'm welcome or not. If I am, I'll tell him about all this. If not, I'll just come back and serve out my time."

"At two D a cycle? Take you I don't know how many years. Besides," Neradis persisted, "it could be just the opposite. He might have looked for you, or had someone trying to find you, on Sancy. Or just wondering what's happened to you since this storm blew up." She paused. "I'd guess he'd not think to check illegal entry records. What's your fine?"

"Five hundred and eighty duats."

Both of them whistled.

"Take you years. Wish I could help, but I just live from cycle to cycle myself." Neradis pondered. "I could call, ask if he'd be interested in news about you. Be easy enough to tell how he feels, just from that."

"I could make you a loan, when I'm out of apprenticeship, two and a half years," Donnil offered.

"I thank you both for your kindness," Tadko said formally. "But no."

Neradis shook her head.

"Take you years," she repeated. "I'll go bond you'll change your mind. When you do, let me know."

"I will," Tadko said, smiling. "And thank you."

They continued to sit, quietly. Big Moon was a fuzzy globe rising in the east. Little Monninet was a pale half circle, almost directly overhead. From here the main part of the city was only a pattern of lights, surprisingly beautiful. The noise of it came as a continuous murmur, almost soothing at this distance.

Around them the hillsides were darkened by the many small gardens and fruit trees surrounding the tiny houses. Windows and a few door lights glowed where other residents sat out on their front steps in the evening. From far down the street they heard a snatch of music, and once in a while there was a cry of "Why!"

"A nice place to live," Tadko commented.

"Right enough," Neradis agreed. "These are all cheapy little houses the Concoras provide, but they're durable and we do have our gardens."

Donnil began to whistle softly, picking up the tune from down the street.

Later, Neradis rose and stretched.

"Best we dock in," she said.

Inside, Tadko followed her up a narrow stair, little more than a ladder. Three doors opened off a landing at the top.

"Middle one's a waste closet so you'll not have to go downstairs during the night," she explained. "This one," she said, opening the door to the right, "was my daughter Thune's."

The room was hardly big enough for the bed, although being built for a Monnan it would be plenty roomy for Tadko. Overhead light, inside wall composed of drawers and shelves, the other three walls mostly screened louvers to let the air through. On one shelf sat a large holopic of a smiling young man and woman, robed in green and wearing crowns of flowers, holding hands.

Neradis beamed at it.

"That's Thune and her husband, Romis Nadvil," she said, clearly as proud of them as she was of Donnil. "Wish I had a place to put that downstairs. That's their wedding picture. They both work on Morneol, diving cell maintenance. Good pay. You can put your clothes on any shelf," she added, "and come down anytime in the morning. Sleep well."

The next two days were leisurely. Tadko learned to brew froile, and to help with the cooking and clean up. He picked ripened toa fruit, to be peeled, pitted, and frozen into a sweet confection for the evening meals. He even became cautiously friendly with Oby.

Neradis worked in her garden. From time to time she sang snatches of a cheerful tune about the ro-o-o-lling waves.

Donnil had much to say about his apprenticeship. Most of his explanations of the work were too technical for Tadko to understand, but it was clear he regarded it with great enthusiasm. Listening to him was pleasant even when barely comprehensible. Tadko responded with tales of life on Elnakt, basking a little in Donnil's amazement and curiosity.

Early on Elevenday, Neradis and Donnil, both dressed in white, went out to the Garden of Memory, where the water and fertilizer made from Ingol's body had been scattered to nourish the trees and flowers. They didn't invite Tadko along, for which he was grateful. He still shrank at the thought of human remains, however transformed, scattered on the surface of the ground instead of buried deep within it—as they buried the dead on Elnakt after the spring thaw.

He spent much of the day dozing in the shade under the to a tree, hands behind his head. Here above the city there was a little more of a breeze. It was warm, like all Monnan breezes, too warm, but pleasant. He took off his smock and rolled up his breeches as far as they would go. He thought he had better not take them off altogether; not in this part of town.

Neradis and Donnil came home bringing coppies to grill for the evening meal, and afterwards they sat, as before, to watch sunset over Tallenport.

CHAPTER FIFTEEN

It was hard to leave. He returned to the barrack as late as he dared, taking the long trotline ride and joining the others as they straggled in from the freedays.

Late that night he still lay tensely awake, fists clenched at his sides, staring at Zhak's bunk above him. Around him were the usual groans, snores, occasional gasps or belches, the metallic squeaks as men tossed in their bunks.

"Hate them," he thought, clenching his fists more tightly. "God of the Galaxy, how I'd like to strangle them all."

"They" were not his fellow prisoners, but the greens, the Concoras, whatever vague entities were responsible for the prisoner system. He turned on his side, still whispering, "Hate them, hate them, hate them." He decided it had been a mistake to spend the time with Neradis and her son, kind as they were. The house, tiny, but clean and pleasant, the garden, even the stupid Why darting around—the contrast was too great. It broke the routine in which he had tried to lose himself.

Sometime during the night he passed suddenly into a dead sleep, only to awaken at the morning signal, feeling groggy and half-sick. Fortunately on a Firstday morning he was not the only one. Mostly silent except for noisy yawns, moans, and half-hearted curses, they filed in for the morning meal and departed for work.

By evening he had recovered enough to notice someone missing from the table.

"Where's Loy?" He blurted.

Rumard shrugged. "Company stropper came to our floor today, transferred a whole line to the pens. He'll be out there in barrack six from now on."

Tadko had heard of the pens, a complex of shallow lagoons along the south coast. There the myriad of tiny sea creatures, fish and plants were raised for the aquaria shipped out of Tallen.

"Can they do that?" He asked, thinking of Loy, wading all day in sea water under the hot sun. "He hasn't done anything, has he?"

"Huh," said Zhak. "They assign you anywhere they like. There's a rumor they got some disease in one of the pens, probably need checkers, clean up crew, anything."

That reminded Tadko of another thing he had puzzled over.

"What do they do with all these fish bowls? Why do they need so many? "

The others laughed.

"Most every tourist who comes to Monna leaves with one. Lots of Monnans buy them too," Rumard explained.

"They ship 'em off world, too, lots of 'em," Zhak added. "An' every year there's a new combination, you'd see if you looked at the tally numbers, supposed to represent a different part of ocean, and people collect 'em."

"Why?"

"Would I know? Tourists."

"Toys!" Homistho's growl made it an expletive.

Tadko shivered a little, in spite of the heat. The packery was bad enough, but working out in the sun, on the water—on Monna even the winds were hot. At least he was used to the packery. He finished his meal in silence, offering up a small prayer to the God of the Galaxy that he not be transferred to the pens.

So the days passed. Once or twice at work Neradis threw him a questioning glance. Clearly she hoped he would change his mind about calling his father. Each time he shook his head, immersing himself again in the constant routine, work, meals, and the game. Only he missed Loy's cheerful enthusiasm. He wondered what Loy was in for. Despite the taboo against questioning anyone about the subject, rumors did circulate about this one or that one. Someone told him Homistho had arrived onplanet legally, but was caught for theft while trying to earn—or steal—departure money. "Some little sun hopper was stranded and paid off here, and he was trying to get home."

So said his informant. Tadko felt a pang of the only sympathy he could ever feel for the sullen Homistho. The man was trying to get home! Still, he could have wished Homistho had been transferred, instead of Loy.

Since theirs was a relatively amicable group, Tadko was shocked one evening when Homistho suddenly threw his marker in Zhak's face and said flatly, "You're cheating."

Zhak caught the bit of metal before it struck him.

"You squatter, you nearly took me in the eye," he cried angrily. "They're your dice, you want to try snaffle some new ones?"

Homistho did not answer. He launched himself across the game and grabbed Zhak by the throat, bearing him backwards. Zhak's head struck the corner of a locker with a loud crack, then blood was flowing. Tadko yelled and moved to pull Homistho away, but Rumard was yelling too. "Back! Back off!"

Then a dazzle of light from above, and a burning smell. Homistho rolled over on his back and lay still. His face had turned blue, his mouth gaped, his eyes were rolled back in his head. His hair had an oddly crisped look. Zhak was still breathing, but he lay in a pool of blood.

Rumard was already running to the entrance.

"Call the sick tank!" He yelled. "Two carriers!"

There were cries of response, and Rumard returned, to shake his head at Tadko's anguished expression.

"You know you can't touch 'em, they would have told you, didn't they?"

"Yes, but—not even to help? Zhak looks like a skull fracture—if we did something right away...."

Another head shake.

"Can't touch 'em. Besides, they'll be here from the tank soon enough. Ugh! Can't stand that smell!" He moved off, to stand up beside his locker.

All around them men were doing the same, grumbling as they came out of bunks, or stepped away from their own games, or were shouted awake by others nearby.

"He's been brewing for it, any route," Rumard added. "Getting more and more stormy all the time. Look at him crossways and he'd go up in a waterspout."

Tadko didn't look at the two bodies on the floor as he stood in the required brace. He couldn't avoid the smell. He was genuinely grateful when the attendants came in with the carriers from the infirmary. Now he pointed at poor Zhak.

"It wasn't his fault at all," he told them. "He didn't do anything. Homistho attacked him."

"True?" said one.

"True," Rumard repeated. "This one went drowno, really sixty fathoms, and just went for Zhak. Didn't give him a chance to get out of the way, or set up—uh—a meeting, or anything."

The attendants grinned slightly. They knew what "a meeting" was—an appointment for a fight down at the pier. The older man turned his head, spoke softly into a mesh attached to his shoulder strap.

"We'll include that in the report," he said noncommittally, then nodded at the floor, where bits of crisped hair now mingled with congealing blood. "You better sluice that off yourselves tonight, the morning flush might not get it all."

Then they were on their way, guiding the carriers between the rows of bunks. Tadko stared after them with a curiously forlorn feeling. Zhak had not really been a friend, but he was the nearest thing to it likely to be found in this prison. At least, after that first morning, he hadn't sneered at Tadko's ignorance as much as the others did.

When the doors closed behind the carriers he sighed and went with Rumard to collect buckets of water and brooms. No one else offered to help. Wearing their work boots, they sloshed the water over the floor and swept it toward the drain line between the bunkroom and refectory, ignoring the mutters of complaint as games were interrupted yet again. They had to return several times for more water.

"They won't just finish Zhak off, will they?"

"I'd say not," Rumard told him. "His record's good, and a skull fracture's not so bad. They won't send him back here, though."

"Why not?"

"Dunno. Just the rules."

By the time they finished the lights had already been dimmed.

Tadko was glad to roll onto his bunk and sleep.

The next evening, he and Rumard examined the game pattern. Blurred, faded patches showed where the beam had struck.

"Could we get paint somewhere, to redo it?" Tadko asked. "It wears out enough with being walked on all the time."

"You can always get end bits of coloring stuff down at Narn Didthow's," Rumard said. "That's where it comes from, mostly. They know about the game. But I think I'll look for another game. It's no fun with only two, and you won't even risk a square."

"I told Zhak and the rest of you. I'm trying to save so I can buy my way out early."

Rumard's nose wrinkled. "You win a few squares, lose a few, what's the difference? Nobody risks much but it makes the game worth something. You'll not find many willing to play with a square-squeezer, but you can try."

He set off down the aisles between the bunks, looking for a new game, with Tadko following. Negotiating these aisles on a work night, with everyone in barrack, was a tricky business. There was plenty of room for two men to pass without touching each other, but where games were in progress the matter was more complex. Players lying belly down and reaching out from the lower bunks could simply pull back. Those seated on the floor had to shift and rearrange legs in order to avoid the walkers. Sometimes they refused to move. Walkers-through occasionally kicked dice or markers out of the way, just for fun, leaving the players to search under the bunks, or even retrieve pieces from another game. When refused passage, the walkers had no choice but to return to the end of the aisle and try to find a way through another.

The etiquette of getting into a game could also be elaborate, at least among strangers. One passed by a group, observed for a while, then asked, "Game?" If the answer was yes, there followed an exchange of names and pertinent information.

"Work at such and such building; used to game with so and so; game broke up (or I quit) because of this or that; I want (or don't want) a game for free days, too."

An unspoken exchange among the gamers would follow; shrugs, gestures, facial contortions. Then one of them would say, "Right enough," and the new man would join the game. Or the answer might be "no room" and he was expected to pass on. In each group, there was always one man who seemed to have the final say. In their group it had been Zhak; how this was determined Tadko had no idea.

This was much simplified if, as often happened, players and would-be player were already known to each other from work, or free day excursions, or simple proximity in the bunk room.

Rumard soon found a group of four at the end of his and the others' bunk row. They looked up as he approached. The say-so in this group was a tall, handsome youth called Chumorden. Unlike most of the others, he didn't wear his hair in a knot, held back by whatever bit of string or cloth he could find. His was always carefully curled, making for more time in the tank than the others cared to spend. Tadko privately considered him a popinjay, but he nodded to Rumard in a friendly enough fashion.

"Want a new game?"

"Right enough. Got room?"

Chumorden glanced around at the others, who nodded in turn. Chumorden then jerked a thumb at Tadko.

"You too?"

"Uh, yes," Tadko began, but Rumard interrupted.

"He won't risk his squares. No betting."

"You're one of those?" Chumorden cocked his head at Tadko with just the hint of a sneer. "What's your fear?"

"I'm trying to save so I can buy out of here early."

A sharp bark of laughter burst from a scrawny, pinch-faced man with age-yellowed hair.

"Think they'll let you? You a new-hatched sprat? When they need the work they'll find some way to dock you and keep you in long's they want."

Tadko felt stunned. No one else had mentioned this!

"Could they do that?"

Chumorden shrugged, sawed his hand in that "either or" gesture.

"Some say yes, some say no. Any route, you sail with us, you risk it."

Tadko hesitated, wondering if it would ever be possible, in this place, to tell fact from rumor.

"You may be right. I'll think about it."

He wandered away to try his luck elsewhere, but found none.

"We got one cheaper already. No more."

"No room."

"No square-squeezers in this game."

At the end of one aisle he found a game with only three players. On the floor lay a long stick with a sharpened bit of shell wedged in one end, but no money. Tadko had heard of this version of the game. While he watched, each man threw the dice in turn, then moved his marker accordingly. The man who moved farthest picked up the stick, waved it gently back and forth.

"My forfeit," he crooned happily. Slowly, caressingly, with a half smile that was almost affectionate, he bent forward and drew five long cuts on the chest of one man, two long cuts on the other. On all three, Tadko could see the ragged scars of previous forfeits on torso, arms and legs. The current losers accepted their cuts with no more than an indrawn hiss of breath. One of them looked up at Tadko.

"Game?" He was smiling, too.

"*No!* Uh, no thanks." Tadko moved away hastily, trying not to shudder, hearing snickers behind him. These were not the first men he had seen with those telltale scars. It was said that games like these were responsible for a good many visits to the fancy houses on the free days, or visits down to the end of the pier. Some said they were careful not to cause permanent injury; others told horror stories of great slashing blood lettings that required a carrier, with more than one man taken away, never to return.

Tadko returned to his bunk and sat down wearily. Play for money or play for blood. What a choice.

He and his friends at home had banged and battered themselves often enough as children, climbing and sliding on the rocky slopes of the steading, chasing each other, learning to ride and care for the oncas, to use tools, throw a hunting knife. There had been injuries and deaths. He himself had broken an arm and a collarbone, sprained both ankles, cut himself under the chin, and fallen any number of times while learning to ride. But this deliberate cutting, with its clearly erotic overtones, made him feel sick.

By the end of the cycle, he knew that his fine resolutions would be impossible to keep, without the game. What else to do, in the barrack after work? He made some efforts to get a group together who would all play without betting. It seemed the obvious thing to do, but no one was interested. Why they preferred to play with others who called them cheapers, he could not understand. But then, he had never tried to move away from his original group until forced into it.

One settled in, he supposed, got used to the others in the group, and didn't care to risk a change.

Reluctantly, when they were paid off that cycle, he collected half his pay instead of leaving it all in his Company Account. That evening he went back to Rumard's new group, and tossed a few zinae in his hand.

"Game?" He asked.

"Willing to risk a bit?"

"A bit."

One of those mysterious exchanges of facial expression all around, and then Chumorden gave him the nod. The others shifted to make room.

He bet as seldom and as little as he could, trying to keep track of wins and losses. There were too many of the latter.

CHAPTER SIXTEEN

On the free days he decided to roam the city, avoiding the game altogether. It was just as cheap, or cheaper, and he stayed away from the wealthier districts.

A mug of froile at the Beached Barge, a cone of sea food down at Rotten Pier, a stroll up harbor to Old Town and the fishing wharves. Not many prisoners frequented these latter areas, and at first he received a good many hard looks from the locals. When they came to know him as quiet, sober, and well-behaved, they simply ignored him.

One could sit for a long time over a cold fizz, watching the passersby and the small bustle of local business, or looking beyond at the toss of water, the reflection of passing clouds. There were bunkhouses where wharf workers could stay overnight for a zina, and they let him in when they had room. He knew he was closely observed, but pretended not to notice.

There were shops offering Repair and Replacement—Purchase of Oddments; he had learned at the barrack that many of these were perfectly honest. If you didn't know the place, they said, stay out.

Once he discovered a branch of the Students and Apprentices Protective League. He was about to pass by when he suddenly recalled his membership badge, and paused.

This branch appeared to be strictly offices, no residences. Only two stories high, built of pinkish coral block, it occupied a space between a warehouse and a boat repair yard. Windows on the street showed the room within. There were the usual desks with comp frames, some comfortable looking benches, a row of booths with drawn curtains, and a middle-aged woman studying the screen at one desk. Tadko hesitated, wondering quite seriously if he was about to commit a crime, then stepped inside. Nothing happened. He took courage and walked over to the woman at the desk.

"Er," he said.

She looked up, taking in at a glance his breechclout and sandals, the locker key on its string around his neck, his prisoner's hairdo. But she smiled, and her tone was kindly.

"Did you have a question?"

"I work for Concoras," he said. "Number three barrack. But I've got a League membership...they told me once I could get a loan?"

Now the smile was sympathetic, but she shook her head.

"You're from offworld, aren't you? Where are you from?"

"Elnakt."

"Elnakt? But I thought all your people were down on Sancy—why are you a prisoner?"

"Illegal entry. And, well, theft. Trying to get there. I thought if I could pay it off?"

Again the sad smile. "I'm sorry. As long as you're a prisoner, we can't authorize a loan. What is your fine?"

"It was five hundred and eighty. I've paid off thirty or so by now. It'll take years to pay off, working. Can't you help me?"

"I'm sorry. I know it must be hard when you're a stranger on Monna. Is there anyone on Sancy, among your own people, we might be able to contact for you?"

Well now; his own people. Would any of them have enough Monnan money to help him? It hardly seemed likely. Or would he want any of them to know what had happened to him? Imprisoned for theft, the Mosor of Daruskan. He considered.

"I'm not sure. I'll have to think about it. If I let you know—would it cost anything to make inquiries?"

"No charge for that. Come back and we'll be glad to find out for you. Or if you wish to resign your League membership and turn in your badge, we will refund half your membership fee."

"Thank you. I'll think that over, too."

He left, feeling distinctly let down. Take all the commercial caste types out and strangle them, he thought. Do the Concoras first, the squatting onca futters. He moved off down the street, leaving the boat yard behind, paused again before a Repair and Replacement shop. He still had his League badge, honestly paid for, and for some reason not confiscated when he was arrested. He walked in and approached the proprietor, a plump, cheerful looking Eilonsader.

"I don't have it with me now, but could I sell a League badge? It's mine, you could check if you want to."

"Prisoner." It was not a question.

Tadko nodded.

"But it's mine, right enough."

"Sorry, those are non-transferable. The League keeps close track of them, and it would be coded to you." He chuckled in what Tadko considered an offensive manner. "Not much good to you now, is it?"

"No," said Tadko, and left.

Evening was coming on, and he headed for a tavern on the beach he had discovered on an earlier perambulation. It was a huge square, with a tent roof staked down on all sides against storm winds. Now the slat sides were rolled up to let the sea breeze through, inner nets left in place to keep out the sand flies that seemed to find this area particularly attractive.

Tadko joined the people drifting in for the evening meal. He picked up a cold fizz and a bowl of coppies at the counter, then returned to a corner table to eat. He ate slowly, relishing both food and ambiance. This was a cheap beach front eatery, but so much better than the barrack.

Someone at the other end was playing a horn of some kind, producing a deep wailing note that wandered up and down the scale, and a few couples rose to dance one of the slow, graceful Monnan dances in a cleared space before the counter.

Two elderly men chose a table near Tadko, and played a game in between gulps of ale and bites of food.

Unobtrusively, he watched them. This game consisted of oddly shaped pieces of wood, which the men took turns piling into a tower. The first man whose addition collapsed the tower, lost. This called for much laughter, another round of ale, and another game. Tadko surmised the gaming would end when neither could balance one piece on another.

He wished this game were played in the prisoner barracks. Played sober, it would be a matter of skill, not chance. You could practice the skill, and have some control over whether you won or lost...on second thought, that might cause more fights than ever. He nodded sagely. Best leave it up to chance.

He sat, relaxing, and watched the dancers. A young woman pulled up a chair at the edge of the dancing space, took out a hexagonal stringed instrument, and began to play, joining the melody of the horn.

From outside came the wheee, wheee of night gliders, sweeping the evening air with mouths open for the clustering flies.

When he was finished he left, heading up the beach for one of the workers' bunkhouses. They charged a prisoner like him two zinae instead of the one for a free worker, nor was he entitled to the morning meal provided for the others. It couldn't even be said the accommodations were a great deal better—bunks, lockers and sanitation were much the same, although chairs and tables were provided for the resident's use. But it was away from the barrack, and the undercurrent of constant tension that he hadn't even been conscious of, until he got away from it at Neradis's house.

In the morning he bought crispbread at a street stand and ate it watching a local barge depart, wishing he could be on it.

It was said in the barrack, among so many other things, that some people had ways of removing the telltale implant in one's hand. Without that, you could escape, free. Only no one knew anyone who had managed to have it done. It was always somebody else who knew somebody else, who claimed to have known somebody who had it done. It was said that if you knew the right place down on the Pier—only nobody did. It was also said to cost a fortune, payable later—and this he could believe. He had begun by asking questions, trying to distinguish fact from rumor, until the others made it clear they were tired of him. Now he just listened and discounted it. Most of it.

This being the last of his free days, he set off for the barrack, but he strolled along slowly. With care, he could make the walk last most of the day. A stop here and there to linger over a cold fizz, a meal in some cheap eatery—always being careful to save a few zinae for betting during the workday evenings.

He bought a bag of ice balls from a street vendor and munched as he walked.

Outside a shop selling used musical instruments he paused to admire the display. On Elnakt they had bone pipes of different lengths and pitches, clappers and rattles, and hand drums. Monnans played a bewildering variety of music makers. Here were shining coils of tubing with complicated arrangements of valves and keys, glass bells hung on wires, stringed boxes of various shapes and sizes, metal strips, oddly bent and curved, hung in wooden frames. He only recognized the drums, a row of small ones down in front, for what they were.

Drums on Elnakt were made of wood. Kuypre was the largest of the water trees that grew in the sinkholes on the halm, and even they were small, with slender, supple trunks. The bark had to be stripped, the wood seasoned, then carved into the pieces that would be fitted together with glue boiled from onca bones to make the base. The drumhead was tanned from onca hide and secured with a network of sinew that also served to brace the frame.

Half consciously, Tadko tapped out a rhythm with his fingertips in the palm of his left hand. These drums were metal, with a pinkish drumhead of unknown material, and a good many studs and ridges that might be decorative or functional. Still, they were about the size of the drums at home, and shaped much the same, in a curve to fit the palm of the hand. He continued tapping the rhythm of a familiar dance, seeing not a shop on Monna but his home steading, firelight and shadows, the rocky slope, the stars overhead, the shouts and calls as the dancers leaped and swung.

On an impulse, he entered the shop. It was brightly lit and smelled pleasantly of wood, varnish, and metal polish. The proprietor sat at a table, his clothing covered by a stained gray apron, polishing the shaft of a long, bellmouthed horn. He looked up as Tadko approached a table display of drums, and Tadko winced inwardly as he recognized the usual glance: "One of those workees. Keep an eye on him."

Aloud, the man said, "Interested in a music maker?"

"I'd like to look at these drums."

The man nodded, but returned only half an eye to his polishing.

Tadko examined the drums with interest. Each one had a wide ridge just below the rim, and several were set in frames using this ridge. The various studs and projections were obviously used to tighten the drumhead, and possibly change the pitch? He picked one up and tapped out a rhythm; the tone was surprisingly resonant for so small an instrument. He turned it over to examine the base.

The proprietor was standing beside him.

"A fine instrument, young man. Four duats."

"Four duats! I'll give you half a D." Tadko gulped. He didn't want to buy the thing at all, did he? *Yes*, he decided, suddenly, fiercely; and he let the words stand.

"Half a—you insult me, young man! I am aware that in your position you have very little to offer, but for a fine instrument—"

"You call it fine? Where is the frame?" Tadko guessed that a frame normally went with all these drums, and it appeared he was right; the man didn't deny it. "Half a D, if you want a sale. You have a whole table full, how well are they selling?"

"Quite irrelevant. Value is value. For the lack of a frame I could reduce it to three and a half— "

"Value? See here, a broken section of rim—"

"Easily mended if you are a knowledgeable musician—"

"Costly, too. See here, scratches, a dent, a stud missing here, you'll not get a knowledgeable musician to pay three and a half for this—"

"This is a playable instrument and I expect a sensible offer—"

Tadko tapped the drum, listened.

"Playable but damaged. I could go another five zinae and you should thank me for taking it off your hands—"

"Now see here—"

Eventually Tadko got it for twenty-eight zinae. He fished the money out of the fold in his clout, paid, and carried the drum out of the shop. He stood there for a few minutes, tapping it, trying to decide why he had done such a foolish thing. He had only ten zinae left for the game next cycle.

That would mean returning to the barrack early enough for the evening meal, he couldn't afford to stop at the Beached Barge. Yet for some reason he felt pleased with himself; he wouldn't return this drum to the shop even if he could. He tucked it under his arm and started off.

That evening, in the barrack, he went up to his new game site. No one was there but Hezrahn, the elderly man with the permanently soured outlook on life. Tadko, wondering how long the man had been a prisoner, could not really blame him, although he found him difficult to like. Hezrahn offered no game, but sat idly tossing the dice from hand to hand. Tadko was not anxious to play. Not alone with Hezrahn, who owned the dice and displayed a remarkable skill at tossing fair scores for himself. No one, not even Chumorden, accused him of cheating; it was supposed to be pure skill, but.... Tadko was about to return to his bunk when Hezrahn looked up.

"Where'd you get that?"

"Bought it today, up street."

Hezrahn snickered. "You going to take it to the House of Many Worlds, go caper for the commercials for a free meal?"

Tadko paused, staring at him.

"I thought they didn't let us in."

"Oh, you got to dress up right, smarten up your hair," he twirled his fingers above his head, "Can't look like a workee, but do you want to, you can get in. Some do."

Sink it, Tadko thought. Would this be the usual matter of someone who knew someone who knew someone?

"Do you know anyone who has?"

"Chumord', young, handsome, and curly haired, he's been there. Can't do it often, or they guess what you are and keep you out anyway. Not me," he added. "Go caper for the squatting commershes for a free meal? Pthuh!" He spat, carefully aiming under the bunk and avoiding the game pattern.

"I agree," Tadko said. It surely wouldn't be worth it just for a meal, however tasty. Not to him, anyway. But it might have other possibilities....

"What did Chumorden perform?"

"Sang. 'The Lonely Isle.' Claimed he had 'em all weeping, but all he got was a free meal, any route."

"What would happen if they tapped him to perform at one of the Houses? Could he get out of here to do it?"

"Dunno. Never heard of anyone from barrack being tapped, and not likely to be. What can a workee do that'll look fresh off the boat? For that you need something—" he paused, waving his arms as if searching for a word. "Something that looks fresh off the boat."

Tadko nodded, picked up his drum, and returned to his own bunk, where he lay thinking. If he wasn't fresh off the boat he was surely as close to it as you were likely to find in Tallenport. Then maybe they somehow knew perfectly well who was a workee, and made sure that such were never tapped to perform at a House. After all, what if they got someone who was in for, well, theft? A real thief, that was, like Dacy. Still, he thought he would ask Neradis. If she didn't know, she could surely find out the real facts for him.

The next day after work, he got Neradis's permission to visit her during the free days. On Nineday, he dressed carefully, took his drum, and set off on the trotline.

Neradis was in her tiny kitchen, sipping a mug of froile, when he came in. She gestured at him to pour a mug for himself and sit down.

"So what is this advice you wanted? If it's illegal, I can't help you."

"It isn't illegal, at least I don't think so." He described his conversation with Hezrahn. "We can get in to perform, then? But what if they wanted someone to entertain them at home?"

Her eyebrows went up.

"Is that how the current sets? I thought you said when you performed on Rowder you nearly died of fright."

He took a long swallow of froile, then scowled at the floor.

"I don't care anymore, I despise them all. But do you know of anyone who got tapped? What if they find out you're a workee? And why do they keep us out if it's really legal to go in?"

"That's a fairly complicated business," she said thoughtfully. "The Houses of Many Worlds tally to House Dakyn, they're eateries, hotels, theatres, all that sort of thing. Their policy is to let in anybody as long as you behave. But Concoras are the power in Tallenport, and they'd rather workees were kept out. So the owner—there's only one in Tallenport—doesn't let in anyone who doesn't look right."

"But then what if you get tapped —"

She interrupted with a tired wave.

"I told you it was complicated. The old lady and the ones actually running things don't do it. But the lazy young sprats with nothing to do, that's part of the thrill. Go and see who floats up. So they get their way. There aren't any murderers or rapists in the work crews, that sort of thing, so they don't have to worry about that. You really want to try it?"

"I would. Not for just a meal, though. According to what they told me, in the League back in the City, they give you money. Might it be enough to pay off my fine?"

She said slowly, "I've not heard of anyone paying off a fine that way. Part of one, right enough. That's not to say it never happened, but if they want you to spend a cycle or so with them, they have to let your work place know, so you don't have to come in. I can't say for certain, but I'll go bond they'd find out how much fine you had left and make sure they don't give you that much."

"What if you didn't tell them. Just went off with them?"

She shuddered.

"Don't try it. As soon as you failed to show up for work or door check they'd activate your tracer," she tapped her palm, "and go after you. Increase your fine would be the least of what they'd do. Flogging—just don't try it."

"I won't, then. But might I make enough to go to the City and back, on my free days?"

"Maybe. I don't see what good it would do—oh. You'd try to see your father, is that it?"

Tadko nodded, still staring at the floor. "I haven't asked the right questions," he muttered. "I could have tried this long ago. Found out, one way or another. If he doesn't want to have anything to do with me...well."

"Well, then what?"

"I stopped at a League office, last free days. They said if I wanted, they could make inquiries for me with my people on Sancy. See if it might be possible to raise money to pay me out. I don't much want to go to them as a paid-off thief, but I'd do it. If that doesn't work out—" He hesitated. "If that doesn't work out, I suppose I'll just have to settle down, try to work out my time without going drowno. Could I play the drum to pick up zinae, down at the Pier?"

"It's legal, but I think you'd not pick up many."

Neradis considered for a while, drumming her fingers on the table.

"I still think you ought to call your father. It would be so simple. Even in a call you could surely tell if he welcomed you or not. Then instead of spending your money—if you do earn any—on a City trip, you start right out by paying off a chunk of your fine."

"No. I want to see him, anyway."

She made a wide, shrugging gesture and shook her head.

"Are all Elnakti as stubborn as you? All right enough, but what would you do to entertain that's likely to get you tapped? That chant you did on Rowder?"

"No, I would dance."

"What sort of dance?"

"This drum I bought, it's about the size of one of our hand drums, at home. If I can fix a way to tie it to my left hand, so I can swing it around, and play it over my head, I'll do one of our drum dances."

"Hm," she said. "And what would that be like?"

"Oh, mostly leaping up and down and shouting to the rhythm, hitting the back of your head with your heels and your forehead with your knees."

She sat up, eyes widening. "I must say! Now that might be just the thing!"

She set down her mug and stood, beckoning him toward the door. "I'd not like to risk it in here, but could you show me outside? Better not do any shouting, though."

He followed her out to the yard, leaving his drum inside. There he paused for a few moments, thinking himself into the rhythm, then began clapping his hands together over his head, springing up and down. He threw his arms up high, whirling in a circle, did forward and backward somersaults, emphasized the heel clicks and knee taps with cracks of his cupped palms, spun again in a flurry of hand claps and kicks. He went through several more measures of the dance, then stopped, panting and dripping with sweat.

Neradis was watching him, open-mouthed.

"My life!" She exclaimed. "That really might be just the thing!"

Back in the kitchen she made him sit down and handed him a wet towel with which to mop up.

"You see," she told him, "they don't get many offworlders here in Tallenport, either in their audience or their performers. It's just a packery, work town, that's another reason there's only the one House of Many Worlds here. Tour groups go out of the hotel complex, on the west side. But something like your dance, and with you an offworlder, ought to make them take notice. What would you wear?"

He looked down at the clothes he bought so long ago at Sandtown.

"This, I suppose. Or the things I brought from the ship. I haven't any others."

"No good. You'd attract more attention in exotic clothes. What did you say your Elnakti gear looked like?"

Tadko described them. "I couldn't stand to wear them to dance here, even if I had them. I'd die of the heat. Bad enough in Monnan wear."

"Hm," she said. "Now let me think...." She stared past him, pondering, then suddenly favored him with a triumphant smile.

"I believe I have just the thing. Come along."

In the other room she climbed a narrow ladder set into the wall, pushed aside one of the ceiling panels, and pulled herself up into the storage space. He heard her rummaging around, then her head reappeared above a large hamper.

"Here, help me get this down."

Together they lowered it to the floor, and Neradis unlocked the catches.

"These are mostly costumes we've worn every year for All Island Day," she explained as she opened it. "Oh dear."

On top lay a once-handsome pair of thigh boots, with their scarlet color peeling off in long strips.

"I told Thune those things wouldn't last in storage." She tossed them in a corner, then took out a long robe, once patterned in silver, blue and green but now considerably faded. She smiled at Tadko's dubious expression.

"Don't worry, these are all made of glit cloth; it's only used for costumes and anyone would know it right away. But there's an outfit in here that Donnil wore once—ah yes."

She lifted out a set of breeches and vest that seemed to be made of a fine, light brown fur.

"What about these?"

Interested, Tadko stepped forward to examine them. Light, very soft, and when he inspected the underside, it looked woven. "What sort of beast did this come from?"

She laughed.

"It's fake, just a cloth. Think ordinaries like us could afford the real thing? Not that we'd ever have anyplace to wear it, anyhow. But it's a standard cloth, mostly used in the far north or south where it is a lot colder. Donnil was supposed to be a sort of primitive hunter, with a spear and face paint."

"It doesn't look much like an Elnakti suit. What would I say if they asked me about it?"

"Not likely they would. If they did, say it's the closest you could come with Monnan wear." She grinned wryly. "That's even true. Here, try them on."

The breeches, made for Donnil's tall frame, hung down to his calves, but the waist was adjustable and Neradis showed him how to snug it up. The vest hung below his hips, and was much too wide in the shoulders. She considered him briefly, then went to one of her wall cabinets and took out a small hand stitcher. It buzzed against his skin as she sewed tucks around the neck, then ran a line of stitching part way up the front. She stood back and inspected him with some complacency.

"Try that now."

He raised his arms, essayed a few cautious steps and leaps. The cloth was warmer than he would have liked, for all its light weight, but loose enough to be comfortable dancing.

"With a dance like yours, that should wake them right up," Neradis told him. "What will you do with your hair?"

"Oh yes. Hezrahn said I'd have to smarten it up. Could I wear it in two braids? That's what we do at home."

"Fine." She opened another wall niche, rummaged a bit, and handed him two lengths of red cord. "Braid it with these."

"That isn't what we do, though."

"No matter, it'll add to the exotic look."

"Right enough." He accepted the cord, then looked at his feet. "We wear boots all the time—could I wear my work boots? Paint them in Elnakti designs, or something?"

"Oh no. Painted or not, everyone would recognize those boots. Wear your sandals, most tourists buy them soon after they come to Monna. You'll need to clean them up, though," she added after a critical look. "And when do you want to try this? The House of Many Worlds is open every night."

He drew a deep breath. "Tonight? If we can fix this drum I'll go tonight."

With elastic stripping, they secured a snug web over the base of the drum. Then while Neradis cleaned his sandals, Tadko showered, washed and dried his hair, braided it with the red cord, and dressed in his new costume. He presented himself for her approval.

"You look fine, very exotic, but don't wear that locker key! You think they wouldn't notice that?"

Tadko shuddered and removed it, rolling it up with the cord and tucking it into his pouch. He fastened the sandals on.

"Anything else? And how will you know if they tap me?"

"I'll be notified." For just a moment, then, a look of near-terror grayed her face. It passed almost instantly, but he understood. Without him, she would be short on her line, and there was the quota to meet. She was kind, and so interested in helping him, perhaps it had only just now occurred to her. He turned away, wanting to promise to repay her somehow, knowing he couldn't be at all sure of keeping such a promise. But to give up his plan...she gave him a slap on the back that nearly staggered him.

"Be off with you then, and don't lose your nerve! You know where to pick up the trotline. Just say, 'House of Many Worlds,' it'll be on the circuits."

CHAPTER SEVENTEEN

Night in Tallenport. Tadko came down Palace Hill and hurried toward the nearest trotline stop, glancing from side to side, on the alert for local, uncaught snafflers. His smock and breeches were violet, slashed with gold. His slippers were gilded leather with scarlet clasps on the turned up toes. Ornamental chains glittered around his neck and wrists. He wore a soft cap of scarlet silk, tugged rakishly over one ear. His embroidered pouch bulged, and he clutched it to his side with one arm while clutching a bundle with the other.

When the trotline car arrived he jumped in with a sigh of relief, pulled off the cap, tossed it to the floor, then thought better of it and tucked it under his belt. He sat nervously during the entire trip though the city.

Would Neradis be asleep? No, her house still showed a light in the front room. Thankfully, Tadko left the trotline car, ran up the steps, and rang the chime. Oby woke up on his perch to call Why? Why? but Tadko ignored him.

Neradis looked dumbfounded when she opened the door; then her face changed as she recognized him.

"Tadko? You look like a strutting commercial! Come on in."

He dropped into a chair.

"Would you by any chance have some froile hot, at this hour?"

"I do; or what about a mug of ale?"

"Oh yes, thanks."

She brought the ale and watched with amusement while he gulped some of it down, then sat opposite him.

"Tell me what happened before I perish with curiosity! They notified me at work that you were at Coral Gold House, one of the Concora mansions! You look rich, but it's only been six days. You look tired, too, so what happened?"

"You'd be tired too if you'd been living with sq—with commercials for six days." Tadko swallowed more ale, and considered. "They really noticed me at the House of Many Worlds. Clothes do make a difference, don't they? All the other entertainers came from Tallenport—well so did I, really, but they didn't know that. So I danced and drummed and shouted, and they certainly took notice, just the way you said—by the time I finished they were pounding the tables and shouting with me. The whole audience, that was, and the man in charge was beaming like a sunrise."

Neradis chuckled.

"You were probably the most unusual act he had in a long time."

"Anyway, four commercials came up to see me afterwards. Two Concoras, Eralto and Fridalla were their names, and I think a Crale, and I don't know the other." Tadko's mouth twisted. "They went on something sickening about how wonderful I was, and would I entertain them at home. So I told them the truth, the way you said to, and they said how awful that a visitor to Monna should be—I forget how they put it, but they were so sorry I was a workee, that was what it amounted to—but they didn't offer to pay off my fine.

"So I've been dancing every day, and singing, and chanting. They gave me the clothes and the jewelry, and a lot of squares." He patted his pouch lovingly. "And there were lots of visitors. Some even wanted to hear about Elnakt, so I told stories. The food was wonderful, too. I've never tasted better." He sighed regretfully. "Then tonight someone came back from Many Worlds with new entertainers—two of them—and they threw me out."

"What!"

"Oh, I don't mean I did anything wrong, they just found some new toys, that was what it was like, and they said, 'oh, dear Tadko, you see how interesting these people are, so we don't need you any more. Good bye!' And a servant came and showed me to the door. They did give me enough time to collect all my things." His mouth twisted again.

Neradis nodded. "Drifters on the waves, that's what they are. Some will grow up eventually into real stroppers and go into management and all, but a lot will just float along and amuse themselves. Who were these new people? I'm surprised they found someone more exotic than you, this soon, anyway."

"Well, I saw them, and they really were very strange. Taller than any Monnan by a head or so, thin and limber as eels, hairless, and painted in wide colored stripes from head to foot." He shook his head. "Hurt your eyes, they were so gaudy. They wore crotch-pieces so I don't even know if they were human, or if that was their natural color."

Neradis was laughing. "They're human, technically so, at least, and it's paint."

Tadko was startled. "You've seen them? You know about them?"

"I've not seen them in person, but there was a program on holovid years ago: People of Distant Worlds. I forget the name of their world, but it's a long way off, and they do paint themselves that way. Strange they would come to Tallenport. Some waterheads want to see 'the places where tourists don't go,' and this is one of them. I can see how they'd be snapped up. Did you get enough money for a trip to the City?"

"Well, I've got—"

"Wait half a jo." She gestured abruptly, stood up and went to the windows. For a moment she looked out into the night, then drew the screening panels and returned to her chair.

"Not like to be anyone looking in, especially at this hour, but best not to take chances." She drew up a little table. "Now let's see."

From his clout, inside his waistband, he took blue squares to pile on the table.

"Blues!" She exclaimed, much impressed. "Worth fifty D! How many of those?"

"Uh—seven."

"That's three hundred and fifty right there. How much else?"

He emptied the embroidered pouch on the table, and together they counted up the total.

"Altogether, that's five hundred and eight D, twenty-three zinae," she said, then scowled ferociously and banged the table with her fist, scattering the money.

"Those eel-sucking squatting cheapers—slime them all!" She raged.

Tadko cringed a little in sheer surprise. Neradis could be harsh and peremptory, but he had never before heard her use barrack language.

"It's a lot of money," he ventured cautiously.

She slumped back with a sigh.

"Oh I know it's more than you've ever seen, Tadko, but they could have given you twice, three times that much and never missed it. Cheapers," she repeated. "How much is your fine?"

"Five hundred and eighty."

"And how much have you paid off so far?"

"Uh, twenty-eight, I think."

"So with this you have five hundred and thirty-six, almost enough to pay you out, but not quite. They do check up and make sure they don't give you enough, I'll go bond."

He pulled at his tunic.

"Could I sell these clothes, and the jewelry?"

"Let me see."

He shed the jewelry, pulled the tunic over his head and handed it to her.

"Oh my," she murmured wistfully, stroking the smooth, shimmering cloth. "That is beautiful, isn't it? Just beautiful. I've not seen anything like it ever before." She examined the label.

"Verala."

"What does that mean?"

"It's the maker. Someone in the City, or maybe even offworld. Is this like what that snaffler in the City wore?"

"No, this is better, although his looked really rich, before I saw this. But could I sell this?"

"Oh, no fear. But getting what it's worth, maybe five, six hundred, maybe more—no hope there. The jewelry?" She shook her head. "I've no more idea than you do how much it's worth. Could even be cheap glitter—would I know? For the clothes you might get a hundred, enough to pay you out, travel to Sancy. Is that what you want to do?"

Tadko leaned back, yawning. He was suddenly very tired.

"Either that or go to the City, to see my father, the way I planned."

She nodded, brisk again. "I agree. That's what you ought to do, no question, and you've plenty of money for that. You could go on the next free days, but tomorrow you'll have to go in to work, then back to the barrack for the end of the cycle."

He groaned. "I do? They said they'd got me for the whole cycle."

"Yes, but when they sent you away, they're supposed to notify the packery and Barrack Control. Maybe they did and maybe they didn't, but if they did and you don't come in, you'll be listed as a runner."

"Do I have to go back to the barrack yet tonight?"

"No, not if they just let you go." She smiled a little. "You can use Donnil's bed tonight, go to work in the morning from here."

He pointed to his bundle. "I brought back Donnil's things. Do you still have mine?"

"Right enough."

"Then could I leave all the rest of this, and the money, with you until the free days?"

She frowned worriedly.

"I'd not want anyone to know I had them; I don't like having all that money in the house—when you get back to the barrack tomorrow night the other men will want to know how much you got, and where it is, and all. Could you tell them you stopped at Rotten Pier and lost or spent it all?"

He understood her reluctance but he hated to take the things to the barrack. Supposedly the lockers were secure, and there were the stun circuits, but still. Besides, they would expect him to do more betting. Hezrahn especially. And buy some rounds at the Beached Barge, on Eightday, after work.

"All the men are locked up until the free days," he pointed out.

"So they are but then they're free, and they mingle, and word gets around. I'm sorry Tadko, but—now what?"

He was sitting up, grinning. "If I took all that money to work, could I put it my company account, even though it isn't payday?"

"Why, of course. Cly could arrange it. Give you a valuation and exchange on the clothes and jewelry, too. It wouldn't be the real value, of course. They might count it enough to cover your fine, and pay you out. Is that what you want to do?"

"No, but it's what I'll tell them at the barrack. They'll believe that sooner than my spending it; they know I'm a cheaper. And I'll go in on a different trotline car in the morning. No one has to know I was here—did you tell anyone you helped me?"

She laughed shortly; then the worried look returned. "They'd not thank me for encouraging that kind of thing. I was totally surprised, and mighty annoyed, when you weren't there on Oneday. Did you mention me when you were at Coral Gold House?"

"No. They thought the clothes were mine, and I let them think it. It made me more exotic, the way you said."

"Well then." She pondered briefly, then spoke decisively.

"All right enough, I'll keep everything here, we can roll it all up and put it in the loft in a utility bag. I warn you, though, you'd better take eight or ten D with you to spread yourself a bit at the barrack. Even for you, it'd be suspicious if you don't. We'll go to work separately. I'll be surprised when you come in, and do some yammering about making quota. You take it nice and meek, no backtalk."

Tadko nodded, grinning.

"On Eightday," she continued, "when you're free after work, go eat somewhere and come out here later. Whatever you do, don't mention where you're going, let 'em think you're going down to the Pier, or some such. You can get a wave jet for the City in the morning, come back here the next day—if you have to. And we'll call before you go, at least make sure your father is there."

She fell silent, and yawned prodigiously. "And now let's both get some sleep."

Tadko was greeted with much surprise when he returned to the barrack after work, the next day.

"You're back!" was the most common reaction, uttered with open-mouthed astonishment.

"You got any back left?" This from a jokester who laughed hugely at his own humor.

"Tried to run and they caught you, eh?" Hezrahn sneered.

Tadko hooked his thumbs in the sides of his clout, stuck his chin in the air, and assumed a swagger.

"No running, no stripes," he announced. "Been entertaining the top castes at Coral Gold House."

"They really tapped you?" Rumard was incredulous.

"Try another," Chumorden scoffed. "That one missed the boat."

Tadko grinned, turning to display his unscarred back.

"Saw me dance at the House of Many Worlds and liked what they saw. Worth capering for the commercials if you get enough squares for it."

In an instant the incredulity vanished.

"How much did you get?"

"What you going to do with it?"

"What's it like, Coral Gold House?"

"Did you see old Vikky?" (This being barrack slang for Vikteborin Esco Concora.)

Tadko was grateful for the stun circuits that kept them from grabbing at him, and grateful that Neradis had been willing to keep his clothes, jewelry, and money. He changed his stance and glowered at them.

"Don't think I'm spreading it all over," he said truculently. "I put it in my company account, help me get out of here."

There were groans and grumbled curses, but all were half-hearted. It was clear that they considered this only what could be expected, from Tadko.

"Cheaper, cheaper," several men remarked.

"More fool you, sprat," Hezrahn muttered. "They'll find a way to fix you out of it."

"Did you put it all away?" Rumard's cry of dismay sounded almost childish.

"Not all." He had taken Neradis' advice and brought some of the money with him. "I'll do some gaming. Stake you a D on anything you want to risk. And Eightday after work, I'll take my gaming partners down to the Beached Barge."

This aroused so much enthusiasm they actually begged him for a demonstration of his dance. He obliged, using the space before the doors, leaping, shouting, and beating his drum, turning forward and back springs in air, and generally showing off to the best of his ability.

Before he finished, the others were shouting in rhythm and pounding their fists together over their heads. Popularity, at last!

After this triumph, he still had to face the rest of the cycle at work. It was hard to conceal the tension he felt, the worry over whether or not Hezrahn might be right—even though his money was not really in a company account—or the fear that the 'company stroppers' might suddenly decide to transfer him away from the city.

Neradis kept her promise and snapped at him. He suspected she was quite serious, for a few times, in his distraction, he lost the rhythm of the work. After those mistakes he concentrated, hard, on what he was doing.

It was a great relief, at the end of the cycle, to take his fellow gamers down to the Beached Barge. He pretended to drink. Later he gave the rest of his money, except for the trotline fare, to the bartender.

"Keep it flowing until the money runs out," he said, gesturing toward the table where the others were singing.

"You leaving?"

"Soon." He managed a leer. "I got someone to meet."

The bartender leered back.

"Right enough."

Tadko returned to the table, played his part until the others were shouting and having a merry old time. Then he slipped away.

CHAPTER EIGHTEEN

Early next morning he stood at the entrance to the shuttle station, trying not to look furtive. Surely someone would recognize him for what he was, a prison workee decked out like a high-caste commercial.

Neradis had advised him not to wear his hair in the Elnakti double braid, for fear someone from Coral Gold might be at the station this morning. Not likely, she said, but possible. Under her critical eye he had washed and combed his hair loose, fluffed it (under protest) with a scented concoction she provided, and pulled on the scarlet cap. The jewelry he packed in his bag, and he wore the good clothes for the trip. Neradis offered him a meal before he left, but he was unable to stomach anything. He did drink a cup of strong froile.

"Wouldn't they know me just by the clothes?"

"No fear. The clothes would come from someone in the house your size, younger than most, and you'd not guess how many clothes those types have. Chambers full, is it. You're probably quite safe just with the hair fixed."

He hadn't liked that 'probably' at all, but here he was. His knees felt wobbly, and his heart seemed to be thudding down in his empty stomach. Nerves, Neradis told him, but there would be food served on the shuttle...first he had to get on it.

Half a dozen people pushed past him into the station, ignoring him completely. He moved on in himself, trying to imitate the lordly, casual manner Dacy Wile had affected, back in the City. He waited until the six had picked up their tickets. Concoras, obviously, from their colors, but different from the ones he had seen at Coral Gold. Their clothing was rich, but less flamboyant; their looks were serious; as they moved toward the waiting lounge they appeared to be in deep discussion of important matters.

Company stroppers, he decided—plotting how to squeeze more work out of the poor scrabblers below. Sink them all.

A few others came in. A woman with two small boys in tow. A skinny, fussy-faced man who looked bound for a holiday, a harried servant behind him towing a mountain of luggage on a float.

Tadko was shocked briefly by the appearance of an Eilonsader in the ridiculous garb that Kheer had sported; after a moment he saw that the man must be at least twice Kheer's age. Looked even sillier, thought Tadko. He breathed deeply, straightened his back, and approached the booth.

"Ticket to the City?" He inquired in a husky voice, swallowed hard, repeated it, and wondered if he looked as guilty as he felt.

Apparently not; the young woman was yawning sleepily.

"Round trip?"

"One way."

This was a risk. If he couldn't stay he would have to pay extra for another one-way ticket back, but he carried his other clothes, along with the jewelry, in a decent-looking bag contributed by Neradis. Presumably he could sell his current finery in the

City for a better price than in Tallenport. Might even look up Dacy...he'd give Unser a real scraping, if he had the chance.

"City departure. City departure." Came the announcement, and he followed the others, hoping no one would speak to him. The skinny man provided a welcome diversion, insisting on personal observation of his luggage stowage, then requiring an attendant to make sure his seat was adjusted precisely to suit him.

Tadko found his own way to an isolated seat. He thought they looked extremely comfortable; built large enough for Monnans, with wide padded arms, they were more than roomy for an Elnakti.

Feeling totally exhausted, he sank back and closed his eyes. He hadn't slept well last night either; in fact, it seemed as if he had been running hard throughout the last cycle. He barely felt the motion as the wave-jet rose smoothly into the air.

A little later, a dulcet, disembodied voice spoke, apparently in his left ear. He started slightly, then relaxed again. Neradis had never made this trip, of course, but knew all about it and had told him what to expect.

"Gooood morning. Welcome to House Ornibeck's City Express. For refreshment this morning we offer hot spiced froile, a golden fizz, sieveral tea, and cumbra tea. Also butterlets poached in wine, grilled stulpin, and sautéed frillets in gleo sauce. Please state your preference."

Tadko ordered froile and butterlets, those being the only items he recognized. He might have eaten some of the others at Coral Gold House, but had been too intimidated to ask for names.

Soon a buzzer sounded from the padded arm rest at his left. He moved, the padded cover lifted back, and his tray of food rose and swung into position. The froile was the best he ever tasted; the crispbread was tasty, familiar from breakfast at Coral Gold House; the butterlets could have used some ordinary hot sauce. He finished, pressed the button that signaled for withdrawal of the tray, closed down the arm rest, and leaned back to wait.

Now they were landing in Monna City, at the onplanet shuttle center. Neradis had tried to explain how he could travel northwest for three hours and arrive two hours earlier than when he left. It sounded absurd; but when he checked the time, he found she was right.

Feeling groggy and fuddled, he located a transit cubicle with cot, left a wake-up call on the convenience circuit, and was finally able to sleep.

The circuit woke him at fifteen hundred hours. He sat up, swung his feet to the floor, and continued to sit, thinking. This was the last part of his journey, and he must go through with it. Slowly he dressed in his old clothes, packing the new ones in the bag. He combed his hair and braided it Elnakti style, then set out to look for a trotline stand.

At Neradis's insistence, he had let her make a call to the College, learning the address of Senior Scholar Osrin Havard, and determining that he was, indeed, in residence.

Tadko left the trotline at a corner and stood looking down the street of faculty residences. The houses were all built of cream-colored stone, two or three stories high, with pale blue tiled roofs rising to peaks in the center. Each place had a square of green turf before the entrance, but most of the yards were filled with flowers and shrubs in every possible shade of yellow-green, sea-blue, pinks, yellows, and lavender, or bursts of deep purple and scarlet. Every yard had its giant umbrel tree, rising to shade the roof with its circle of green, feathery branches. A few children played on the plots of turf, and many people worked among the garden stuffs. Were they servants, or owners of these faculty houses? None wore anything he could recognize as a livery, so he could not tell.

He started down the street, checking the house numbers, turned in at what was supposed to be the right one, and rang the bell. The door was opened by an elderly woman in a green smock and yellow trousers.

Tadko cleared his throat.

"Is—uh—Senior Scholar Havard in?"

"Yes."

"I'd like to see him, if I may."

Her look was skeptical.

"Are you a student? These are the free days. Have you an appointment?"

"Uh, no. I thought, since this is a free day—"

Her mouth drew down at the corners.

"Don't you have authorization? Who are you, boy?"

Tadko winced and tried to stand taller.

"Could you please tell him someone from Elnakt is here, would like to see him. It's business," Tadko added, hoping this would sound a bit more impressive.

"Wait here." She closed the door, leaving Tadko feeling like a fool.

Presently the door opened again, and yes, this was Osrin Havard, much older than in his mother's pictures, with lined face and fading hair, but unmistakable.

"From Elnakt?" He asked, surprised.

"Yes, Siro," Tadko began, quite unable to say 'father.' "Siro, I thought—I'm Tadko. Tadko Darusko. Seiare's son."

"Tadko!" The man exclaimed, stepping out of the door, peering closely at Tadko. "Why, yes, my boy, you've quite a look of your mother! Is she with you?"

"No, Siro," Tadko shifted uncomfortably, feeling obscurely guilty. "I'm sorry. She died—before I left Elnakt. I'm sorry."

"I see." Disappointment crossed Havard's face. "It wasn't the Rhionny—"

"No. Siro. It was a pain inside. She died just before they came down on us, but she'd been sick a long time. I'm sorry."

Havard shook his head. "I am sorry, too." Then he was brisk again. "But come in, my boy!" His arm was around Tadko's shoulders, drawing him into the house. "Come in! Where have you been? I looked for you on Sancy as soon as I returned from Eilon-sad and heard the news about what was happening on Elnakt, but no one there knew anything."

Tadko felt dizzy and just a little sick. Neradis was right, then, and it had all been unnecessary; most of it, anyway. He allowed himself to be guided inside and seated on something. He realized that Havard had sat down opposite, his expression worried.

"Tadko, are you all right? You don't look well. Zena," he called, turning. "Bring us froile, and something to eat."

He waited, silent, with Tadko unable to speak, until the woman brought two mugs and a pot of froile, with a plate of spiced pastries. She set the tray on a small table, glancing at Tadko with astonishment before she left.

Gratefully Tadko drank the froile Havard poured for him, and gazed around the room. It was large and airy, the walls paneled in cool, translucent greens and blues. A fountain played in the center, rising from a circle of pale green stone, and a wide window, shielded from the direct rays of the sun, overlooked the garden.

Tadko finished his froile, and leaned back on the couch.

"Thank you, Siro. I am...tired."

Havard nodded. "Call me Father, my boy. You do look tired. Worn down. Tell me where you have been."

Tadko drew a deep breath. "First of all, I had better tell you I landed on Monna illegally, after the others came, and—it's a long story—I'm here in the City illegally, too. I'm a workee—a prisoner—at Concora's on Tallen, in there for illegal entry and...and petty theft, and if I'm not back to go to work on Oneday morning, they'll activate my tracer—" He held up his hand, the code visible through the skin on his palm. "And send the greens for me. Uh, the civic orderlies."

Havard looked shocked, but less so than Tadko would have expected; the look soon changed to one of concern. He poured more froile for himself and drank it thoughtfully.

"This would be a difficult environment for someone from Elnakt," he said finally. "But this is still Nineday. We have the evening ahead of us, and two more days before you must report back. Why don't you begin at the beginning, and tell me."

He refilled both mugs. Tadko drank, and munched up several pastries, thinking.

"I suppose for me, it really began a long time ago," he said at last. "When I was too little to go out with the herds. Grandfather hadn't gone that year, either, because of his bad leg, so Keldat, his second cousin's grandson, led them out.

"I was in the school room with Mother when we heard people shouting outside, then Grandfather came in and told us they'd captured a Rhionny, a cub, snooping around the steading. He said they would let him go in the morning and we could have a real Rhionny hunt like in the old days, and I could ride with them. We were proud of that, you see, the Daruskos, the ones who pushed farthest east, the Rhionny hunters."

Tadko hunched his shoulders, not looking at Havard.

"I know," the man said quietly. "All that was long ago."

"Any route, my mother—I had seen her angry with Grandfather, but never like that. She said she wouldn't have it, that it was all a lot of nonsense from the past, that grown men shouldn't be so foolish—I forget all the things they both said. But it ended with grandfather going to have his hunt, but I wasn't to go. Of course I was disappointed. I thought they were treating me like just a cub, myself. But I knew if Grandfather agreed, I'd have to do what Mother said.

"But that night I sneaked out, because I just *had* to see a real live Rhionny. I had heard all the old hero chants, you see. You know how the steadings are built, on those rocky hills that rise above the halm?"

Havard nodded. "Old, old volcanic necks," he said, "worn down and all extinct long before humans ever arrived. But go on, my boy."

"Well, they had him in a cage up near the crest, that big level spot where we have the dances and festival fires, and all. All three moons were up and none of them are as big even as Monninet, but they give a pretty good light.

"I went up to the cage, and the Rhionny came up to the front—and he was just a boy, almost like me. Paler." Tadko paused, gulping. "I don't see how Grandfather and the others could see him as—a kind of hairy animal—even though he was naked. I didn't know what to think. I knew I couldn't have hunted him. I'm not sure why, but I tapped my chest and told him my name, Tadko Darusko. They hadn't said anything about him talking, but then he tapped his own chest and said, very clearly, 'Yarron.' So I opened the cage and pointed over toward the river, and he ran. Quiet as a shadow, down the hill, and then I lost sight of him. I hurried right in and went back to bed.

"Grandfather and some of the older men were furious in the morning, and they went out to hunt anyway, but they didn't find him."

Tadko munched another pastry and looked, puzzled, at Havard. "Why couldn't they see that he was just a boy?"

"People see what they expect to see, very often," Havard said quietly. "What they have been taught to see; and your grandfather and the others had all their lives been proud of their ancestors, the Rhionny killers, who took Elnakt for their own. Did anyone ever suspect you?"

"No. And I never admitted it either, even to my friends, or to Mother. Then last spring," Tadko resumed, "at least the last spring I was home—it was early, the herds were pretty well all out of hibernation, but not ready to go out.

"Mother had been sick, most of the winter. It was a pain that started in her hip, and got worse, spreading all the time. The doctor gave her sikonet to drink, and it helped the worst of the pain, but it got worse. After a while, she couldn't eat much."

Listening, Havard seemed to have fallen into a reverie. He held his mug in both hands, his gaze far off, his face drawn.

"God of the Galaxy," he muttered. "If only—but then I knew what it was like—ah well." He shook his head, returned his attention to Tadko. "She died before the Rhionny came, then?"

"About the same time. We were deciding whether Keldat should lead out the herds with both Grandfather and I staying, or should one of us go.

"It was about midday when Tered Ossek rode down from Ossikor, north of us. We saw him coming, riding as if a hunting slaen could be after him, and we went down to meet him. His onca was nearly foundered, and he told us the Rhionny had taken Ossikor.

"At first we couldn't believe it. I suppose you understand. He said there were twenty or thirty of them, wearing leather and even metal plates, riding little hard-hoofed mountain beasts. Later I think they would have sunk in the halm, but it hadn't bloomed yet, and the ground was still hard frozen. They must have crossed the Ice River farther north, somewhere, although by Daruskan the ice was going out.

"Tered said the people at Ossikor saw them coming from the north, and they were puzzled because Ossikor is the northernmost steading along the river. He said about forty strides from where the steading rises, all of a sudden they yelled, and started galloping all together. People at Ossikor, well, they didn't know what was happening. Then the Rhionny were close, and they rode right up the hill and started throwing heavy darts, and they had some kind of missile firing guns that shot round balls that knocked people down dead. Tered's people started trying to fight back, but the Rhionny shot or stabbed everyone in their way. Tered's father, the Mosor, sent him off and he managed to get away. He said when he left he heard them shouting something; first he couldn't make it out, but then he knew it was 'Daruskan.'"

Tadko paused for another deep breath, swallowed more froile, and wiped his face on his sleeve. Talking had brought it all back, the mixture of terror, bewilderment and disbelief, the crashing break in a way of life that had come to seem eternal; the only right way for Elnakti people.

"Grandfather," he began again, and stopped, biting his lip. "I think—I'm not sure—I think maybe he thought—it would be wonderful to fight them. Like a hunt. After all, we had about forty men able to go against them, and the Ossikor people had killed some Rhionny. So we mounted up and got out the slam guns we use for hunting slaen, we had a dozen of those, and the slings for small stuff, and I said good-bye to my mother. I told her what was happening. I could see how badly upset she was, even in her pain; she didn't want me to go. But I was the heir of Daruskan, you see? I really had to go.

"So we rode out and met them coming south. I was one of the men with slam guns, and Grandfather and Keldat of course. The slam guns have a long range. I got two of them and the others got some, but they kept on coming, and then they got close with their pellet guns, and I don't know how they threw those darts so hard and so far. We couldn't control the oncas when the darts started coming. I don't know how many of us were killed. Or wounded. Oncas too. I didn't even have time to make a count—well, we just turned around and ran.

"Grandfather was shot, and Keldat. Grandfather was still able to ride, so when we turned to run I held him up on one side and Bartos, Keldat's brother, on the other. We rode home as well as we could. My mother had died while we were gone, and Grandfather died that night. I don't know what happened to Keldat; he didn't come home with us. So many didn't. I hope someone was able to bury them decently, sometime. The slaens—anyway, so that made me Mosor of Daruskan," Tadko finished bitterly. "Supposed to guide the people."

"Where did they get the metal, the guns?" He asked Havard bewilderedly. "Even the darts had metal heads. We get all our metal from the traders, and it's all made goods, knives, pots, harness fixings, things like that."

Havard rubbed his chin, looking equally puzzled. "I do not know. When I first heard the reports from the refugees on Sancy, I thought they were, perhaps, the exaggerations of frightened people. There was still much confusion, conflicting stories. But guns, pellets, metal headed darts, the metal plates on their leather—you saw them for yourself?"

"Oh yes." Tadko's voice was still bitter. "Later I saw them up close and there's no mistake. Where did they get such things?"

"I have no idea, and I would very much like to," Havard said. "To my knowledge, no traders have been into the mountains of Elnakt. I looked into that myself. If they have been smelting their own metal—but go on with your own story, my boy."

"I'd go bond they have. And we bought from offworld traders, sink them." Tadko scowled, then sighed, and continued. "I'm not sure why the Rhionny didn't follow us straight to Daruskan. Having a good time at Ossikor, I guess. But I knew they'd be coming. Six more people died in the night. We wrapped all the bodies, and said the first prayers, and carried them down to the coldest room to wait until the ground was soft enough for proper burial."

Tadko did not see Havard's momentary shudder. He was seeing his home, under a dull orange sun.

"Then I called the rest of the people together, and told them what I wanted to do. Maybe we could have fought them, I don't know. I didn't think so. I still don't. So I decided when we saw them coming I would ride out to meet them alone. Tered had said some of them could speak our language, so I would try to tell them that I was the Mosor, the leader, and they could take me, and do what they liked, if they would leave the rest of my people alone."

Havard was staring at him, wonderingly.

"You were willing to do that?"

"I didn't know what else to do," Tadko said apologetically. "They might have killed me and gone on to kill the others too, but I thought I could try. And I was Mosor. We lost five of the slam guns in the fight, so nobody thought we could fight them any more."

Tadko paused, and rubbed his face tiredly. "Any route, two days later we saw them coming and I rode out, with Bartos and Tered a way behind me, to see what happened. I had named Bartos as Mosor after me, not that it meant anything. We both knew that. So some of them did speak our language, and I made them understand, and they agreed. Then we rode back and they stripped me and put me in a cage—like we did with Yarron. But as much as I could see, they were treating my people all right. So I thought they'd hunt me.

"But that night, one of them came to the cage. He tapped himself on the chest and said, 'Yarron.'"

"The same boy?" Havard exclaimed.

"He had to be, I think. At first I was too surprised to think. Then I tapped myself, and said, 'Tadko Darusko.' He smiled, and opened the cage, and beckoned me to follow him. He took me down the hill with him, around to the west.

"There was an onca there, not one of those we usually ride but a well-freshened one, frisky and ready to go. Also a saddle and bags and some clothes. Yarron pointed to me, and them, and west, and said, 'You go. Run.'

"Well, it took a while, but I made him understand I was afraid to escape, for fear of the others harming my people. He waved up the hill and grinned.

"'They my people now,' he said. 'This my place. No harm to them. Old Tadko dead?'

"I didn't like that much, but I said yes, old Tadko was dead. He was so sure that my people would be all right. So I ran."

"Were you hunted? By any of the others?"

"I don't know. I saw some of them, right enough, riding oncas which they couldn't manage very well, but they didn't seem to know how to look. I hid out in the thickets where the halm grows tall, and the water trees, by the sinkholes, or I just lay down flat with Yarron beside me. They didn't seem to see very well out on the flat."

"Yarron?"

Tadko grinned. "That's what I called the onca he'd fetched for me. We always name the ones we ride.

"So I kept going west. Herds started moving out but there were always Rhionny with them, besides Elnakti, so I did a lot of dodging. Coming toward Port Town I saw a lot of oncas without herders. It was after midsummer that I finally got there. I could see where the ships had been, and a lot of people had tramped around, but it was empty. I stayed for a couple of days. I thought I might keep going, maybe southwest, try to find a steading where no one knew who I was, and Yarron and I could spend the winter. But then a little ship landed. They'd been down in the south continent, getting a load of bloodwood for the jewelers here, and they let me come with them. I sent Yarron heading back east, and the last I saw of him he was making good speed. He would know where to go for hibernation.

"The ship people were kind. It wasn't until I got here that I found out so many of my people had already arrived, on the trading ships. They weren't allowing any more in, so—the ship people helped me sneak in.

"Oh yes. I tried to get Yarron to understand about burying my people properly, when the ground was thawed."

Havard leaned back, rubbing his chin, shaking his head.

"I must say, my boy, you had a good many adventures before you ever arrived on Monna. I believe it is too late to continue your story tonight, you still look very tired.

"We should have a late supper; I am sure Zena left something for us, and we can begin again in the morning. How much is your fine?"

"I have more than five hundred, still to pay off."

"We will take care of that in the morning." He smiled and clapped Tadko on the shoulder. "Come along, son."

CHAPTER NINETEEN

Tadko woke and sat up. After a moment, he slid out of bed and began padding restlessly around the room.

The struggle and uncertainty were ended. He had achieved his goal. His father was a kindly man who welcomed him most gladly.

Why, then, did he still feel so...uncertain? Out of place, that was it. He looked around. Although definitely not in a class with Coral Gold House, this was also very different from Neradis's tiny home. Large, high-ceilinged, airy rooms. This one had a floor of cool, multi-colored tiles, slightly resilient underfoot. The windows were opaqued at present, but open louvers with their nearly invisible screens let air currents though three sides of the room. Lights were recessed in the ceiling. Chairs, a table of smooth, blackish-green stone, a study center similar to the one he had been shown at the League; wall panels of fine-woven matting alternating with inset cabinets for clothing, bedding, book films and the like.

He made use of the adjoining lavatory, reveling in the streams of cool water in the shower, so different from the stingy sprays available at the barrack tank. This place smelled much better, too, in spite of the cleanser poured through the tank every cycle. After some thought, he dressed in the fine clothes from Concora's, omitting the silk cap and jewelry. He found the control panel Havard had explained the night before, pressed the plate to clear the windows, and found the lift to the lower level.

His nose led him to the breakfast room, where Zena was laying out spiced crispbread, grilled fish wrapped in tartleaf, bowls of fruit, and froile.

Havard was already there; he looked at Tadko in astonishment.

"Where did you get the glittering scales, my boy?"

Tadko grinned apologetically. "They were given me, and I wore them for the trip here. It's another long story."

"I can see that it must be." Havard waved him to a chair. "Sit down and eat first, and then I will have to hear the rest of your adventures. You will be glad to know," he added, "that your fine is paid, and you are now a free man. I contacted the Immigration Records Office earlier, claimed you as my son, notified them of the birth record, and had the necessary funds transferred to the Tallenport office."

Tadko gaped.

"It's all done? I'm free?" He looked uncertainly at the tracer in his palm.

"You are free," Havard confirmed. "The tracer has been deactivated, and on Oneday we will go down to the local office and have that removed."

"Thank you. Thank you...Father." It sounded totally inadequate to Tadko, but Havard smiled and reached over to lay a hand on his shoulder again.

"Eat your breakfast, my boy, and then I must hear the rest of your story."

Later, in the fountain room, Tadko described his attempt to find Havard, and his discovery that Havard was on Eilonsad. A question had been lurking in his mind that he really hated to ask, and yet he felt he must know.

"If I had come here right at the start, would they have accepted me as your son?"

"I have many friends here who know of my marriage, and how my wife returned to Elnakt, taking you with her, because she could not stand the climate of Monna. Not in this latitude, anyway, and I am here most of the time, now. Had you any proof with you? Identification? I know Seiare took such things with her."

"No, I had nothing. I left in too much of a hurry. Yarron wouldn't even have known what to look for."

"Then, with so many others coming as refugees, they might not have believed you—but I think someone would have arranged for you to join the others on Sancy, illegal entry or no, and of course reported to me as soon as I returned."

Tadko nodded gloomily.

"I might have guessed—I suppose I should have guessed—but I didn't. I decided I had to look out for myself. But I admit I've learned a lot, and survived. In fact, I really enjoyed the barges; even crossing Tallan was an adventure, until I got sick. I don't think I regret much of it, except the packery. But Neradis was awfully kind. I wish I could do something for her."

"This may be possible," Havard said. "The College can do some investigating."

Tadko was silent for a moment, trying not to think of what-ifs, while he finished his breakfast. Then they moved into the fountain room, and he began on the rest of his experiences.

It took a while, with Havard stopping him often to ask questions. He showed no surprise when Tadko told of his theft at the League. They had explained that when he called to arrange for payment of the fine.

They stopped for a short snack with plenty of cold fizz, but it was evening, with yet another meal ready, before he finished.

"And I do thank you again, Father," he said, "but I think I can pay off my own fine."

"You can? I thought your collection at Coral Gold did not cover it, and you bought your ticket to the City."

"I bought a one-way ticket," Tadko explained. "So I have money left from that. I can turn in my League badge for twenty-five D. Neradis thought I could get a much better price for these clothes here, maybe enough by itself to pay me off, and then there's the jewelry. She said she couldn't even tell if it was valuable or not."

He opened his bag, and spread his jewelry collection on the table for Havard's inspection.

"I am no expert on such things myself, but I would say yes, these are valuable. By no means the finest those people could afford, naturally, but very good. I know a reliable jeweler who could give us an honest valuation, and you may not even have to sell your clothes. But this isn't necessary, my boy. I can take care of it."

"I know, and I really am grateful. But this is my fine, to be paid by me," Tadko said firmly. "Even to that rasper of an Eilonsader. I did steal from him, and this is my debt to pay."

Havard set his fingertips together and pondered judiciously, like a teacher considering a student's thesis, before offering any final comment.

"Taking all in all, Tadko, I would say you managed very well for a stranger on Monna. You could not have known that it would be safe to come to the College, and every reason to think it would be unsafe. Of course it was a help that this is such a tourist world, with strangers very common in most places." He chuckled. "I must say, under the circumstances, I cannot really blame you for stealing from that young Eilonsader." He paused again. "Yours is an honorable decision, Tadko, and I will accept it."

"Are they really all like that? Willen said those from the—the—"

"The diarchate? Not all, but many. I have dealt with such, myself."

"And I'd still like to know where the Rhionny got their ironmongery," Tadko finished.

"That is a very interesting question," Havard said. "And one that should be in my own field of study. Flyover surveys would have spotted such things, if any had ever been made. I must check the records, but I would guess not. Not in many years—since long before I went there myself."

Briefly, Havard appeared to be thinking to himself. Then he looked up, and smiled.

"I take it you do not care to go back to Concora's and try to hire on as a free worker? Or apply at the League for casual unskilled labor?"

"Well, no, not if there's anything else. Although I don't think I'd mind casual labor if I was free and not having to hide. Willen had some kind of apprenticeship?"

"We are both fortunate that you came now," Havard said. "This is a break in the school year, and we will have plenty of time to decide these things. You see," he continued seriously, "Your mother appears to have done an excellent job of educating you as far as she was able, but I fear you lack the formal qualifications possessed by most of our students. I will arrange for an evaluation series to be taken some time next cycle. You had better have a medical evaluation as well. You may already need a booster for the bubble lung."

"I haven't been coughing," Tadko said.

"Best to take care of it before the coughing starts," Havard said. He chuckled again. "of course there is no question of casual labor—not for my son! We will find out what classes you need for an apprenticeship, or to qualify for an entry level commercial position of some sort."

To Tadko this sounded hardly more appealing than the packery. But then, he reflected, he still knew so little about these things.

"With a commercial house?" He asked dubiously. "Like Concoras or Crale, or one of them?"

"Not with Concoras," Havard laughed. "Most definitely. Wait until the evaluation is complete, and we can examine your options."

"Right enough!" Tadko said. "Uh, yes. Could you tell me—" he paused. "I would like to call Neradis. Let her know how things turned out."

He thought he would like to repay, her, somehow, although he wasn't quite sure how he could manage. She would be short on her line until they brought in another prisoner—he had no idea whether that would take another cycle, or another year. He had no idea how regular the supply of prisoners might be. Or what kind of repayment Neradis would accept. She had a prickly sort of pride.

"I'd like to call her," he repeated. "She helped me a lot, and she always gave me good advice, even though I didn't take it. I wish I had—I thought she'd like to know."

"Do you have her number?"

"Oh yes."
"Then I will check the time difference."

"Luxane here."
"Neradis? This is Tadko."
"Tadko! How went it, then?"
"My father was glad to see me, and I can stay. I'm calling from his house. You were right. I should have called when you said I could, from your house."

Neradis chuckled. "Ah well, we're told the hard learning is the best learning. All set up, are you then?"

"Right enough. And thank you for everything. I—" he hesitated. He wanted to say, *I'll find a way to repay you*, but he mustn't. Instead he said, "If I come to Tallen again I'll come to see you, if I may."

"Come and welcome, right enough. Luck of the catch, Tadko, and by the way, I've got a replacement already—an experienced replacement—so you won't have to go back to Concora's!"

Tadko signed off, feeling that curious emptiness once more. "I would like to see her again," he said aloud. "She was kind."

"I am sure it will be possible to arrange sometime," Havard said. His own smile was kind, as if he understood something of Tadko's feelings. "She was a real friend, was she not?"

"Oh yes. A real friend. I'm glad she has someone experienced on her line, now. She's got her quota to make."

The following day, he accompanied Havard to one of the Gardens of Memory. He would have preferred not to go, but didn't know how to refuse tactfully.

Before they left, they paused at Havard's memorial alcove. This was larger than the one Neradis had, but not nearly so much as the one he had glimpsed at Coral Gold House. Instead of a plain white wash, the walls of this were finished with a raised scrollwork design; the floor was a pattern of white and silver tiles. Above, in oval white frames, were the small portraits of Havard's forebears. Only one oil flask and lamp, because the dead whose larger portraits hung directly above had their oil mingled for burning.

Tadko had had visions of these flasks of oil accumulating over the generations. Where would you keep the things? But of course there was only so much oil from each body and eventually it would be used up. It was the family lamp that was handed down. Ugh! What a custom.

But he bowed and touched his forehead respectfully, and followed Havard out to the latter's private floater, for the trip to the Gardens of Memory.

He had to admit it was beautiful. Gardens of white flowers. Paths, paved with closely-set white stone flags, winding among them. Shade of tall trees, occasional deep pools also filled with white flowers. White birds in roomy cages of filigreed white metal sang, "What cheer! What cheer!"

He thought the song was hardly appropriate, but supposed the birds were chosen for their color—or rather lack of it—and not their song.

Here and there along the paths were slender white domed buildings, each having a slot where contributions for upkeep could be left, and sheltering an enclosed, rollable scroll bearing the names of those whose remains, in the form of fertilizer and water, had gone into these gardens. One could start the scroll by touching a plate at the side and letting it run until the names of one's departed came up.

Tadko found it all...what? Not blasphemous, certainly, or sacrilegious. Just...not right. He knew perfectly well that the bodies of the dead on Elnakt eventually returned to the soil. That was why the soil around each steading was so much richer than out on the halm. But there were proper ways of doing these things.

The dead should be buried, returning slowly into the land's keeping, not scattered over the surface like this.

He could tell from their expressions that his father and the few other people they met strolling the paths found a sense of peace and comfort here, and he tried not to walk gingerly, or to let his thoughts show. Still the idea that he might be treading on someone's remains, in the dust on the walk, was most unpleasant.

Afterward they went to lunch at a campus eat shop and tavern called The Drunken Scholar. It was a low round building with paneled walls of a green-gray wood, and a round peaked roof like an enormous red and yellow hat. This tilted almost to the ground on one side, to give it a definitely tipsy appearance.

Havard smiled indulgently as they entered. "It should really be called the Drunken Student," he said. "Much more of a student's rendezvous than a scholar's. The food is reasonably priced but good, the drinks are reliable, and they offer a very effective soberstim for those who overindulge."

The food and ale were very good. Lunch was followed by crisp fruit tarts of various flavors and bowls of fruit ice. There were few other customers at this time. Havard explained that when the school term began, it would be crowded every afternoon and evening.

While they ate, a gaunt-face young man in scholar's dark red robe stalked in the door. Both robe and hair were rumpled; he seemed to see nothing but the bar as he strode up, slapped it for the barman's attention, and ordered gruffly, "Ale. And shoot some lava into it."

Tadko watched with interest as the barman poured the ale, then brought a hose extension out from under the bar. From it he squeezed a large round scarlet globule into the ale. The scholar paid, took a long swallow, choked a little, then carried his drink to a booth, where he sat drinking and staring at nothing.

There had been rumors of this stuff around the barrack. You could get it at Rotten Pier, if you knew where to go. Made you drunk really fast. Cost the ocean full. Rotted the belly, too. He looked questioningly at Havard, who cleared his throat.

"This is the period for dismissal of those who have been judged inadequate for one reason or another. There are those who do find it extremely difficult to face." His tone was embarrassed. "I do not recommend the addition of lava. Soberstim will clear up the immediate effects quickly, but continued use is extremely harsh on the digestive system."

"No fear," Tadko said. "I've heard about it."

They spent the evening at home, with Tadko telling much more of his childhood on Elnakt, and Havard a listener who wanted every detail. What did he really think, Tadko wondered, about a son growing up so far away, in such a different world? His interest appeared genuine and caring. He made no comment about "savages" or "primitive living conditions." He was clearly both saddened and pleased with all that Tadko could tell about his mother and the lessons she had given him.

* * *

The following cycle was busy. On Oneday, they went first to the League where he received his twenty-five duats, fortunately without meeting anyone he knew, and he paid Kheer's money directly. Kheer would be notified when he returned, and the League would call the Civic Orderly Office.

Next they went to the jeweler, where his collection was indeed valued at more than enough to pay him out.

"Wise young man," the jeweler said. "Most of these poor young fools would take their gifts to some back-of-the-hand passer and not get a quarter of the value."

So much for a visit to Unser, Tadko thought, almost regretfully.

Then they were off to the nearest office of Civic Orderlies, where the tracer was removed from his hand, which felt strangely light without it. He was now a full, free citizen of Monna, Havard explained, and his name was registered as Tadko Darusko Havard.

On Twoday he went to a clinic for a full medical evaluation. He and Havard were told that he was underweight, and his lungs were developing congestion again. A booster was recommended for the bubble lung and treatment for the existing condition.

He spent the rest of the cycle going in during the morning to inhale medicated vapors at the clinic, followed by a visit to the college offices for "academic evaluation." This last involved tests, tests, tests, both oral and written, and was worst of all.

Evenings were better. There was time to sit with his father over cold fizzes and talk, to ask questions and have them answered, to learn something of Havard's own experience on Elnakt. He began learning to drive the private floater, and found, much to his surprise, that it was a pleasure; no more difficult than running the machines at Concora's, and much more enjoyable.

At the end of the cycle, the academic evaluator recommended that Tadko be entered to study for a commercial clerk's position. If he finished adequately, after a year, he could surely find a place, possibly an apprenticeship, with one of the commercial houses.

Tadko and Havard talked it over and decided this would be best. If he aimed for House Wintollen, he could probably get a place in one of their offices on Dorra. The cold climate would be best for Tadko; he could come to Monna for vacations; and service on Dorra was not terribly popular. If he did even reasonably well, he should be able to get such a posting with little difficulty. Also, Havard assured him, other options might open up during the coming months. If they did, they would alter their plans accordingly. Tadko felt uncertain, but cautiously hopeful, and willing to try.

When classes reopened, he had to report, on a Oneday, to Ilrue Nebas, the scheduler for commercial entry students. With the help of a campus map and some instructions from his father, Tadko managed to find the Primary Building. He took the lift up and eventually located Room 808A, Nebas's office. At 808A the doors were open; the man behind the desk chatted with another, who occupied what looked like the most comfortable chair in the office. This person was more stooped and wrinkled than anyone else Tadko had seen on Monna, but he wore a dark red robe with the gold collar of an Elder Scholar. There were only six of these at the College, Havard said, who ran the place—along with the Chancellor.

"—totally unqualified," this person was saying. "Are we scholars, or are we common traders?"

"We are attempting to initiate a new policy," the other began, then took note of Tadko.

"Yes?"

Tadko hesitated to interrupt; both men cast annoyed glances; but after all, he did have an appointment. He checked his new timepiece, just to make sure.

"Ilrue Nebas?" He inquired.

"I am Ilrue Nebas, yes."

"Tadko Darusko Havard. I was given an appointment." Tadko stepped in and handed over his admission qualification forms. "My father arranged for me to take the first level clerk's preparation for Wintollen Commercial House."

"Ah, yes. That would be the eighth hour class...." Nebas spun out an assortment of symbols on his comp screen. "Daily?" he looked curiously at Tadko. "Oneday through Eightday?"

"Right enough...yes. He...we thought it would be a good idea." Never mind going into Havard's explanation that the daily repetition of material would be best for someone without the usual preparation.

Nebas made no further comment. "Dordien House Four, Room 206B," he said, handing Tadko the foil strip. "You have missed the class today, but you are now entered and will be expected to attend tomorrow—Twoday at eighth hour."

"Dordien?" Tadko asked uncertainly.

Nebas looked irritated. "Commercial applicants begin their studies at Dordien, whatever their eventual House affiliation," he said. "You have your campus map? Then that will be all."

Tadko took the foil and left, pausing as he heard the wrinkled elder say, "That boy is the son of Osrin Havard?"

"Adopted son, of course. His mother was Elnakti and we've drifted too far apart genetically to produce offspring any more. Elnakt is a harsh world."

If more was said, Tadko did not hear it. He stood rigid, unable to move or breathe, on the other side of the half-opened door. Adopted son! Adopted son? Why was he here, then? Who was his blood father?

CHAPTER TWENTY

It seemed an age before the paralysis left him, and moving slowly, furtively, he stole away from Room 808A. He stood for a while outside the building, still trying to think, and failing. Then he headed for the Drunken Scholar. It was barely past the ninth hour now; as he had hoped, few other customers were there; most booths were empty.

"Ale," he said to the barman. "And shoot some lava into it."

The man opened his mouth, ready to engage in the usual banter with a reckless student. Then he saw Tadko's expression, and desisted. He filled the order silently.

Tadko carried the mug to an isolated booth and watched as the fiery red syrup diffused though the liquor, forming tiny bubbles that rose and burst. Then he took a long swallow, and choked as the stuff burned down through his insides. Awful stuff, he told himself. Impossible. Then the burn faded, giving way to a lovely warm glow, a wonderful contented feeling. He leaned back with a sigh, and took another swallow. This went down much more easily. The table was supplied with a tray of salt sprats and kelp buttons. He munched a few, trying to fill the unpleasant hollow that still occupied his stomach.

Time passed.

Eventually students from the early classes began drifting in, ordering lunches and snacks. The morning sessions were over. He supposed he ought to go....

He hailed one of the waiters now moving among tables and booths, and pointed to his drink.

"Another," he ordered.

Time passed.

It dawned on him at last that his second drink had never arrived. That meant.... Yes. It meant they wanted him to go.

He considered that for a while, decided he would, and stood up.

The room reeled around him and he sat down again quickly, swallowing bile. Something he had better order before he left. Oh yes. He gestured at the waiter as he passed again.

"Shobershtim," Tadko managed to get out. "An' crip—crishp bread, plain."

This time the waiter returned promptly with his order, waiting with a smirk while Tadko fumbled the coins out of his pouch.

After the soberstim and the crispbread he felt better. Sober, no longer dizzy, his stomach settled. Still miserable.

He left the Drunken Scholar and headed home. But was it home? Tadko almost wished he could have stayed at the Scholar, just sitting, not having to think. All night, and all the next day. Until when? No, Havard had no classes today and would probably be still in his office, working. Best to find out what was what, right now.

He brushed aside Zena's hasty gestures indicating that his father was extremely busy, and walked into the office where Havard was comparing notes on the texts displayed by four different screens.

"Siro Havard," Tadko began loudly.

Havard turned, his expression first impatient, then concerned. "What is it, my boy?"

"I understand you aren't—you cannot be—my blood father. Who am I then?" The last was a cry although he hadn't meant it to be.

"Oh Tadko, my boy!" Havard's face had crumpled, gone gray. He sprang up from his chair and held out his arms to Tadko, then dropped them to his sides again. "Oh my boy, I assumed you knew," he said sadly. "I had no idea—I thought your mother would have told you—I know she meant to."

Whatever Tadko had expected, it wasn't this. He slumped onto an old couch that Havard used sometimes for naps.

"I don't understand anything," he said flatly. "I don't even think I know anything. Why am I here then? You thought she would have told me—but she was lying, all those years? But she was your partner—I was born here—is that a lie, too?"

"No, no, not at all." Havard had forgotten his work. He sat down beside Tadko. "I loved your mother very much, and you as my only child. I was the first person from Monna in many years to spend any time on Elnakt, and she, I think, was the first Elnakti to try to live on Monna. I knew of the genetic difference, but neither of us knew how difficult it would be for either of us to live on the other's world. You know that my field is ethnic research—human variations and history on varied worlds."

Tadko nodded indifferently.

"Is that important?"

"Yes, because this was the reason I went to Elnakt. I learned through my own studies that except for the few traders who went there, Elnakt was an almost forgotten world. No one had deemed it worth the study. I'm sorry, Tadko," he finished apologetically.

Tadko twitched a shoulder. "I've been learning that ever since I came here," he said. "So you went to Elnakt, then."

"Yes." Havard paused a while, as if lost in his own memories, before continuing. "I went as a researcher, of course, with recorders and translators and a fully equipped floater from the College. I did have a survey map from decades before, showing the location of Port Town and most of the steadings. Some shipmaster had been asked to do it on behalf of the department. It was still accurate. Nothing seemed to have changed. I intended to see the year through.

"They landed me in early spring, with an autoship left in orbit for me to call when I needed it. It was at a southern steading, before the herds were out of hibernation. The place was called Aldukska. I learned the language, observed, and recorded. I moved to other steadings, went up to Port Town to watch the trading in midsummer, spent some time out on the halm with the herders, and then went to Daruskan."

He was silent, briefly. Tadko said nothing.

"That was before the herds came back," Havard went on. "Your mother was in charge. She was such a striking woman. Tall for an Elnakti, intelligent, a natural graciousness." He sighed. "She made me welcome. She was the first Elnakti to be as interested in my world as I was in hers. So I stayed at Daruskan. Then I began to notice that she was looking worried, even frightened. I thought it might have something to do with my presence, so I asked her to explain, and she finally confided in me." His smile was bleak. "Better an offworlder than a fellow Elnakti."

"Are you trying to tell me that my father was one of the other men at Daruskan?" Tadko interrupted. "No need for worry or mystery there—she could have had her choice, and declared him her partner, whoever she wanted!"

Havard shook his head. "No, Tadko. Your blood father was a man of the Rhionny."

Tadko jumped up, fists clenched, glaring at Havard.

"My father! A Rhionny! How can you—how—you're lying!"

Havard only looked at him, his face tired and sad.

"You—" Tadko tried to go on, then stopped. No, he thought miserably. Havard would not lie. Even in the short time they had known each other, he had learned enough of the man to be sure of that. And after all, why had his mother left Elnakt? He sat down again and asked dully, "What do you know?"

"She told me it was in early spring. The river was still frozen, but it was warmer. The days were growing longer and brighter. A few of the oncas were fully out of hibernation, and she rode across the river with some friends to hunt groungers. A late, sudden blizzard came up, and she lost the others. She was trying to reach the river when someone took hold of the onca's harness, and began leading her. When they reached a cave, out of the wind and snow, she saw this stranger. They were there for several days. He built a fire, and he had food. I would imagine, now, that he was a scout; that they had been watching your people in secret for some time. He was handsome and gallant, and it was a remarkable adventure. He asked her to go with him into the mountains, but when the storm was over, she came back to her own people."

"And then she found out about me," Tadko said. He thought of his grandfather, bluff and swaggering in manner, but so kind to his only grandson; so proud of him. "Grandfather would have killed her. Both of us."

"So she feared. And of course she couldn't know what her child would look like. Too pale? Too much hair?"

"That was why she wouldn't let me join a Rhionny hunt, why she was so angry. For all I know, he might have been my half-brother. But they didn't look all that hairy to me, not like poor old Homistho back on Tallen."

"His was dark and coarse, although he was light-skinned. Theirs, she told me, is fine and smooth, almost invisible against the skin, but it is there."

"So you brought my mother to Monna."

"Yes, my boy. I thought I had the perfect solution. I had come to love her, she was so different from the Monnan women I had known, and I know she had at least come to care for me. I had also concluded, by then, that I would have to leave before winter. There was the heated floater to sleep in, and supplies, and I had both thermoclothing graded for use on Dorra, besides Elnakti gear I had been given, yet I felt half-frozen all the time. Going through a winter—anyway I asked her to come with me to Monna, and marry me. I explained that we could not have children together, and I would be glad to adopt her child as mine.

"When your grandfather came back with the herds, he was outraged, of course. But as you say, she had the right to declare her partner, even when it meant leaving Elnakt. Then I signaled the shuttle that had been left in orbit to receive my reports, and we came home.

"I know, when she returned to Elnakt, that she was going to teach you about me, and about Monna. She hoped you could come to see me, in time. But I know she also meant to tell you about your blood father. Perhaps she wanted to wait until your grandfather was dead."

"There wasn't time," Tadko reflected. "I think at the last, maybe she was trying to tell me." He thought of his mother, gasping with pain, plucking at his coat. "Tadko," she had said, "don't go—your father—your father—" He had thought she was urging him to go to his father on Monna, but there was no way of knowing.

"What was his name?" Tadko asked Havard.

"I do not know. She never told me, and I never asked." For a moment Havard's brow furrowed, as if in pain.

"But she did tell me, many times, that she wanted me to come here, and learn to know you. You are my father, as far as I'm concerned. I don't want any other," Tadko said, and Havard smiled.

"I wonder, though," Tadko went on, "if I should go back—maybe all we Elnakti should go back there. Dorra would be better for me, but what about the others?"

Havard regarded him quizzically. "Back to the old life?" he asked.

Tadko felt an overwhelming longing for just that. The slow, changeless round of the herding, sleeping under the stars and the dim little moons, the closed-in winter months when they slept and told stories and worked on the many tasks needed to keep the steading going. The long, long, open reaches of the halm.

...and the cold, an honest part of his mind prompted. Elnakti or no, there were times when they all felt half-frozen. There was the hunger at winter's end, and the people lost every year to sickness, or attack by knifeclaw or slaen, or in sudden freezes or storms. He remembered, too, people carrying waste buckets down to empty into the rock-lined cesspits. Or carrying water up from the river, or ice chunks to melt inside rock hollows during the winter...here it was all available at a touch....

"I guess not," he said aloud. "Not back to the old life. I've gotten more used to Monna than I thought, even the food. Besides, I'm not Mosor of Daruskan anymore. Yarron is."

"I think the college, especially my department, will be looking into the changes on Elnakt, in time. Meanwhile, shall we have something to eat? I hope you will be willing to try going to school tomorrow."

So, the following morning, he went to school. He sat in class, listening to the instructor drone on about trade compacts, relative costs, currency exchange rates, transport allowances, favorable—or unfavorable—balances, and economics of space—no; it was economics of scale.

So much of the vocabulary was so strange and specialized it hardly seemed like the same Monnan language he had learned. Havard had given him a portable glossary, designed for this class, but even with this for reference, he thought that prisoner jargon was easier. The definitions were often as bewildering as the original words or phrases.

He sat before screens trying to make sense of graphs, lines, lists of figures and complicated diagrams that changed continually. These were simple comps, he was told, operated by voice commands; but you had to remember the right commands. Worst of all was having to just sit. The class was two hours; it seemed more like twenty before it ended, and they all must rise for the instructor's departure.

His buttocks ached, his legs were stiff and one was almost asleep, he felt cramped all over. The other students left rapidly; most had other classes to attend. Tadko was glad of a few minutes to stretch hugely, unkink, and straighten his back before he departed. He picked up the tiny cube that contained the day's lesson for home use, dropped it in his pouch, and went out.

That afternoon, he plodded through it again, doing his best, with Havard's patient, sympathetic help.

"I don't think I can do this," he admitted finally. "There's so much to learn, and it's harder sitting down all this time than it was in the packery. Even on the barges we could move around and stretch out. Maybe I should join the League again, and look for casual unskilled labor."

Havard, looking worried, ran his hands through what was left of his hair.

"You may be right, my boy, but I hope you are willing to keep at it at least for the rest of this cycle. Considering your lack of previous formal schooling, you have actually done very well for today."

"Right enough then," Tadko said resignedly. "I'll keep trying."

It was a long and difficult cycle, not least because he was assigned after class to a scholar from Havard's department to answer questions about Elnakt. Havard suggested this, he told Tadko, because he felt his own section should have this information. But with Havard's patient help, Tadko began to make sense of both class and stupid questions about Elnakt.

On Eightday, after school, Tadko went home feeling totally exhausted. Even if he was beginning to understand a little, he dreaded the prospect of sitting at that desk, cycle after cycle. Worse than the packery.

When he came down late the next morning, Havard had already left for the College.

Tadko ate, drank two mugs of froile, and carried a cold fizz into the fountain room to sit. He supposed he should work at his studies, but for now it was easier just to sit, watch the garden, and listen to the sound of falling water.

Presently he heard the floater, and then Havard came in, having stopped in the kitchen for a glass of ale.

"You still look tired," he said, "but for your first cycle of classes, you did very well. Are you recovering?"

"I think so. I even think I'm beginning to understand some of it. Trade is more complicated than I thought, at least if you want a fair price for your goods."

Havard raised his glass in a gesture of salute.

"Very good! Before you came, were your people still getting paid for their fleeces in those cheap gold rings?"

"Yes, we were." Tadko exclaimed sadly. "And there was the timber from that southern continent! We never even tried to settle there. We burned dung and turf because there's no real timber in the north, not on the halm, anyway. Just the skinny little whips that grow in the sinkholes. Father, why have we stayed so—so backward?"

"Elnakt is a bitterly harsh world, my boy, barely marginal for human beings. Your own chants tell of what conditions were like, in those five ships, by the time they reached it. They must have come from across the gap in the galactic arm. They could get no further than Elnakt, and they landed where they could. As for the timber, you can be grateful the traders have been wise enough to take small loads only, rather than stripping the forests. Of course they have done it that way only to keep the price up. It is beautiful wood, used only for inlays, jewelry, and the like."

Tadko sighed. "So I learned from Dacy. We thought the Rhionny were not much more than animals, and nearly extinct. The few that were seen, and hunted, were naked, like Yarron."

"Those few may have been sent out to give that impression, and possibly act as spies, also."

"And we never tried to explore. I know," he added before Havard could speak. "We just survived. Where did the Rhionny come from? We thought they were natives."

"So did we, when your people began to tell their stories. Now we know they, too, may have came from some much earlier settlement of humans. This is another thing I would like to know. Have they records, or traditions?"

"I couldn't even guess. It still seems unbelievable, that they were living up there in the mountains, then suddenly attacked us, after all this time. Have they killed all my people? If they're making their own iron, do they need the traders? I've been thinking, too. We didn't give a very good account of ourselves, those of us who came to Monna. We just ran. If any of my own people are left, they may despise us. Not want us back. This class I'm taking," he added. "Does it include, well, primitive planets—how to do things fairly?"

"It will, eventually. But it would take a careful analysis of conditions on Elnakt, an exploratory group, before any trade or assistance mission could be set up. Your information has excited my colleagues, and such a group should be going to Elnakt after this term is over."

"Will you be going with them?"

"Yes, indeed, and if you wish, you may go to, as a paid professional assistant, what's more, because of your local knowledge and experience."

"I could?" Tadko sat up eagerly. "Are you sure?"

"Absolutely. I have discussed it with the others, and they agree. But I hope, my son, you will also be coming back to Monna with me." Havard's smile was somewhat wistful.

"No fear, I'll do that." Tadko grinned, realizing with some surprise that he meant it. Elnakt would still be home, in a way, but so was Monna—and there were all the other worlds he had heard about since his arrival, if only in bits and pieces...all the strange people.... "You've gone to worlds even beyond the three suns, haven't you?"

"Oh, yes, a good many. If you like, I can show you all my records."

"I'd like that very much." Tadko was silent for some time, thinking. Havard drank his ale, and waited.

At last Tadko said slowly, "If I were to study and learn enough, not just the requirements for a commercial clerk, but—all that was necessary—could I become a scholar, like you? I think I'd like to see other worlds, some day. And I'd like to see all of Elnakt, and learn enough to really help my own people, and the Rhionny, too. If they would let me."

"Yes. my boy. This you could do, given time." Havard beamed, as if at an apt student had made a particularly bright remark. "Given your initial evaluation, and your performance so far, I am sure it would be possible. It would take time, as I said. Many other classes besides this one. You would have to work very hard."

Tadko drew a deep breath. "All right," he said decisively. "I'll go to school, and I'll sit in class, and I'll work hard. Somehow, I'll do it!"

Havard's smile grew broader, and he clapped Tadko's shoulder. "And don't forget, my son, you'll have all the help I can give!"

APPENDIX

Funerary Pyrolysis
by Ellen R. Kuhfeld, Ph.D.

Here's s how the oil for the memorial lamps might be made:

Organic chemicals, in a reaction vessel with hydrogen gas under high temperature and pressure, react to form simple compounds, stable in a reducing atmosphere. This process has been used experimentally to turn organic waste into a kind of crude oil, capable of being refined into gasoline and motor oils. Oxygen reacts with hydrogen to form H_2O, sulfur will form H_2S (hydrogen sulfide), nitrogenous compounds produce NH_3 (ammonia), and phosphorus compounds can form PH_3 (phosphine)—poisonous, corrosive, and explosive. These things happen with geological petroleum also, and refineries can deal with them. With catalytic cracking and/or polymerization, we can produce methane, ethane, octane, and so forth. Organic substances become fuel and oil. Adjusted properly we would get a hydrocarbon about the weight of kerosene—a good lamp oil.

Corpses are, chemically, a rich source of organic compounds. In a pyrolitic reaction chamber, a human could be reduced to petroleum plus residues. Assuming a 100 kg man (a large but reasonable size), and taking the customary figure of 95% water, he would reduce to about 95 kg water. The rest would be solid residue, perhaps 10 kg of petroleum (the added weight would come from hydrogen absorbed in the reaction), a few kilograms of mineral ash, and trace quantities of ammonia, phosphine, and other gases.

The mineral residue, and most of the gaseous impurities, could be processed into a rich fertilizer. With care and efficiency, our large man could become five or ten pounds of fertilizer, about nine gallons of clear water, and a gallon or so of kerosene.

Imagine a funeral garden, tended in careful ritual and getting much of its fertilizer and water from the dead of the city. There would not be enough kerosene to significantly affect society's energy budget—I see that gallon being handed over to the family. It would be stored in a reliquary flask, and used to fuel an oil lamp which would be lit when the spirit of the deceased was to be invoked.

Appropriate times might be birthdays and death-days, anniversaries, marriages of children, celebration of religious festivals, and celebration of the deaths of enemies. Old grudges or feuds could be given final settlement by mingling the oils of the deceased combatants and lighting a lamp in the proper ritual. Old grudges could be carried on by using the kerosene for arson. The uses are many, and far more interesting than a hole in the ground.

ORDER FORM

FTL Publications
P O Box 1363
Minnetonka MN 55345-0363

Order from this form (or a photocopy of this form),
and FTL Publications will pay the postage!

Please send me _____ copy (copies) of *The Wrong World*.

I am enclosing $9.95 for each copy. $_____

Postage   PAID

Minnesota residents
please add applicable sales tax $_____

Total enclosed $_____

Please make check payable to FTL Publications and send to the address above.

Name: _____

Address:_____

_____

E-mail (optional):_____